W9-ABS-684

Strip Search

Other Gabe Wager Mysteries by Rex Burns

The Alvarez Journal
The Farnsworth Score
Speak for the Dead
Angle of Attack
The Avenging Angel

Strip Search

A · GABE · WAGER · MYSTERY

Rex Burns

THE VIKING PRESS

NEW YORK

First published in 1984 by The Viking Press
40 West 23rd Street, New York, N.Y. 10010

Published simultaneously in Canada by
Penguin Books Canada Limited

Library of Congress Cataloging in Publication Data
Burns, Rex.
Strip search.
I. Title.
PS3552.U7325S7 1984 813'.54 83-40220
ISBN 0-670-67905-4

Printed in the United States of America
Set in Gael

To

CECIL THOMAS SEHLER

Strip Search

· CHAPTER ·

1

"Mr. Sheldon, if you have need of an attorney, you can call one."

Max Axton's voice rumbled like distant thunder. From down the carpeted hall came the muffled ring of a telephone and the mutter of the duty watch answering. Like Max's voice, the sound deepened the silence of the almost empty Homicide offices.

Sheldon, his eyes blurry behind thick lenses, looked from Axton to homicide detective Gabe Wager, then back to the big man who rested his elbows on the desk.

"You think I did it? You think I killed my own wife?"

Wager shifted his gaze from Sheldon and the mustache that straggled across his suddenly gray and vulnerable face. In the daylight, the office windows looked out over southwest Denver toward Pikes Peak some sixty miles away. On good days you could see its humped outline, powder-blue snowfields, and rock against the slightly darker horizon. Ten, maybe twenty times a year, you could see it sharply etched with its own glow; most of the time you couldn't because of the smog. Now, you could only see the freckled lights of office towers thrusting up at the south edge of Denver—the other downtown, local boosters liked to call it. Even this late, there were those columns of glowing dots. Cleaning crews, probably.

"I didn't! For God's sake, I loved her! I been nearly crazy —she didn't come home from work and I called and then

I called you guys, the cops, and for five days . . . I didn't kill her! I loved her!"

"All right, Mr. Sheldon. All right, now." Axton's voice didn't rise or accuse. It stayed as calm as a stone—like, Wager thought, Axton himself. "All right, we're not saying you did anything. We're only saying you can have an attorney if you want one."

"But then why—"

"Because the law says so, Mr. Sheldon. If, while we interview you, something comes up that might possibly incriminate you, then the law entitles you to have a lawyer present."

That wasn't quite accurate, Wager knew. Sheldon wasn't under arrest, so he didn't need the *Miranda* warning. But it sometimes shook information out of people who confused the warning with an accusation, and it covered anything let slip by a witness-turned-suspect. It was a good idea, and he guessed that Axton felt the same way Wager did: this grieving husband wasn't telling the truth, the whole truth, and nothing but.

"If you can prove indigency, Mr. Sheldon, then a public defender will be provided for you. Do you understand?"

"I understand." The man's cheeks pulsed with weak anger as he tugged at the few hairs that formed the corner of his mustache. " 'Indigency'? That's 'poor'? I ain't poor! And what I don't understand is why you guys are laying it on me! Why don't you look for the son of a bitch that did it!"

That's what they were doing. When a husband was killed, you looked at the wife; when the wife was blown away, you looked at the husband. He or she didn't always turn out to be the murderer, but the odds were in your favor.

Wager flipped open the new manila folder labeled SHELDON, ANNETTE E., and glanced at the crime report sheet. The victim had been found at twilight by one Marie Voiatsi, who had returned home from a week-long business trip to

Omaha, Topeka, and Kansas City. She decided to look around her backyard before dark—check on the irises and tomatoes and hollyhocks that grew tall along the waist-high fence lining the back alley. But she found more than aphids. She found a hole mashed in the hollyhocks, and, filling that hole, the sprawled, half-nude body of a female: Caucasian, twenty to twenty-five years old, long bleached-blond hair, eyes of unknown color because the magpies had eaten them. By late evening, Ross and Devereaux—the two detectives on the four-to-midnight shift—had surveyed the crime scene, interviewed the neighbors, and finally got a lead on the victim from the Missing Persons file. Official identification came just before midnight when Kenneth Sheldon was taken to the morgue, where he named the victim as his wife, Annette. When Wager and Axton reported in for the midnight tour, they found Mr. Sheldon sitting alone, bent under the weight of the cold fluorescent lights.

"That's the victim's husband," muttered Devereaux. "We just brought him from the morgue and haven't asked him a thing yet. He needed some time to settle down."

"Thanks." Under the new team concept in the Homicide Division, cases were no longer assigned exclusively to individual detectives, but were worked by each shift in the division. It was supposed to provide more continuous coverage of the cases. Maybe it did. But to Wager's mind, something was lost: the tenacity that a detective brought to "his" case. Some detectives, anyway. A lot of people liked the new system because it helped ensure a forty-hour week. When quitting time rolled around, you just turned to the oncoming shift and said, "It's all yours."

Wager studied the slumped figure sitting beside one of the half-dozen metal desks that the homicide detectives shared. The man was just out of earshot, but judging from the unblinking way he stared at the floor, he wouldn't have heard them anyway. "How'd she get it?"

"Back of the head. Small caliber; .22's my guess."

Wager nodded once at the seated man. "Suspect?"

Devereaux half-shrugged. "Looks like a rape-and-dump. But he is the husband. And he's all yours. Ciao."

• • •

"When was the last time you saw your wife, Mr. Sheldon?"

He looked at Axton, and his watery blue eyes blinked back the feeble anger that had stirred him a moment before; then they shifted to the flat white of the wall. It was as if Sheldon preferred to talk to that blank surface than to the man who loomed patient and massive across the desk. "Saturday night. Last Saturday. She went to work like always." His gaze dropped to the carpet—the gray color and pattern were designed to hide dirt but couldn't quite manage it. "I told her I'd see her after work. She never came back."

"She worked nights? Where'd she work?"

"The Cinnamon Club." Wager caught a faint lift of pride in his voice. "She was a dancer there."

The Cinnamon Club was the latest name of a topless-bottomless joint on the East Colfax strip. Wager knew it under three or four earlier names from as long as ten years ago when he worked Assault. That was before exotic nude dancing was legal, but the owners had provided equally suitable entertainment in the back rooms. Now it was done up front.

"How long had she worked there, Mr. Sheldon?" Max asked.

"A year and a half. She was good. She was real popular. One of the stars in the revue."

"Do you know of anyone who ever threatened her?"

He quickly shook his head and Wager saw Max's eyelids drop just a shade. "No. She was popular," he said again.

"She made more money than any of the other girls. The owner, he was always saying what a good dancer she was."

Axton's voice softened. "Did she have any male friends that you know of, Mr. Sheldon?"

"Male friends? You mean was she"—he groped for the polite term—"seeing other men?"

"That's right."

"Hell no! She was my wife! What kind of question is that? What are you trying to say, man!"

"All exotic dancers get asked, Mr. Sheldon. You know that."

"Not Annette! I mean, she got asked, sure. Like you say, they all do. But she didn't go down for nobody. She was clean. She did her sets and came straight home after the last one. She was a dancer—legitimate—you can ask anybody!"

They would. Axton shifted the topic. "What time did she usually get home?"

"Two-thirty or so. I always waited up for her and we'd have some tea and she'd unwind." His gaze moved away again. "When she wasn't home by three, I knew something was wrong." After a short silence, he said, "Do you know that the people in Missing Persons don't even take messages until eight in the morning?"

"Did she have a car? How did she get to work?"

"She drove. She had her own car." Again that little swelled note. "We got two cars. Both paid for."

"The car disappeared, too?"

He nodded.

"Can you describe it?"

"A Ford Mustang. Black with red stripes. A year old." He added, "It had a stereo, too. A good one."

"License?"

He pulled it out of his memory. "CB 4827. I told the Missing Persons lady all this."

With one ear Wager listened to Axton go through the series of questions that would fill in as much as possible about the victim's life, her routines and acquaintances, her actions on that last day. And, through constant oblique probing, her husband's attitude toward his wife and especially her job, toward the people she worked for and those she danced in front of, trying to find out what was behind that little odor of mendacity that had come again when Axton asked if she had been threatened by anyone.

The reports and photographs in the folder told Wager what the actual scene had told Devereaux: the woman had probably been killed elsewhere and dumped over the fence into the yard. The autopsy wouldn't be held until tomorrow morning, but from the corpse's lividity, from the absence of a footpath leading to the body among the blossoming stalks, from the nearby residents who, in that quiet neighborhood, told Devereaux they'd heard nothing, Wager was pretty sure what had happened: she had been raped, shot, and driven down an alley to be tossed. As Devereaux said, it wasn't the kind of murder a husband would do—not the rape, anyway. Maybe one of her admirers got a little too heated up and just had to have the girl of his dreams—and then was afraid of being recognized by his victim or her husband.

He studied one of the large black-and-white glossies. There was also a small plastic case holding a videotape of the location in sound and more-or-less living color. It was a new technique the department was trying out, along with the team approach—one that gave a better overall depiction of the site. It was good, but it was expensive, and storage was a problem. Wager didn't know how long the department could afford it. He and Axton would wait until Sheldon was gone to view the film. When the hand-held television camera played over what was left of a loved one while the flat voice of a narrator described the scene and the corpse, relatives tended to get hysterical.

From the contorted sprawl in the still photo, Wager could not tell if she had been attractive. She was female and did not seem overweight. The half-unbuttoned blouse showed one breast that had deflated like the rest of her body into that vagueness of detail that death brought. Her long hair was snarled among the broken stalks and half-tangled under one shoulder. Her face, with its ragged, empty sockets, had begun to decay, and even the harsh glare of the camera's flashbulb could not bring sharpness to those surrendering features.

In the background he heard Axton's gently persistent questions and Sheldon's mumbling, groping replies. Once, the man's voice was squeezed thin and nasal as an answer carried a pang of memory, and he half-choked into a wet sob. Axton held out a box of tissues and Sheldon, blowing his nose, took half-a-dozen deep breaths before going on in his soft monotone.

Wager closed the file and telephoned the Traffic Division. If the car had not been found since the Missing Persons report was filed, then it was probably gone, cut up by a chop shop into parts and pieces that would be resold for three times its whole value. And absolutely untraceable.

A woman answered with one of those defensive voices that civil servants on the night shift seemed to share.

"This is Detective Wager in Homicide. Can you tell me if you have an abandoned vehicle report on a Ford Mustang, red on black, Colorado CB 4827?"

"Just a minute, sir." The line went blank for a short while, then the voice came back. "Nothing on the city-county list. I can't check the metro list until morning, sir. You want me to have the day watch do that?"

"Yes."

"That was CB 4827?"

"Yes."

"All right. I'll tell them."

Wager hung up and, catching Axton's glance, shook his head.

"Do you have a recent photograph of your wife, Mr. Sheldon?" Max asked. "It will help our investigation. We'll return it to you."

Sheldon hitched up on one thin ham and pulled out his wallet. Flipping through the plastic windows, he drew out a glossy square. It showed a statuesque woman nude from the waist up. Looking more closely, Wager saw that she wore a sequined G-string and a large, feathered headdress. Her slightly awkward arms were raised high, and she smiled over the camera as if she were a Las Vegas chorus girl. At one side of the photograph, almost trimmed out of the picture, the edge of a kitchen chair showed. "It's a publicity photo. It was her favorite." Sheldon gazed at it before handing it to Max. "I took it for her portfolio. She was beautiful. Really beautiful."

Wager put it on top of the victim's folder. "We'll make copies of it and get it back to you, Mr. Sheldon." Unless some horny bastard in the division lifted it for a pinup.

"Thank you, Mr. Sheldon." Axton heaved to his feet and Sheldon's head swayed back as he watched the man keep rising. "You've been very helpful. I hope we're soon able to catch the person who did it." He handed the slender man a business card. "If you think of anything that might help us—someone who might have threatened your wife in any way—please give us a call, any time of the day or night."

Sheldon held the card in both hands and stared at it before he, too, stood. "Is that it? You're not going after nobody?"

"We don't know who to go after, do we?" said Wager. "But if you have any ideas, tell us."

The man's mouth chewed for a minute, then clamped into bitter wrinkles. He shook his head and carefully put the card in his wallet. "It just seems . . . I don't know . . . It seems the cops—the police—somebody—should be doing something."

"We will do something. We'll be going over to the Cinnamon Club to ask questions. But if there's something you know," Wager insisted, "no matter how slight, and you don't tell us, then you're going to slow things down. Maybe enough to let the killer get away."

"I don't know anything, goddamn it!"

"Do you need a ride home?" Max asked.

"Ride? No. My car—it's out front."

Max's large hand brushed Sheldon's arm in a nudge. "Come on, I'll walk you down there."

Wager followed, pausing to lift a key ring from the transport board. He flipped the little slides by their names to show the duty watch where they were. The personnel board read In, On Patrol, In Court, Off Duty, and a few other less popular locations. It didn't seem necessary to Wager; all the detectives were tied by radio to the dispatcher, who could reach them anywhere in the city. But the board looked impressive and up-to-date and filled one wall. And they were ordered to use it. It was part of the team concept.

"I'll bring the car out," he told Max.

• CHAPTER •

2

"What do you think, Gabe?"

Wager drove while Max shoved back hard against the passenger seat as he tried to find room for his legs in the small, underpowered sedan. The department saved money by buying year-old rental cars, the economy models. But no matter how well they were taken care of, the guts were always run out of the engine by the time the detectives got them. Fortunately, they were seldom involved in hot pursuits.

"I think he's lying about something."

Max grunted assent. "He's keeping something back, anyway. But I don't believe he killed her. I didn't get that feeling." He said after awhile, "He's not a good liar."

"He's what, ten, fifteen years older than she was? And she must have met a lot of men," said Wager. "A lot of men every night."

"Yeah, I understand that. But this doesn't look like a jealousy killing. Rape his own wife? Shoot her in the back of the head? And carry a picture like that! What kind of husband carries around that kind of picture of his wife?" Before Wager could reply, Max answered his own question. "Maybe he wants to brag about what he's got: money, new car, sexy wife. Things he never thought he'd have."

"Maybe he wants to show how jealous he's not," said Wager.

Max thought that one over and came up with some of the

sociology crap that always irritated Wager. "That's convoluted psychology, partner. But it could be, I suppose. A defense mechanism that he doesn't even recognize." He gazed at the dim shine of the gold leaf on the state capitol dome, no longer illuminated in an effort to save energy. "Leave it to a Mex like you to come up with the jealousy motive. But still, it doesn't look like a jealousy killing."

That was true, but it was the truth of experience, not some half-baked college-class theory. Most jealousy killings came during a fight. First a few drinks to loosen up the bitter questions and the short, defensive answers; a few more drinks and a sneering exchange to blame each other and to hurt as deeply as possible; a few more drinks as dinner's forgotten in the circle of endless quarreling, and then the explosion. The shot, the butcher knife, the head clubbed against a doorframe. And then the fear. The frantic effort to make it look like something or someone else: she ran off; a burglar broke in and shot him. Those were the easy ones. A homicide cop could almost have fun cracking a suspect like that.

"He didn't seem very shook up over her murder," said Wager.

"He said he knew something had happened. After the second day, he said he knew she was dead." Axton thought back over the man's statement. "It's like that sometimes—you know bad news is coming and you get ready for it. He had five days to get used to the idea."

"What's his alibi?"

"He was home waiting for her."

"Alone?"

"C'mon, Gabe. What the hell else would he be doing at two in the morning?"

"Coming from another woman's house, wise-ass. Or," he added, "following his wife after work."

Axton whistled a tune softly between his teeth, a habit he had when mulling something over. There had been that note of evasiveness in some of Sheldon's answers. True, that wasn't unusual—a lot of honest citizens had a lot of things they didn't want cops to pick up on. And they had nothing to do with a homicide. But neither Wager nor Axton liked to see evasiveness, not in a murder case, not from a man who said he wanted so badly to have his wife's killer caught.

"Maybe he planned it. Maybe he threw her into the flowers to make it look like a garden-variety rape and murder," said Wager.

" 'Garden variety,' ha." Axton half-smiled and the green of a traffic light glimmered over his teeth. "Have all you Mexicans got such twisty minds?"

As usual, Wager hadn't intended the pun. "It runs in the family. My cousin's a Jesuit."

"At least your family's got somebody to be proud of."

They were, too. More of his cousin than of Wager, who was not only a cop but one who had divorced his Catholic wife. And who was now running around with an Italian woman who had no religion at all and who didn't care if she slept with a man she wasn't married to. "It's because he's a coyote," said the more rabid cousins on his mother's side of the family. "Aunt Ynez shouldn't have married his father —she shouldn't have married outside the people; that's what's wrong with him." Cousin Gabe the mixed-breed—half-Anglo, half-Hispano; neither dog nor wolf: a coyote.

Wager steered the white sedan through the tangle of heavy traffic near the state capitol and its oval of dimly lit trees and paths. The area was now known as Sod Circle because of the male prostitutes who strolled these paths to pose and smile at the cruising cars. A monument to Colorful Colorado and the equality and majesty of the laws Wager was sworn to uphold. He turned onto East Colfax, one of the few corners of the city that still held life after dark, and joined the slowly moving cars nosing down the tunnel of neon and pin spots that made headlights unnecessary. Colfax Avenue was one of the longest sex strips in the country.

The west end went four miles toward the mountains and was dotted with drive-in restaurants, a plentiful scattering of bars, and a line of motels that did business by the hour rather than by the night. It was mostly the teenie's drag strip. The east end was called adult—adult films, adult bookstores, adult arcades, adult live shows. It went across the prairie in the direction of Kansas, leaving Denver around mile eight, and then staggering on as far again before fading into the bug-spattered neon of all-night truck stops and cut-rate gas stations with their scratched and scarred "adult dispensers" on the grime-streaked walls of men's rooms.

At this, the lower end of the strip, a short walk from the capitol, the Cinnamon Club's glowing pink-and-green sign hung out over a sidewalk crowded with night people. The car glided past a Laundromat, half-filled at one-thirty in the morning with customers hunching their shoulders against one another. Across the street, a dark-colored van sat in the unlit parking lot of a small group of closed shops. Around the van half-a-dozen men of various ages clustered wearing the street uniform of the dope world: tattered fatigue jackets, Levi's, hats of several styles, vests. One, standing at the open door, carefully counted out his money while the driver, glancing anxiously at Wager's unmarked car, snapped his fingers.

"You recognize that dude?"

Axton craned his neck. "No. New pusher in town."

Wager tried to see the plates on the van, but they had been bent and smeared with dirt; besides, it was an item for Vice and Narcotics. If they had the time, if they had the manpower, if they had the interest, Vice and Narcotics might set the dealer up for a buy-and-bust. Had Wager and Axton swung around to arrest them for what was plainly a rolling dope market, the money and the dope would disappear into the vehicle, and so would the case—in some kind of constitutional infringement. It wasn't enough anymore to witness a crime in progress; you had to get a warrant to investigate a homicide if it was on private property. There was a lot of talk about some pendulum swinging back toward law enforcement, but Wager hadn't seen it yet.

He pulled into a yellow zone near the corner, half-aware of the cautious eyes slanting their way from the strolling crowd. Their car caused a subtle undertow among the people walking or standing and talking, or alone and watching the action along the street. A teenaged whore in white shorts turned away abruptly to wander toward the other end of the block, her legs awkwardly thin and bony on tall sandals. From the shadowy landing of a stairway leading up to the cheap apartments above the stores, a figure withdrew into the darkness. Wager and Axton locked the car's doors and walked toward the glare of light. Along the curb, eyes slid away from them, and a grimy pair of panhandlers eased out of their path.

The Cinnamon Club advertised its shows as Sweet-n-Spicy. A glass case at the brightly lit entry showed a fly-specked collection of nude girls standing at the edge of a stage, smiling regally down at the camera. At the top, near the center, stood one who looked like Annette Sheldon; it was hard to tell, though, because the stiff poses and the harsh light made them all look alike, except for the various hairstyles.

"Let's get some culture," said Max.

The white glare of the entry wasn't only to illuminate the come-on shots; it was to keep exiting customers from being mugged, at least until they stepped off the club's property. It was also a kind of barrier: the inside was almost black; anyone—customer, cop—had to pause a moment to let his eyes adjust and give the bouncers and B-girls a chance to look them over. Wager's ears told him that the room was not very crowded tonight, and when his vision cleared, he could pick out empty chairs along the runway where customers sat and drank and watched. Of the faces he could see, most were young; but at least one gray head near the wall caught a remnant of pink light. Here it was, a half-hour before closing—one of the busiest times of the night—and the place was half-empty.

Voices were muffled by the thudding crescendo of stereo music while, on the runway in a dim glow of red lights, a dancer writhed under the stroke of her hands and snapped her long hair back and forth whiplike across her torso. Her thumb edged under the narrow panties and began to slip them down one pale hip with a slow, pumping motion to show a corner of dark hair to a man who held a bill out and tucked it into the girl's garter.

Axton led Wager to the bar dotted with faces that seemed rubbery and smooth in the glow. As he stepped to the serving station to catch the eye of the bartender, a heavyset man in a sport coat materialized from the back and tapped his arm.

"Not there, friend—that's the waitresses' stand."

Axton looked down at the bouncer. "Police. Where's the manager?"

Hesitating until Axton showed his badge, he said, "Come on, gentlemen." His tongue had trouble with all those syllables, and it came out "gemmn."

He shoved through empty tables and chairs and past the end of the runway, where a man stared with a lax smile at the dancer who had now turned her back and was looking over her shoulder. The music's volume was lowered. The other side of her panties inched down and she ran her tongue in circles over wet lips as her shiny hips ground in the glow.

"Just a minute," said the bouncer. "I'll see if he's in." The man's hairy knuckles rapped twice on the door and he opened it to peek in. Then he stepped back. "Go ahead, gemmn."

The manager was in his fifties and wore a Hawaiian-print sport shirt that bulged out over a stomach as tight and round as a bowling ball. Graying hair tufted above his ears;

the rest of his head was shiny. He took off a pair of horn-rimmed bifocals as he stood in the dimly lit office and held out his hand. He had a wide smile and guarded eyes. "Police? What's the problem, gentlemen?" He waved toward a wide couch that filled one wall. "Sit down. You want some coffee? A drink?"

Wager folded his badge case; they remained standing. "Did Annette Sheldon work for you?"

"Shelly?" The man's baggy eyes blinked. "She's been found?"

"She's a homicide victim," Wager said.

"Ah. Well, shit. Well, that's really bad."

"She worked here, is that right?"

"Yeah—a long time. Longer than me. . . . How'd it happen? Who did it?"

"She was shot. We don't have a suspect yet. What's your name?" asked Wager.

"You got to ask me like that? Like I'm a suspect?"

"That's not what we meant, sir," said Max. "We need your name as her employer."

"Berg. David Berg."

"You're the manager?"

"Manager, owner, chief accountant—you name it. I don't dance. That's the only thing I don't do around here."

Axton looked up from his notebook. "I thought Irv Sideman owned this place."

"He used to. He sold out to Jim Parmelee, what, a year ago. Parmelee couldn't make it, and I bought it from him six months ago." He ran a palm across his shiny head. "I should have waited another six months. Parmelee would have paid me to take it."

"How long did Mrs. Sheldon work here?"

"She came when Sideman had the place, I think." He glanced at the steel filing cabinet against the shadowed wall of the small room. "I could find out from the pay records. It'd take some time, though." The telephone clattered and a light winked under one of its plastic buttons. "Excuse me." Berg sat back in his swivel chair, the soft glow of the desk lamp catching a film of sweat on his face. "Yeah?" He listened a moment. "How much and what bank? . . . Okay, get the number and go ahead and cash it. If not, give him a free drink and say we're sorry." He hung up. "Out-of-state check," he explained. "I got to okay every one. People are pushing a lot of bad paper lately. Bad times, bad paper."

"It's not too big a crowd tonight," said Max.

"Listen, I'm not knocking it—I wish all of them were this good." His head wagged sadly. "Weeknights, I'm lucky to make the overhead."

"When did you see Mrs. Sheldon last?" Wager asked.

"Last weekend, what, Saturday? Yeah. She showed up Saturday for work and then Tuesday her husband, what's his name, he called to ask where she was. First I knew she was missing, I swear."

"You didn't see her Sunday or Monday?"

"We're closed then."

"Mr. Sheldon didn't call until Tuesday?"

"My private number's unlisted. In this business . . ." He ended with a shake of the head.

"Do you know Mr. Sheldon?"

"I seen him once or twice. He seems like a real gentleman. But I can't say as I know him."

"Did you see Mrs. Sheldon leave the club last Saturday?"

Berg shook his head. "Unless it's payday or unless they got a problem, I don't see the girls come and go. We have a business meeting once a week—Thursday morning. That and payday's about the only time I see all of them."

"She was at last Thursday's meeting?"

"She was still working Thursday night. You miss a meeting, you're out on your sweet ass." He smiled, "That sounds hard, maybe, but some of these young ladies, they never had discipline in the home, you know?"

"Did she have any men friends other than her husband?"

"You mean was she cheating on him? Not with my customers! The young ladies dance for the customers. When they're not dancing, they serve the customers their drinks. The rest of the time they leave the customers alone and vice versa. This is a clean establishment, gentlemen. Wholesome exotic dancing, you know? You could bring your wife or mother here. Some broad tries dating up the customers, out she goes on her sweet ass."

"No one ever asks the girls for a date after the show?"

"Well, sure—that's human nature, right? But all she's got to say is she'll lose her job. It gives the girls an excuse they appreciate, you know? I find out somebody's hustling customers, she's through. Period. I make this very plain at the hiring interview. I tell them the rules and tell them they can be replaced like that if they break the rules—it's simple as that." He thought a minute. "Of course, what they do on their own time away from here, that's their business. I'm not a fascist, right? But this is a clean place; if Shelly had something going on the side, it wasn't from here." The telephone rang again and, after a terse conversation, Berg hung up. "Things get real busy about this time," he hinted.

"Annette Sheldon never broke the rules?"

"Not here. But like I say, away from here . . . But she was a real nice young lady, Annette. This is a terrible thing, a real tragedy to happen to such a really talented and lovely young lady."

"Who might have seen her last?" Max asked.

"The other girls. I guess you want to talk to them?" At Wager's nod, he pressed a button under the lip of the desk. "Sure. The place is yours. Anything I can do . . . a real tragedy." A knock on the door and the bouncer's wide head poked in. "The last set's just going on now and the bar's closing," Berg told them. "The girls should be in the dressing room soon. Cal, take these gentlemen back to the dressing room. You gents want a drink, it's yours. But—ah—try not to shake the young ladies up, okay? They got artistic temperaments, you know? Real prima donnas, every one."

Cal the bouncer said "Follow me" and led them back across the edge of the dark floor where, with intermission, waitresses in hot pants over Danskin leotards moved from table to table getting the last orders before the final set. In his glass-faced booth above the stage, the disc jockey had shifted tapes and in place of the stomach-punching thud of the previous music, the ripple of a quiet jazz guitar flowed over the gradually rising voices and sharp tink of glass.

This door was down a short alley separated from the main room by heavy drapes. Another curtain arced away and led to the rear of the dancing ramp, so the girls could make their entry high upstage. Once more, Cal knocked and stuck his head around a door. He mumbled something indistinguishable, then said, "All right, gemmn," and headed quickly back toward the noise. Closing time was busy for him, too.

Wager and Axton stepped into the hot and heavily perfumed air of a dressing room smaller than Berg's office. Two light mirrors formed one wall above a shelf littered with makeup and wadded tissues. Along the facing wall was a series of narrow metal doors with combination padlocks and a long bench holding bits of clothing and street shoes. It looked like a gym locker room. An opening at the far end led to a toilet stall, its metal door crayoned in lipstick graffiti.

Four young women looked at them as they came in, one quickly turning her back to snap her bra in place before tugging on a blouse. At one light table, a girl whose bright red hair formed a corona of tight curls wiped cleanser across her face and tossed the tissue near a garbage can.

"We're with the Denver Police," Wager announced. "We'd like to ask you some questions about a homicide victim who worked here: Annette Sheldon."

"Who?" A girl wearing a short, stained dressing gown looked up from tugging on her pantyhose.

"Shelly," said Axton. "Annette Sheldon. She used the name Shelly."

"Oh—Shelly's dead? God!"

Axton and Wager asked them to please wait around until they could be interviewed, then each chose a girl and started the questions. Wager, trying to ignore the glimpses of pale flesh, began with the curly-haired redhead who sat on the bench and smoothed her short robe over her knees. She smiled widely but nervously at him.

"Can I have your name, please?"

"You mean my real name?"

"Yes, ma'am."

She crossed her legs tightly and tugged again at the robe. "Is this going to be published? I mean, like in the newspapers?"

"No, ma'am. But whenever we take a statement, we like to get names and addresses in case we need to verify something later on." He did not mention the possibility of subpoenas for court appearances.

"Myrtle Singer. 1423 Clarkson, Apartment 2-D." She spelled her name for him.

"Miss or Mrs.?"

"Ms."

He wrote it that way. "Do you use an alias, Ms. Singer?"

"You mean a professional name? Yeah. Scarlet." She patted her hair, making her gown gap slightly. "Because I'm a redhead. A real one." She had large breasts and that very white skin that a lot of redheads have.

"Did you know Annette Sheldon very well?"

"Shelly? Not real well. We work—worked—together is all. How'd it happen?"

"She was shot."

The curls shook once. "That's too bad. Really."

"Can you tell me the last time you saw her?"

"I guess it was Saturday . . . yeah, Saturday."

She stopped as a sweating dancer pushed abruptly into

the crowded room, looking with surprise at Axton and Wager and yanking her thin robe tighter. "What's this shit?" she asked. "What's these men doing in here?"

"Cops." One of the waiting girls looked up from filing her fingernails. "Shelly got killed. They're asking about her."

"Oh yeah?" With a flourish, she dropped the robe from her shoulders and tossed her folded costume on top of her locker. "Well, cops or no cops, I'm taking a piss." She turned around once to face Wager and Axton aggressively with her nude body and then strode through the open door. Large butterflies tattooed on each rear cheek flitted away in alternating bobs.

Wager cleared his throat. "Saturday," he said. "How late did she work, Ms. Singer?"

"Scarlet. She stayed until closing, a little after. She always worked the floor for the last set." She caught Wager's glance and explained. "Serving drinks. Girls with seniority get the best times on Fridays and Saturdays. New girls get Tuesdays and Wednesdays—the slow nights."

"She worked here a long time?"

"Almost two years, she told me. That's a real long time in this business. I came six months ago when Berg took over and hired some new girls. I'm not going to stay much longer, though. It's not worth it."

"How's that?"

She shrugged and focused on her long, fake fingernails. One had slipped and she reglued it over the chewed nail beneath. "The money's good, but you get, I don't know, hard. At first it's kind of new and even exciting—all those men watching you, and you can just feel what they want: you. Then you get kind of . . . superior. You kind of enjoy teasing them because it makes you feel better than they are." She shrugged. "After a while, you kind of want more . . . I don't know how to say it. It's like, well, you got to have that kind of excitement all the time or you don't feel like you're anybody." She aimed a dagger-nail toward the sound of the shower. "Then maybe you go stale. You do it, but you really hate the customers even while you're up there doing it. Like Rebecca. She's a real bitch."

"Rebecca's all right," said the girl filing her nails. "You just keep your fucking mouth shut about Rebecca."

Scarlet's lips tightened and she hissed to Wager, "That's her girlfriend—they're lesbians."

The girl filing her nails looked up with a little sneer and then shrugged.

"What about Mrs. Sheldon?" Wager asked. "How'd she feel about the customers?"

Scarlet was still angry and lowered her voice so that Wager had to strain to hear. "Her name's Shelly. We use our professional names, you know?"

Wager nodded. He'd seen it before: personal names revealed a self that people liked to keep distant from what they had to do. An alias, a nickname, a stage name let them move into a different personality, one that felt no guilt for whatever chance or ignorance or greed led them into. "How did Shelly feel?"

"I think she still liked it—she came across that way when she danced, you know? She acted like she was on Broadway or something. But she was a good dancer—really." Speak no ill of the dead. "I learned some good moves and steps from her." Her voice rose a bit, "Not like some of the cows that just go out and swing their butts around."

The fingernail file paused. "You knew all your moves by the time you were ten years old, honey."

"Did she have any boyfriends?" Wager asked. "Anybody she'd go out with other than her husband?"

"Dike," muttered Scarlet. Then, "She better not. Not where Berg could find out about it, anyway. He really keeps an eye out for that—the Vice people would have his license tomorrow if he let that get started." She added, pulling her robe together again, "Her husband, I don't think he'd know if she was two-timing him or not."

"Do you know Mr. Sheldon?"

"Yeah. He's a wimp. I met him once at the club picnic. We have this picnic at Washington Park once a year. Beer and steak, you know? And live music. It's real nice—if certain types of girls don't show up to spoil it."

"Was he jealous of her?"

"You think he did it?" Her blue eyes blinked surprise.

"We don't know who did it. Do you think he might have?"

"No way! He's not one of these people that do things. There's two kinds of people—the doers and the happeners. He's a happener. You know, things happen to him instead."

Wager nodded but thought otherwise. Anybody was capable of murder. Burglary, rape, extortion, embezzlement—not everybody could do those crimes. But murder was democratic. "Do you know anyone who might have wanted to hurt her?"

"No. Some weirdo in the audience, I guess. I mean, they're out there." A note of worry tinged her voice. "That's another reason not to date them—most of the customers you feel sorry for, but there's always a few . . ."

"Do you know of any?"

"Weirdos? Not their names—they come and go. But you can kind of tell the way they watch you dance. Their eyes . . ."

"Were any of them in last Saturday?"

She gave a helpless shrug. "I can't remember. Saturday's so busy."

"Did you see who Shelly left with Saturday night?"

"No. We settled up with Nguyen—he's the night bartender—and came off the floor. By the time I finished changing, she was gone."

Wager thanked her and motioned for the girl who was filing her fingernails. She was a leggy brunette whose hair fell in thick curls and caught the glare of the dressing table lights with a ruby tint. She wore stained Levi's and had pulled on a baggy sweatshirt that read HERS.

"Is this going to take long?" she asked.

"Not long. Can I have your name, please?"

Her stage name was Sybil. She had worked here four months. She knew Shelly only at work and that was all she knew. She had no idea who might have killed her. Now could she go?

Wager's third witness was Clarissa—Nadine Bell—who had been working at the club for six weeks. Before that, she worked in a roadhouse up north in Boulder County. That was her first job, and she worked there only two weeks.

"Why?"

"It was a rough place—a biker's place. Their girls did the dancing and they really didn't want me around." She admitted with a slight shudder, "They scared me. Besides, the money's a lot better here. And nobody's always, well, you know. It's just a lot better place."

"How much do you make?"

"I can pay the rent and have a little left over. And I just bought a new car." She added, "I paid cash."

"How much do you think Shelly made?"

"She did all right for herself—she was a good dancer, and she knew how to work the tips. Berg gave her the late sets, too." She figured silently. "I guess as much as a thousand in a good week."

And most of that would be tax-free. "Do all the girls do as well?"

"Not me, that's for sure. You have to get the good sets on Friday and Saturday to do that well." Clarissa's hair was long, too, and had been lightened; it was parted by a dark streak in the middle and swept back behind her ears and was clipped in place by two tortoiseshell hairpins. "With Shelly gone, we'll all move up. Another two or three months, and I should get the good ones."

"What did you do before you started dancing?"

She smiled. "I went to college. I want to be a writer. Another year of this and I'll have enough stories to last a lifetime." Her chin lifted. "And enough money to let me write for a while, too!"

"Did Shelly have any boyfriends?"

"No. She was married."

"Did her husband ever come here? To check up on her, maybe?"

"I never met him if he did. But I don't think he'd be the jealous type."

"Why's that?"

"She worked here a long time. Anybody who was jealous wouldn't let their wife work here that long, even for the money. Besides, there's Berg."

"What about Berg?"

Clarissa hesitated a moment, her dark eyes expressionless beneath the pale yellow of her hair. "Berg gets first ride. That's part of the 'hiring interview.' "

"He what?"

"You know what I mean. That's all he wants—it's a macho thing with him. After that, he leaves you alone."

"Mr. Sheldon knew this?"

Clarissa shrugged. "It's no secret. Call it show biz. I've heard of people doing a lot worse for a lot less money. And it doesn't mean a thing—except to Berg. It's his own ego he pumps, not you."

• • •

Wager and Axton worked through the dozen or so girls as they came into the dressing room while the club emptied out. But the information did not vary: Shelly received grudging respect because of her earnings and because she knew something about dancing. Some of the girls liked her, some didn't, but no one knew her very well because she seldom talked to anyone except about club business. In fact, few of the girls knew each other very well, and most seemed to want it that way. Axton finished before Wager did and motioned that he'd wait outside; a few minutes later, Wager joined him in the tiny hallway. Axton sniffed at the lapel of his jacket. "I smell like a French whorehouse —I hope I can air out before I get home."

They watched the tight designer jeans on one of the girls as she walked on spiked heels toward the bar.

"Just tell Polly the truth: you were interviewing nude dancers."

"Right—thanks. What'd you get?"

Three of his interviewees had started this week, after Annette Sheldon had disappeared, and could tell him nothing. Two others who had worked last Saturday night had since quit, but the other responses indicated they hadn't been special friends of the murdered woman. "A lot of zilch."

"Me, too. Annette was a good dancer. She made good money. She apparently had no boyfriends. And she stuck strictly to business."

"That's my picture, too," said Wager. "Let's talk to the people up front."

In the now-empty club room, a busboy quickly dumped litter from the tables and stacked the chairs in front of another busboy, who pushed a broom in urgent thrusts across the floor. A colorless glare fell from the ceiling where a rheostat had turned up the lights, and the Vietnamese bartender, gray in the pale glow, stood at the cash register carefully entering totals into a ledger.

"You're Nguyen?" Wager asked.

"Yes, sir." He closed his account books over his thumb. "You want to know about Miss Shelly?"

His English still had that oriental singsong that held so many echoes for Wager, and he half-wondered if, in some dusty, pungent village, he had marched past this man. "Did you see her leave last Saturday?"

"No, sir. She checked her accounts. Table accounts. Then she went to dressing room. After that I was very busy. I didn't see her leave."

"You didn't see anyone follow her? No customer paying special attention to her?"

"Special? No, sir." He smiled, showing a row of gold-streaked teeth. "All the girls have regulars, yes? But not special like you mean, no."

"Did you see any of her regulars? Or anybody spending a lot of time with her in the last couple weeks?" asked Axton. "Maybe spending a lot of money on her?"

"No, sir."

"Did you ever meet her husband?" asked Wager.

"No, sir. He never come here. Mr. Berg, he don't like husbands coming here."

"Anybody give her a specially big tip that night?" asked Max.

"Not that she tells me. Maybe Ed knows."

"Who's Ed?"

"Disc jockey." The bartender's slender hand gestured toward the booth above and behind the runway where a light shone dimly through the ceiling glow. In the shade beneath the booth, a busboy whistled shrilly between his teeth and called to someone in the kitchen, "Let's go, Carlos—andale, man!"

Wager started toward the dance ramp.

"Please, sir!" The bartender waved a nervous hand. "No shoes on stage, sir! You please walk around, yes?"

Wager did, following the curve of the waist-high platform into a shadow where a narrow stairway led up to the booth. Behind him, Axton asked the bartender more of the now-familiar questions.

At the top of the straight stairs, a door hung open, spilling light and stale, sweaty air into the club room. The disc jockey, in his mid-twenties, with a drooping mustache and blow-dried hair, looked up from a pile of tapes and records and shook his head. "Not up here, man. Off limits."

Wager showed his badge. "I'm investigating a homicide. A girl named Shelly. I'd like to ask you some questions."

"Homicide? Shelly? Does that mean murder, man?"

He nodded. "Can I have your name, please?"

"Man!" The brown eyes widened and stared at Wager. "Shelly . . . !" Absently, he reached for a cigarette and lit it, drawing deeply and hissing out a thin stream of smoke. "Man!"

"You were working Saturday night, right?"

"Huh? Oh—yeah. Every night."

"Can I have your name, please?"

His name was Edward Gollmer and he had been the regular disc jockey since Berg bought the place. "That's quite awhile in this business. People burn out. It's really a lot harder than people think."

Wager nodded. "Did you see her Saturday night, Ed?"

Gollmer had. She danced her three sets of three dances each and worked the floor as well. One of the better dancers, she was scheduled late in each round of sets. "That's when the tipping gets heavy. And Shelly always did pretty good when she danced."

"How do you know?"

"I get ten percent. That's part of the deal—minimum wage from Berg and ten percent of the girls' take. It's not like I don't earn it, man—it's my job to establish the mood for the sets. I cool things down and then build them up a little bit, give a girl her introduction. Then I run their music the way they want it and handle the volume. That's an art—you have to run the volume up a little at a time through the set, you know? It's no easy job."

"Did you do the music for Shelly that night?"

"Sure. She was real particular about it. A real artist, you know? She talked once about going to dance in Las Vegas or maybe she'd been there—I'm not sure. But she was good."

"Did she ever talk about any friends of hers? Or her husband's?"

"No. She was strictly business. She told me what she wanted and I did it, and that was it."

"Did she give you her ten percent last Saturday?"

"Sure. A girl doesn't give it over, I have a word with Mr. B. She either feeds the kitty or she's out on her sweet ass. Unless I screw up—then no ten percent." He shrugged. "It happens once in a while. We're all human, man, and some of the music the girls want . . ." He shook his head and fingered the gold chain around his neck. "A monkey couldn't hop to some of the music they drag in."

Wager asked, "Does the bartender get ten percent, too?"

"Sure. He's got the same arrangement I do. That's where the real money is in this racket. It sure ain't in the salary."

"Any of the girls ever skim?"

"It happens once in awhile, sure. But you can usually tell—you have a pretty good idea what each night brings. Things have been dropping off lately, though. The depression, right? But it's overall, if you know what I mean. A girl skims, she stands out."

"Shelly?"

"No. Never. What for? Shit, she could pick up two, three hundred. And a few nights she even made half a grand."

"In one night? Five hundred dollars in one night?"

"Right. You get a Saturday-night house pretty well oiled, they can put a lot of bucks on the table. It's amazing what some guys will pay just to look up a girl's snatch." He shrugged. "Like I say, minimum wage, that's for the IRS, you know?" A thought struck him. "Ah—you guys don't talk to them, do you?"

"Only about my own taxes, Ed."

Gollmer smiled with relief. "Right. What the IRS don't know won't hurt us."

"So Shelly paid you Saturday. Was that before or after she changed clothes?"

"After. They go in and count the tips and then settle up on their way out."

"You saw her go out?"

"Right. I was sitting at the bar and having my drink, like always. She says, 'Here you go, Ed,' and hands me my money, and then out she goes."

"Alone?"

"Yeah—right."

"You saw her go out the front door alone?"

"No. The back door. Over there." He pointed off across the vacant ramp whose waxed surface threw back the ceiling's cold glow like a strip of ice. "There's an employees' lot out back where we park."

"Can you think of anyone who might have wanted her dead?"

Gollmer shook his head.

"Nobody in the audience who showed special interest in her? Gave her a big tip? Asked her out after the show?"

"No more than usual. You know, 'Can I give you a ride home?,' that kind of crap. The out-of-towners do that, not the regulars. She got her share of it—she was a good-looking girl. Really a good figure." He shook his head again. "Murdered. . . . What, was she raped and killed?"

"It looks that way."

"Well, I guess I'm not all that surprised."

"Why's that?"

"You do get your share of sickies coming in here. Some of them . . . well, Cal has a tough job, you know?"

"That's the bouncer?"

"Right. Mr. B. keeps the place clean; nothing rough, nothing dirty. It's not like some of the other skin houses. Still," he added, lighting another cigarette, "we do get our ration of sickies."

Wager went through the rest of the questions, asking the same thing a couple of different ways, but getting the same answers. Shelly left for the parking lot a little after two. She had been alone. No one seemed especially interested in her. Gollmer knew of no trouble between her and her husband. He knew of no one who might want her dead. And he could think of no sickie that stood out in the audience Saturday night.

When Wager came back down the stairs, Axton was waiting for him.

"Anything?"

"It looks like the disc jockey was the last one to see her leave."

"Alone." It wasn't a question now.

"Yeah. Let's go out this way—it's the employees' parking lot."

It was a dirt square tucked between the windowless brick walls of the adjoining buildings and open at the back to an alley that glittered with crushed glass. Across the pavement, a high wooden fence with a board broken here and there guarded someone's backyard, and beyond that a darkness of thick trees protected an old neighborhood from the noise and gleam of Colfax. High on the club's wall above them, spotlights flooded the parking area with light. A black Mercedes sat in the slot closest to the door. Its license plate read MR. B. and on the wall in front of it was stenciled *Reserved for Numero Uno.* Other slots were numbered in older paint half-hidden under sprayed graffiti. Only four cars were left in the lot by now. They were all late models and one other had vanity plates reading D.J.-1.

"Not much hope for any witnesses," said Axton.

He was right. It was, despite the openness and light, a secluded spot. Wager glanced again at the solid brick walls boxing in the lot. A girl could step through that door and, crossing suddenly into another world, simply disappear. "Looks like another wait-and-see killing," he said. Wait-and-see if anything would turn up, because there sure as hell wasn't much to help them right now.

• CHAPTER •

3

Annette Sheldon was autopsied the next day. Parts were taken out, weighed and measured, sampled and tested, then tossed back into the body cavity, which was tacked together for burial. Golding and Munn, on the day shift, interviewed Mr. Sheldon again to see if he could remember anything else after a night's sleep. They handed their report on to Ross and Devereaux on the four-to-midnight, but those two were called to a shooting on the west side. A Chicano gang had squared off against a Vietnamese gang over the question of who was getting a bigger share of the welfare cut. So Ross and Devereaux had no time to follow up on Sheldon. When Wager and Axton came on at midnight for their eight hours, Sheldon's second interview lay unread in the case file and the thick autopsy report was still in its brown routing envelope. Axton picked them both up when he gathered the day's mail.

The pages of procedural steps and blanks were filled in by the medical examiner's findings. It was, as usual, a detailed and comprehensive job. Doc Laban had been at it for over thirty years, and though some people outside Homicide might wonder at Doc's continued fascination with the mangled and the mutilated, the division had a lot of respect for him. When he retired, it was going to be hard to find somebody as good.

"Gabe, Doc says there're no sperm traces."

Wager looked up from pouring his first cup of coffee. "She wasn't raped?"

"No medical evidence of it. No bruises, abrasions, or sperm in the vaginal, anal, or oral areas. No sperm traces on thighs or buttocks."

He thought about it for a moment. "We still don't have all her clothes." Sometimes a rapist got his kicks before he could go all the way. But not usually. More often, the rapist needed to feel a woman's writhing terror and pain, even her hatred, as part of his pleasure.

"We probably never will have them," said Axton, and added, "still—"

Wager agreed. "Like I said, why would somebody want to make it look like a rape?"

"You and your twisty mind." Axton turned to the section on internal organs and read through the findings. "Approximate time of death, four to six days before the autopsy." He counted back. "That could fit early Sunday morning—she got off work and got killed the same night." His finger skipped down to the next paragraph. "He located a cocaine trace in her body fluids. The organs are normal, though. No evidence of long-term abuse."

"Recreational chipping?" Wager wasn't surprised. It was fairly common for a customer to offer a toot instead of a tip to a nightclub waitress. She either used it herself or sold it later.

Axton read further. "Looks that way. No other foreign substance. Generally a healthy woman." He looked up. "All that dancing—she got a lot of exercise. Wasn't Golding in an aerobic dance class?"

"Golding's in everything. Did he and Munn ask about any insurance coverage?"

Axton turned to the follow-up interview. "Let's see. . . . 'Mr. Sheldon stated he could remember nothing more concerning . . .' No, Sheldon said there was no insurance at all, on either of them."

So there went that theory. Wager tested the heat of his coffee with a cautious tongue. "Where does Sheldon work?"

"He was interviewed at home . . . here we are: 375 Oldham, Nickelodeon Vending Repairs. He's the owner of a vending machine repair service."

"The owner?"

"Owner and manager, it says here."

"Anything else on it? Partners? Employees?"

"Nothing. What sly convolutions are going on now?"

Sometimes Axton made preppie-sounding jokes, maybe to show that he went to college. But he was still a good cop despite the sociology degree; besides, he was Wager's partner. You let your partner get away with things like that now and then. "If there was no insurance on the victim, and if there was no other man involved, then what other reason might Sheldon have for doing it?"

"Gabe, I think you really don't like the guy."

What he didn't like was the odor of a lie in some of the man's answers. "He's a suspect."

"So is anybody in the club that night. And half the people outside, too."

"But it was made to look like rape."

"It happens that way sometimes, Gabe. You know that."

But very seldom with guns, and not to the back of the head. Strangulation, sure: sometimes a rapist got a little more persuasive than he intended and the victim's throat was crushed before he could complete the act. But weapons, pistols especially, were something else. No one tended to argue with a pistol, so the rapist would have gotten his way and left the evidence of it. Still, Axton's point was the right one. Even if the man shared the same suspicions as Wager, he was offering the right objection: lack of evidence. There was nothing to point to Sheldon or to anyone else. Only that feeling. Wait-and-see. And perhaps wait-

and-no-see, like too many of those red-tagged files in the steel cabinet of cases labeled Open.

"Anything from ballistics?"

Axton riffled through the pages and shook his head. "Not enough for a report. The slug fragmented. Doc says it was probably a .22 hollow-point."

Which didn't tell them much. There were maybe half-a-million .22-caliber pistols in Denver; they were cheap and easy to buy and most of them were unregistered. They were also the professional killer's favorite close-range weapon because the slug tended to rip apart and was unsuitable for a ballistics trace.

Axton glanced at his watch. "Want to eyeball some skin? Maybe some of Annette's regulars will be there now."

Wager nodded and drained his cup. The taxpayers weren't getting their money's worth while he sat on his rump and drank coffee. No, sir, he should be out there sitting on his rump watching naked women.

• • •

Cal the bouncer remembered them, but there was no happy smile of welcome. "You gemmn need something more?" Behind him, on the runway, Scarlet was smiling in front of a man whose glasses winked pink sparks as he stared up at her. It was her first dance of the set and she still wore her costume, a strapless bra and a sarong slit high up her thigh. It flared teasingly when she braced her fingers against the ceiling and spun sharply.

"We'd like to talk to some of Shelly's regular customers," said Axton.

"The customers? You want to start talking to the customers now?"

"Something wrong with that?" asked Wager.

"Well, yeah! It might scare them off. How'd you like to have cops come up and start asking you questions?"

"It happens all the time," said Axton.

"We could get a warrant," said Wager. "We could do a lot of nasty things with a warrant for this place."

Cal chewed his lip and then said, "Mr. Berg's got to hear about this. You guys wait right here—I'll go get him." He turned away and then turned back, remembering his manners, "You gemmn can have a drink if you want—on the house." He hustled off into the red glow. Nguyen, the bartender, smiled widely and raised his eyebrows. Axton shook his head.

Berg came out a few minutes later, a worried frown wrinkling the wide strip of flesh above his eyebrows. "Cal says you gentlemen want to start hassling the customers now?"

"Not 'hassling,' Mr. Berg," said Max. "Just ask Shelly's regulars a few routine questions. We don't have much else to go on."

"I don't know that any of them are here now."

"We can keep coming back until they show up," said Wager.

"I see." He glanced around the dimly lit room. It was Friday and busier than last night; chairs on both sides of the runway were filled and a haze of cigarette smoke thickened the red glow. Scarlet was into her second dance; with pirouettes and pauses, she slowly unwrapped her sarong and opened the bra that strained to hold her breasts. "Let me ask the young ladies if they recognize anybody." He strode toward the runway and tapped a waitress on the shoulder. She listened a moment and looked at Wager and Axton, and then nodded and came over, with Berg right behind her.

"All right," he said. "Sybil says a couple of them are here. But look—let's do this with a little couth, all right? Sybil offers them a free drink and asks them to come over and talk to you. No rousting, okay?"

"That's couth enough for me," said Wager.

"Okay, honey," said Berg. Then to Wager, "I'm cooperating, right? But I got a business to run, too. I'd appreciate it if you gentlemen remembered that."

"We will, Mr. Berg," said Axton.

Wager watched as Sybil threaded between the tiny tables and up toward the chairs along the runway. She bent beside a man who smiled up at her and then stopped smiling as she spoke. He glanced toward them and then asked Sybil something. Then he nodded and followed her back to Wager.

"This is Jim," she said. "I'll go ask the other one."

"Hi, Jim." Wager rested a friendly hand on the back of his arm. "Let's step over here out of the noise. I'm Detective Wager and I'm investigating Shelly's murder—it's nice of you to help me out."

Max waited for the second one, a pleasant smile on his face, too. Couth.

Jim was as short as Wager but wirier; in the dim light, he seemed in his late thirties. His black hair was long on top and short on the sides, and he had long, narrow sideburns that came far below his earlobes and ended in little shaggy points. His full name was James M. Hugo and, yes, he liked to watch Shelly dance. "She knew my name," he said. "She always said hello. She was really a good dancer—better than anybody else here."

"You came to see her a lot?"

"Three or four times a week. I'm a regular, I guess." He shrugged apologetically. "I like it better than watching television."

"You live alone?"

"Yeah. I drive short-hauls. I like this place—the people's nice. They're not always hustling you like in some other places."

"You were here last Saturday?"

"No. I was over to Durango to pick up some cows."

"Can you tell me where you stayed there?"

"Sure." He did. Wager noted it for later corroboration.

"How long did you know Shelly?"

"A year, I guess. She was a real lady."

"Did you ever ask her out?"

"Me? No! I liked her dancing—that's what I come here for. We'd say hello, but, no—I wouldn't ask her or nobody out!"

"Did she ever go out with any of the customers?"

"I don't think so."

"Do you know any of her other regulars?"

"Know them? No. I see some guys here a lot and she talks —talked—to some of them, but I don't know any of them."

"Anyone special she seemed interested in?"

"Not that I know of. She was real popular. She said hello to a lot of guys. But she never went out with any of them that I saw."

"Did anybody get angry when she turned him down?"

"No. It's a rule, you know? Like 'No touching.' You can't date the girls or they lose their jobs. They're nice girls."

"Did you know her husband?"

A pained look crossed his eyes. "She was married?"

Wager nodded.

"I didn't know she was married." He added, "I guess most of them's married, ain't they?"

Jim said little after that, and there wasn't much left for Wager to ask. He thanked the black-haired man and sent him for his free drink and caught Sybil's eye as she made her way to the bar with a tray of empty glasses.

"That's the only two here tonight." She wasn't any friendlier than she had been yesterday. "There's maybe two or three more, but that's all that's here now."

"You don't know the names of any of them?"

She shook her head. "A few first names, but that's all." Her voice dropped and so did the corners of her mouth. "We don't even want to know their names. We've got our own names for them—you know, the Fat Man, or the Crip, or Whitey or Mr. Cool. Or the Drooler. He's a real winner. I got to go, I'm on."

Wager thanked her and waited for Axton to finish talking with his man. Max did, and gave a friendly wave toward Cal, who returned a stiff "Goodnight, gemmn." Wager followed the big man out of the smoke and thudding music, and they paused in the glare of the entry. A grime-encrusted panhandler started to approach, smelled cop, and quickly faded back into the weekend crowd that had begun to fill the sidewalks.

"Anything?"

"Just sheer wonder," said Max, "that anyone would waste his time and money night after night doing the same damned thing."

"It sounds a lot like police work."

"Don't it, though. What about you? Your man have an alibi, too?"

Wager told him. "I'll check it out in the morning."

"Better turn it over to the day watch," Axton reminded him. "Bulldog Doyle's hot for this team concept."

Wager spat on the sidewalk. "Right. I guess Golding can handle that much."

"He gets the same pay you do," agreed Max. Then, "I don't think it would be a regular."

Wager didn't think so either, but he asked, "Why not?"

"For one thing, they can be traced—they'd know that. But the stories are all the same: she was never overly friendly with any one of them. And you get the feeling the regulars are happy with what they pay for, a little extra attention from a woman that everybody's looking at."

"Yeah." But there was another angle, one that Wager hadn't fully groped his way through and that he did not yet want to trust to his partner or anybody else on the team.

• • •

Nickelodeon Vending Repairs was a pale-brick building of one story and two wide panes of glass that flanked a recessed entry. Apparently, it had been built as some kind of retail store—clothes, shoes—before the original owner discovered that a neighborhood shop was not a good investment in most places, and was a definite loser on the north side of Denver. The flanking buildings had also been converted to light industry or service trades, and the few private homes that made up the rest of the block—large houses with peaks and cupolas and turrets—now advertised Rooms by the Day, Week, Month. The curb in front of the building was empty, and Wager pulled his Trans Am to the doorway of the shop, where he sat for a moment to study it.

The blank display windows opened to an interior half-filled with the hulking shapes of vending machines. In one window, a square red machine glinted with fresh enamel; beside it, an unlit pinball machine lifted its back panel like an ornate tombstone, reinforcing the feeling that the store was empty.

Wager crossed the wide, vacant sidewalk in the hot sun and tried the door. He was a bit surprised when it opened with the jingle of a bell whose sound bounced slightly among the machines scattered around the tile floor. Most had their backs off or showed gray steel racks in place of removed front panels. No one answered the door's ringing.

"Sheldon? Anybody here?"

A distant voice echoed back. "Who is it? Who's there?"

"Police, Mr. Sheldon. Detective Wager from Homicide."

He heard a shoe scrape somewhere in the rear of the store, then Sheldon, wiping his hands with a rag, appeared between two of the upright boxes.

"Detective Wager? You found out something about Annette?"

"No, Mr. Sheldon. We still don't have anything. But I'd like to ask you a few more questions."

"Jesus. Didn't those other two guys ask enough?"

"Just a few more, Mr. Sheldon. Things they overlooked."

"Well, is it going to do any good? All these questions, and

nothing coming of it. . . . I'm busier'n hell. I don't have time for—"

"We're trying to catch your wife's killer, Mr. Sheldon."

His narrow shoulders rose and fell with a deep sigh. "Yeah. I know. Come on back."

He led Wager into the rear section, which had been a stockroom. Now it was a machine shop; a long bench down one wall was lit by fluorescent tubes and held a steaming coffeepot. Above the work site, framed on the wall, was an enlargement of Annette Sheldon's publicity picture with a small silk cross tucked behind one corner; beneath, on a shelf of newly planed wood, were several sympathy cards in a row. At each end, a white vase held a single fresh rose. Sheldon saw Wager look at the shelf.

"Some of the girls sent cards," he said. "It was nice of them—they didn't have to. Mr. Berg even came to the funeral."

Wager glanced at the names under the black script; one was signed by Rebecca and Sybil, another by David Berg, a third said "a friend." A larger one had four or five girls' names in different-colored inks. "You put up new flowers every day?"

"Yes. Annette loved roses. Every day."

Wager felt uncomfortable in the aura of sentiment and pain that seemed to pool in front of the little shrine. "What can you tell me about Berg? Do you know him well?"

"Mr. Berg? He's a nice guy. He gave Annette the good sets—the late ones. Because she was such a good dancer. He knew real talent."

"Did your wife ever talk about him?"

Sheldon's eyebrows bobbed. "Just business talk. Who he put on the afternoon shift. Who he moved up to night work."

"She never told you he tried anything with her?"

Two red patches rose on his cheekbones. "Hell no. He didn't, either! Annette didn't have to put up with that kind of crap from him or anybody! She was too good a dancer. She even got offers in Vegas—the Dunes, the Sahara—to dance in the reviews. That's real big-time and that's how good she was, man!"

"She got offers but she didn't go?"

The anger died as quickly as it came, leaving his pale eyes wide and aching behind their thick lenses. "She said we were doing too good here—her business and mine. . . . We were making better money here, she said."

"Better than she'd be paid in Vegas?"

He nodded and swallowed and tugged at the thin mustache. "You got to figure the cost of living there. They pay good, but it costs a lot, too."

"You visited Vegas?"

"Every two or three months. Gamble a little, lay around the swimming pool and get some sun. Annette liked to see the new dance routines." He stared at the plumed figure on the wall. "She liked the costumes, too. She got ideas for her own routines from watching the reviews."

"How'd you meet your wife, Mr. Sheldon?"

"Meet her?" He didn't face Wager but talked to the photograph and smiled slightly with the memory. "She was tending bar at a place I used to go when I worked for Precision Metals. We just got to talking and hit it off. We liked the same things. . . . After awhile, I asked her out. I didn't think she'd go with me, you know? I figured she thought I was just full of bar talk, and I'm not the best-looking guy in the world—believe me, I know that. Somebody was always hustling her, though, and she was tired of that trip. I didn't; we just talked. Maybe that's why. . . . Anyway, it took me a long time to get up the nerve to ask her out, and when I finally did, she just said 'Sure' like that and smiled, and I almost fell off my stool!"

"How long ago was this?"

"Three years and six months. We were married three

years and four months." He straightened one of the sympathy cards. "I figured out all the dates."

"She wasn't dancing then?"

"No. But she always wanted to be a dancer, ever since she was a kid. Her parents bought her lessons when she was little, and she was in all her high school shows—the musicals." He glanced at Wager. "That's what we talked about when we dated. I didn't know anything about dancing then, but she was crazy about it, and I talked her into taking lessons again. At first for the exercise, you know, but she was good at it and liked it. The Cinnamon Club was my idea—she didn't want to at first, but I told her, 'Look, a professional dancer's an entertainer, and it's something you've wanted to do, now's your chance.' She could have been . . ." He stopped talking, mouth squeezed in a hurt line and eyes shut against the rise of pain from within.

Wager strolled a step or two away and gazed out through the half-open delivery door at the graveled alley and the wire fence and the carefully mowed backyard beyond. In the center of the yard, someone had put up a birdbath; beside it a pink plaster flamingo stood on one leg and curled its neck toward the water. Around the base of the pedestal, a froth of bright petunias caught the morning light. At the far end of the yard, the white stucco wall of the house held metal awnings that shadowed the windows. The distance of that sunny yard from the little shrine behind Wager stretched far more than time or space could measure; it was a distance that made heavier the weariness of a long tour of duty, and now he felt the added drain of groping his way through this man's defenses, one question at a time.

He took a deep breath and pushed back at the surge of weariness. "She worked at the Cinnamon Club a long time. Didn't she ever talk of finding a dancing job somewhere else?"

"Sure. We talked a lot about moving to Vegas or LA.

There's not much going on in Denver for dancers, and what there is, is pretty amateur."

"But you stayed here."

"You mean why? Like I said: the money." Sheldon started wiping the bits and pieces of a vending machine drive. "She made good money at the Cinnamon Club and she was still learning more about dancing. We figured one, two more years at the most, and then we'd have enough saved up to try somewhere big."

"You were working somewhere else when you met her? Precision Metals?"

"Did I say that? Yeah, right. We bought this place maybe a year ago. Annette invested a lot of her money in it—she said she wanted me to have a place of my own." He looked around and sighed. "We figured we'd sell this place and go wherever."

"The shop makes a good living?"

"Yeah. Annette did all the bookkeeping. She was real good with numbers and paperwork—she liked it. I really don't know how much this place made last year. I haven't felt like going over the books yet."

Good money dancing, good money from the shop. They lived at a very good address, too—a condominium in a new tower near City Park. "We haven't found any trace of her car yet."

"I figured I'd hear from you if you did. It's probably in Mexico by now."

"Mr. Sheldon, what we think is that somebody in the club followed her out to her car and pulled a gun on her. Then forced her to go with him."

He wiped again at the drive shaft. "I think so, too. The bastard. The dirty bastard!"

"Did she ever say anything about anyone at all who might have been after her? A regular customer? A stranger? Anyone at all?"

The anger drained away. "No. . . . I mean, she had her

regulars; all the dancers got fan clubs, you know? That's show business. But they tip good and they mind their manners. She'd tell me about them and we'd sometimes laugh at them and even feel sorry for them. In bed, we'd talk about them and—ah—feel sorry for them, like."

"You don't know much about any of them, though?"

"No. Mr. Berg didn't like me to go there too much—the customers don't tip as much if they know the girls got husbands or boyfriends in the audience. But Annette never told me about anybody who was after her that way." He looked up as if begging to be believed. "And she'd have told me. If anything like that happened, she'd have told me, so I could take care of it, you know?"

Just like she'd told him about Berg's hiring interview, Wager guessed. "How, take care of it?"

His thin shoulders pulled back slightly. "Well, I'd tell them first, 'Leave my wife alone.' I mean, most people go there to enjoy the dancing, not to hassle the girls. If that didn't work, I'd tell Mr. Berg. He don't put up with stuff like that. He'd heave that dude out on his tail."

"And you never had to do that to anyone?"

"No! Annette said she could take care of anything like that." His eyes turned back to the picture of the girl standing with arms upraised and smile frozen. "She told me never to worry about anything like that, and I didn't."

Wager said carefully, "The medical evidence shows she was not sexually attacked before she was shot."

"She wasn't?"

"No. It looked that way. But she wasn't."

Sheldon leaned on the bench as if his stomach hurt. "I'm glad for that. I'm glad she didn't have to go through that."

"Yes. About how much money did Annette bring home each week, Mr. Sheldon?"

He came back from wherever his thoughts had taken him. "How much? Oh—sometimes two thousand dollars a week. Any week she didn't make fifteen hundred was a poor week for her. I told you, she was real popular. There was a bunch of Arabs used to come in sometimes and see how high they could stack twenty-dollar bills before she finished a dance."

"What did you and your wife do with all that money?"

"Do with it?"

"Did you spend it? Save it? Invest it in something?"

"Well, ah, we spent a lot—the condo, that's expensive. And the cars. Video stuff—working nights, you miss the good programs. Vacations—a little gambling in Vegas." He looked around the cinder-block walls of the machine shop. "And a lot of it went into this business. This whole set of tools and machines . . . all new . . ." He shook his head, "Like I said, Annette kept the books and I just haven't had the heart to go over them yet."

"Did you lend money to anyone who might not want to pay it back?"

"No," he said definitely. "We never lent money. We saved some and we spent some. That's it." His voice rose. "And I don't see what any of that's got to do with some son of a bitch killing her. Why don't you just go out and find what crazy son of a bitch followed her out of the club and killed her! Why don't you do that instead of coming around here and bugging me with all these questions that don't mean shit! Go on—go on and find out who it was, and leave me alone!"

· CHAPTER ·

They rode that night, and the next, and all the following week, too. The Sheldon file moved an inch or so toward the back of the Open drawer as later homicides, farther up the alphabet, crowded in. Some of those files were open-and-shut within an hour and moved to the Action drawer for legal disposition; others sat longer while the detectives methodically interviewed witnesses, gathered physical evidence, and put together cases for the cadre of young assistant DAs, who would face the accused in court. It was during busy times like these that Wager had an occasional image of himself as swimming just above an ocean floor and fingering the detritus that settled into the murky slime. High above him, the people who could afford to be near the light passed each other, surrounded by comfortable space that cushioned their jostle for money or power. Farther down, where things got darker and more crowded, the jostling wasn't so polite or so well governed. There, when species bumped, they tore at one another for other reasons besides greed. It had more to do with reflexes or terror, or even the pleasure of destroying another living being. Below that was the turbulence of a continual struggle of one against the other, and against those above who pressed down. There, the occasional leviathan swam out of the gloom to feed when hungry, to awe when not. There, those smaller than the leviathan, but quicker, more savage, dipped to feed on the easier prey at the bottom. And there, too, was where Wager swam. While, beneath it all, the bits and pieces, tattered remnants of the struggle, spun slowly down to lie in the sludge and serve things that could only crawl to their dying feed.

By now, almost two weeks after her death, Annette Sheldon had become just another piece of jetsam on the floor of this sea, and other, more recent victims demanded more attention. There was the four-year-old boy who was beaten to death by his mother's live-in; no confession yet, but good medical evidence that the bruises and the ripping loose of the child's brain from its skull did not occur when he took a little tumble out of bed, as the mother claimed. There was the enraged shooting of two teenagers by a third, who was now known as Pepe the Pistol Aguilar. Five .25-caliber bullets into one corpse; reload; six into the other. Pepe the Pistol was still hiding in the shadowy corners of the city, but it was only a matter of time before one of the friends of those he had killed spotted him and made a quick, anonymous phone call to the police. There was the knife fight between two drifters along upper Larimer Street; one died from a severed artery—and, a witness swore, the shock of breaking his wine bottle. Wager and Axton picked up the other one ten minutes later, painted with his own blood and that of the victim. Most of that night's tour was spent taking statements from the soberest witnesses and fending off the gabble of the drunkest. There was the killing and burning of an old woman by a neighbor's son who had only been looking for some loose change in the lady's bureau when she caught him. It wasn't fair for that old lady to have more money than she knew what to do with and not give any to him—it wasn't fair for her to start yelling like that when all he wanted was her fucking loose change. So he thumped her and then tried to burn the evidence, which wasn't quite dead yet, and had shrieked the neighborhood awake. All these and more came into the night watch and were rotated through the division as each team picked up the cases in turn, and handed them on to the relief shift while the clock swung through another twenty-four hours. Except for the infrequent times when Wager's eyes paused at the name on the manila folder in the Open drawer, Annette Sheldon was left farther behind. In the minds of the Homicide detectives, she had become another wait-and-see, another victim of a stranger-to-stranger murder whose solution, if it ever came, would depend on luck. Right now there was a stack of corpses in the morgue whose slayers were within easier reach of the Homicide team. And the team invested its time where the payoff was most likely.

Wager was already at his desk and checking the crime reports of the preceding watch when Axton, the latest mail dwarfed by his fist, came on duty. Max liked to deliver the letters and Wager let him; it was a kind of ritual for the big man. It helped make the homicide business routine and put some kind of psychic distance between the fact that Max and his family and friends were human, and the things he investigated had once been human, too.

"Ross tells me there's another one."

Wager looked up. Ross preferred to talk to Max because Wager had refused to join the police union. Max had joined —"We need some protection, too, Gabe"—but never urged it on Wager. But Ross was the union rep for the division and believed that if a cop wasn't for the union, he was against it. To which Wager agreed: anything Ross was for, he was against. "Another what?"

"Exotic dancer." Axton tossed Wager's letters to him and began leafing through his own. "She's not ours—she was found out in Adams County. But she lived and worked in Denver."

Wager's envelopes were always the kind that had postage meter franks instead of stamps, and those little plastic windows with his name preprinted on the easy-return, postage-paid acceptance card. He shoved them unopened off his desk into the circular file. "Let's hear it."

Axton thumbed through his letters. He liked to look at the pictures of all the prizes and free gifts he could win. "One shot in the back of the head, probably from a small-caliber handgun." He tossed most of his mail after Wager's and poured a cup of coffee from the stained Silex. "Got a dime?"

Wager rattled it into the dish with the coffee-splattered card that read PLEASE.

"Half-nude, dumped along a roadside in Adams County. The sheriff's report came in a couple days ago, but it went to Missing Persons. Our copy came in today."

"The same m.o. as Annette Sheldon?"

"It looks like it." Axton sipped. "Which means that your buddy Kenneth Sheldon isn't such a hot prospect anymore."

"Maybe there's a connection—it's worth checking out. Where'd she work?"

"Foxy Dick's." Max handed Wager a small pile of papers. "Here's what the Adams County Homicide people came up with."

Wager leafed through the Xeroxed sheets, scanning the less important information and spending more time on the narrative sections. The only witness was the man who found the body. There were the medical examiner's reports summarized, a coroner's report, a responding officer's brief report. It was a spotty dossier, and Wager did not recognize the investigating officer's signature.

"I hope it's not a loony," said Axton.

This victim's name was Angela Sanchez Williams. Twenty-one years old, divorced, one child. She had danced at Foxy Dick's for six weeks. Before that, she had worked as a cocktail waitress at a restaurant out at Stapleton Airport. She had no known enemies; she did have a boyfriend, Brad Uhlan. He had a confirmed alibi. She left work and didn't arrive home. Her mother, who lived with her and baby-sat for the child, reported her missing early the following morning. However, no results on the Missing Persons bulletin came in until five days later when a body matching Williams's description was found by a mower crewman along County Road 44, northeast of Denver.

"It does sound familiar," said Wager.

"Don't it though."

The medical reports offered little more than the cause and approximate time of death; the body had lain too long in the sun to determine rape or assault, and the internal organs had decayed. Given the lack of clothing, however, and the probability that the woman had been killed elsewhere and tossed beside the road later, the presumption was rape and murder.

"Anything on NCIC?" asked Wager. One of the services of the National Crime Information Center was to list crimes with a similar m.o.

"Ross sent a query this afternoon, but no reply yet."

Nor would there be for a while, and the crime's characteristics were so common nationally that whatever did come back would probably be useless. Wager scanned the list of telephone numbers pressed beneath the glass top of his desk, then he dialed the Adams County sheriff's office. A quiet-voiced man answered.

"This is Detective Wager, Homicide, DPD. I'm calling about that shooting death out on County Road 44. Is Detective Lee on duty?"

"Yes, sir, I know the one you mean. But Lee's not here. He's our Homicide man, but he won't be in until around eight-thirty, Detective Wager."

"Thanks." He hung up and shook his head at Axton's inquiring glance. "Have to wait until morning."

Axton grunted. "Let's go look for Pepe the Pistol."

• • •

They turned the watch over to Munn and Golding at eight. As usual, Munn was a few minutes late coming on, just as he would be a few minutes early going off. Every minute away from this job, he once told Wager, meant an extra day of life for him. But he was too close to retirement to quit now. It was a race, he said, chewing on a chalky tablet, between retiring and dying, and sometimes he thought dying would be a hell of a lot easier in the long run.

Golding came into the stale office like a brisk whiff of after-shave lotion. "Gabe! Christ, you look sick, man!"

"I've been on duty eight hours."

"And drank a gallon of coffee and filled your belly with pure crap. No wonder you look green." He pulled a magenta sheet from his vest pocket. "Look here"—he unfolded it and slapped it on the desk like a high card—"this is it! This is the real thing. Biofeedback was good, but it used a machine. This is one hundred percent organic, and it works!"

The bright sheet of paper had a Navajo design of some kind at the top and in flowing script below said "Aura Balancing."

"What the hell is 'Aura Balancing'?"

"The electromagnetic field that surrounds the body. Everybody's got one—it can even be photographed. This guy balances your aura for you. Look at Max there—you can just look at him and tell his aura's pretty good." Golding squinted. "But I bet it could use a little tune-up. But you, Gabe. Christ, you're really turbulent!"

"Golding—"

"No, read it now. It really works, I'm telling you. Right

here." He pointed to a hand-lettered paragraph which explained that a turbulent or unclear aura gave one a turbulent and unclear relationship with the world. Aura Balancing through dialogue and through action of the Light (a pure force of spiritual energy) would clear the aura; negativity, judgments, and disturbances held in the aura would be released. All a person had to do was drive up to Boulder once every three months for an adjustment session.

"I'm supposed to give this man fifty bucks every three months so I won't make judgments? What kind of cop would I be then?"

"Well, he means prejudgments—you know, prejudices and things that don't let you see the world as it really is."

"Right—Boulder's just the place to see the world as it really is." He stood and pulled on his sport coat. "I'm off duty, Golding. See you tomorrow." As he went past the personnel board and flipped the slide by his name, he heard Golding shift targets, "What this guy does, Max . . ."

• • •

He was off duty, but he didn't go back to his apartment. Instead, he swung his black Trans Am into the last half of the morning rush hour and nosed his way through the tangle of downtown streets blocked by the flashing lights and boarded sidewalks of constant construction. Even in depression or recession or stagflation or whatever bad times were called now, Denver kept putting up more office towers and buying up more residential and retail blocks around the downtown core. A few scattered groups were making efforts to preserve some blocks for homes and apartments, but the pressure of big money was always there, and gradually winning. His old neighborhood, Auraria, was long gone; street after street of frame houses that had been home and kinfolk and shortcuts through neighboring backyards as familiar as his own, all were gone. In its place a university sprawled—a collection of factorylike buildings as ugly as they were cheap. The whole downtown, following the same path, was becoming an area no one could grow up in: crowded and uncomfortable by day, blank and cold at night. And on weekends the empty streets were dotted here and there with straggling tourists who showed their uneasiness in the face of all the dark, locked doors. If a city had an aura, then Denver's must be totally maladjusted—torn between the commuter life of nine-to-five, and the rest of the day, which was dead. Even the Colfax strip, with its drifting filth, was better than being dead, and Wager could understand the need of those who returned night after night to the busy lights and constantly moving feet, even though they did not like the pimps and pushers who jostled them. They were turning their backs on a dying city.

He guided the low-slung car onto I-76, angling northeast. Now, most of the traffic was going in the opposite direction, and he could focus on trying to outstare a sun that made the concrete glow like copper against his eyes. Gradually, the highway swung farther north and the glare lessened; he pushed the accelerator closer to the floor and felt the car hunker a little nearer to the pavement. The road arced gently through an unending series of bedroom communities punctuated by glittering shopping centers where only a few years ago wide harrows had carved the heavy earth. Billboards flashed smiling families or gigantic split-level homes nestled under trees that the bare prairie never had. Other signs offered creative financing that anyone could afford if they were willing to sell themselves to a bank for forty years.

The only thing Wager was willing to sell himself to was his job, as his ex had gradually discovered after many tears and angry words. In fact, that very phrase was hers. He didn't think of it as selling himself; he *was* his job—he was what he did, which was the thing Lorraine could never accept. Maybe some of these people felt the same way about those split-level houses. Maybe those forty years of payments was what they were. Maybe they were really happy to fuss over a different paint scheme every decade or so, to drop their sweat all over the skinny saplings that they scratched into the hard clay, to quarrel with their neighbors about the kind of fence that separated their kingdoms. Maybe they were busy and happy making a neighborhood, one that would not be scraped away like Wager's own. But he could not escape the feeling that these were one-generation neighborhoods, that their roots were far shallower than those of old Auraria.

Well, theirs was the choice, what choice they had. Wager was very seldom surprised anymore at the ways people claimed identity. Or, for that matter, snuffed out the identities of others. Right now, it just felt good to know that none of these homes or struggling trees or growing families anchored him to a tiny square of earth. He was glad he was not buried before he was dead, and he found deep satisfaction in the wind tugging through the open window against his hair and the sound of its restless boom against his ear. It felt good to floor the accelerator and leave behind eight hours of stuffy routine, to follow the spread wings of the gold eagle traced on the hood in front of him. True, he was taking his work with him; but that was okay—his work was what he was—and the thirty or so miles to the Adams County sheriff's office went quickly in the mindless relaxation that lonely driving often brought him. He did not once think of the words "team concept."

Detective John Lee greeted him with a reserved smile and an offer of coffee. Somewhere in his mid-twenties, the man's mustache was more neatly trimmed than Wager's, and he had the habit of tugging his shirt cuffs from the sleeves of his blue herringbone jacket. Then he would hunch his shoulders and the cuffs would suck back in again. Wager didn't know the man but he knew the type: three or four years in uniform, possibly in a department back East. Maybe another year as a detective; more likely, given his age, Lee joined the sheriff's office right out of a patrol car, seeing it as one step up the long ladder to becoming a police captain by the time he was thirty-five. Wager had heard that, because of the rapidly growing population in Adams County, the sheriff's office was upgrading its staff. Promotions came quickly when that happened.

"I'm not sure what more I can tell you, Detective Wager. I sent a report over to you people last week. It's all there."

It was never all in a report, and that report wasn't too good in the first place. But that wasn't what Lee was telling him. He was saying he did not want another lawman poking around in his homicide. Good murders were hard to come by in Adams County, and the successful solution of this one would make a nice entry in an ambitious cop's personnel file.

"Maybe if you told me about the crime scene," he said. "Maybe something didn't get into the report."

"My report's complete, Wager. And this is an ongoing case." Which meant that the notes and evidence which usually held the real information were hidden from any eyes except the detective assigned to the case.

Wager sipped at the thick mug of coffee. A gilt seal on its side said Adams County Sheriff's Department and reminded him that he was a guest, which was next to being a civilian. In Denver, the sheriff's main duty was to assist the court in the care and handling of prisoners and to serve papers; in the unincorporated areas of outlying counties, the duties had to include all the other areas of law enforcement, whether an agency was capable of them or not. "We have a similar homicide, Lee. Maybe you got a flier on it: Annette Sheldon, exotic dancer. One round to the back of the head, suspicion of rape. It happened less than a week before this one."

Lee shook his head. "I might have seen the report. I can't remember."

"It looks like the same m.o. It's possible that a special metro unit will be formed to take over the investigation of both homicides." That was unlikely. Metropolitan task forces were expensive and unwieldy, and the casual murders of a couple of nude dancers wasn't important enough politically to squeeze the effort and money out of the state attorney general's office. But Lee was new; he might not know that. "Our district attorney's talking about it. Naturally, the senior man would come from DPD."

"The body was found in Adams County!"

"But it's possible that the crime originated in Denver—she was probably abducted after work, in Denver County." And in Colorado, the origin of the crime dictated the responsible agency. Wager gave him the option: "If we work together, of course, then the DA probably won't see the need for a task force."

"You think it's the same killer?"

"I don't know. You haven't told me anything yet."

Lee didn't look happy as he felt his case start to slip between his fingers. But he finally shoved back from his imitation wood desk and pulled open a file drawer. Lifting out a dark folder, he laid it open in front of Wager. The photographs showed the body facedown on a bed of weeds and buffalo grass. It was a half-disrobed female, and very dead. That was all one could tell from what was left.

"No identifiable tire tracks or footprints?"

"I checked all that personally. We found what might have been tire tracks, but we couldn't get an impression—the scene was too old."

Wager leafed through the colored glossies and noticed, without saying anything, that the sequence of photographs showed minor disturbances in the evidence: in one photograph there was a cigarette butt; a similar shot later showed it was gone. Another pair of photos taken at different times revealed that the victim's head had been moved. The crime scene, in short, had been violated before the photographic record was complete, so none of it would be worth a tiddly-fart in court. "What about the cigarette butt?"

"Nothing. It was older than the crime. I told you, Wager, everything I found is in the report."

"Where'd you work before coming here?"

Lee's dark eyebrows lifted in surprise. "Newport Beach, California. Why?"

"I thought it might be back East. DPD gets a lot of applicants from there." Wager had heard some gossip about Newport Beach and its PD—the kind that warms the laughter-filled coffee breaks at three in the morning when patrols gather for their fifteen minutes around a café table. It was a playground for the rich, a tourist trap where little was spent on nonessentials such as police training. The department hired walk-ins because they were cheap, issued them badge and pistol, and told them to go out and bust tourists to keep the city treasury solvent with fines instead of tax money. Maybe it was to Lee's credit that he wanted to move away from an outfit like that. But poor training always showed up, and now Adams County would be the worse for it.

At the bottom of the folder, Wager found a sheet describing the subsequent investigation. Lee had interviewed the victim's mother, had visited Foxy Dick's, had appended a list of friends and acquaintances. At the top of that list was Williams's boyfriend, and there was a little check behind his name.

"The check means you interviewed the person?"

"That's right. And if there's nothing there, it means he didn't have any information to give."

"The boyfriend's alibi is good?"

"He's a night clerk at a gas station. He was working the night she disappeared."

"Did any of these people know Annette Sheldon?"

Lee blinked and tugged his cuffs out of his coat sleeves, then he shrugged them back in. "I didn't ask. There wasn't any reason to."

There was reason to. Wager's silence said as much. Lee, lips thin, poured himself another cup of coffee. "Have you had any reply from NCIC?" asked Wager.

"I put in a request this morning."

Or he would as soon as Wager left. Sighing, Wager tapped the file together and closed its cover. "Where do you go from here?"

"Just like you, I wait and see if something more turns up. There's sure as hell not much to work with now."

"Yeah. Well, let me tell you what we've got on Sheldon." He waited for the detective to take out a pencil and paper, but he didn't. Instead, his face settled into an expressionless stare that told Wager the man did not believe that the two homicides were related, that he did not want to pool his information with Wager or anyone else, and that he would be happy to see the Denver detective drive off into the sunset. So Wager kept to facts and away from hypotheses. "We still haven't found Sheldon's missing clothes, money, or car. She might have had as much as five hundred dollars when she left work. There's no medical evidence of rape. The only suspect we had was her husband, but he has no motive. The rest of it's just like your case—no one saw her leave work with anyone, no one knows of any enemies she had." A thought struck Wager. "Did Williams have a car?"

Lee said grudgingly, "A '79 Caprice. It hasn't been found yet."

Wager gave the man a description of Sheldon's missing automobile and a list of people he and Axton had interviewed. And that balanced out the exchange between them. Any more information he might need about the Adams County slaying would be Wager's to find, and they finished their cups of coffee talking about fishing streams.

• • •

The drive back seemed much longer than the ride out. The morning's freshness was gone from the wind, and Wager began to feel the drag of his duty tour heavy on his weary eyelids. It wasn't just the overtime—he was used to that. It was the burdensome knowledge that even with people who were supposed to be in the same business, there was competition and jealousy—and the result was inevitably a half-assed job that made you ask the equally inevitable question: Is it really worth the effort?

He pushed the radio buttons until a voice wailed in a nasal tone, "Does your love for me grow stronger or is your hate just plumb wore out?" Well, it was worth the effort—to Wager, anyway. He was subject to fitness reports and annual reviews, promotions and ratings, even the opinions of the men he worked with. But the only judgment that really meant a thing was what Wager thought of his own work. Not his team's work or his division's record, but his own. He knew when he did a good job or a poor one; nobody else's blame, nobody else's satisfaction really counted.

Which was why, despite the tired sting in his eyes and the heat that sapped his remaining energy and pulled him toward sleep as he drove, Wager did not go home. Instead, he turned off the freeway and cut across the northern part of town for one more stop.

This time, he approached down the alley. The service door at the rear of Nickelodeon Vending Repairs was open to catch any late-morning breeze, but there was none, and the dust that his tires raised from the gravel settled like a thin mist on the glossy enamel of his car's fenders. Sheldon turned from his workbench as Wager's car coasted to a stop, and now he watched without moving as Wager opened the door and got out.

"You're back soon enough," the man finally said. "You got news?"

Wager paused in the cool silence of the shop and looked at the two new roses beneath the shrine. "Nothing on Mrs. Sheldon. Did you or she ever know an Angela Sanchez Williams?"

Sheldon frowned and tugged at the corner of his mustache. "I don't think so. Why?"

"She's an exotic dancer. She was killed sometime last week, in the same manner as your wife."

Large and blurry behind their lenses, the blue eyes stared at Wager.

"Mr. Sheldon?"

They blinked rapidly and turned to the picture. "So it is some nut. It's some goddamned nut with a thing for killing dancers."

"It looks that way. But you're sure there's no link between your wife and Angela Williams?"

"Was she from the Cinnamon Club?"

"Foxy Dick's."

The man shook his head. "Annette never had anything to do with that place. It's a dump." His eyes met Wager's and held them. "Some sick, crazy bastard . . ."

· CHAPTER ·

It was Wager's turn to drive. As usual, they cruised the two northern districts of the city, with an occasional dip into the southwest quadrant where the West Ridge projects huddled in the smoky glow of a generator plant. They looped through those neighborhoods where trouble often burst out of sagging, crowded houses and apartments, filling the streets with blood and curses. But tonight, midweek, was a quiet one for Homicide, and the partners rode in a silence that had become as easy as conversation between them. Once, Axton mentioned that he was going to take his oldest boy camping on his next day off; Wager recommended Red Feather Lakes.

"This time of year they're still stocked. And it shouldn't be too crowded if it's not a weekend."

It had been one of his favorite spots when he was a kid and his old man was still alive. You could camp and then fish the small lakes for trout, casting your bubble almost silently on the glassy water just after sunup. Then, on the long drive back to Denver, you'd take that steep dirt road down into the Cache La Poudre valley and stream-fish. That was the best kind. It was a swift river with occasional deep holes where the big trout liked to hold themselves against the current. Wager had never caught one of those. But in the shallower parts of the stream, where the water widened over polished stones, the smaller trout would hit a tiny spinner with that solid thud that only stream fish have. A lot of the river was restricted to artificial lures, and the state wildlife agency was trying to bring back the green trout that so long ago had been fished out of the waters of Colorado. They'd have to be quick, though. There was more talk of damming the stream across a narrow part of the canyon. An Arab investment company had bought a million or so acres of high desert and suddenly discovered they'd need water in order to farm that land. The Cache La Poudre was one of the last undammed rivers along the east face of the Rockies, and to some it now seemed a shame to let all that water run free as far as the reservoirs on the prairie.

"The Cache La Poudre's up that way, isn't it?" Axton asked.

"Yes."

"That's a nice canyon. One of the prettiest."

It was. He hoped it stayed that way: free of dams and wild enough to worry people every spring with its runoff. But a lot of things never stayed the way they should. Maybe nothing did. Maybe when things stayed, they were dead. Still, he wondered why change so often seemed to be for the worse.

Turning into an ill-lit alley, he cut behind one of the newer housing projects for the evening's first routine sweep. These buildings were among the better offered by the city, and a hell of a lot finer than some of the places he had lived in as a kid. Two-story brown-brick townhouses, they had grassy lawns trimmed by the state and fenced playgrounds and a subsidized daycare center. It reminded him of the married housing provided for the NCOs at some of the military bases where he had been stationed. But Wager did not want to live here. Despite its surface placidity, maybe nobody wanted to live here. It was as if the place dammed the people up into a reservoir and they, without knowing why, rose with periodic restlessness against the barriers that held them. Especially the kids. The variety and type of crime the kids of this project committed were far more savage than anything Wager and his various street gangs had ever gotten mixed up in. When he was a restless kid who roamed the barrio with his buddies looking for excitement, people still laughed at the old ladies who locked their doors at night. Now, if you didn't, you were knifed. It was another of those changes.

Axton leaned forward to peer against the square shadows of the dark buildings. They were nearing the home of Pepe the Pistol, the kid who pumped all those .25-caliber bullets into his amigos. A call had come in saying that he was still in town and had sneaked back to his mother's house regularly for a home-cooked meal and condolences.

Wager flipped on the spotlight and swung it across the lawns, catching a gray cat whose eyes flashed green before its head and tail dropped into a quick trot. Nothing else moved in the roving finger of light. He clicked it off and turned out of the alley. If things stayed quiet, they'd sweep the area just before dawn. Then the next shift would cruise past a couple times. And the one after that. And so on. If Pepe didn't skip town, they'd get him sooner or later; when every officer in Denver knew who to look for, it was only a matter of time. Persistence, patience, time. The suspects you didn't know—the increasing number of stranger-to-stranger killings—those were the ones you measured your skill against. Like Annette Sheldon and now Angela Williams. At least that's how the rest of the Homicide team classified them—stranger-to-stranger. Calling them that made it easier to accept the fact that they were still unsolved. Some—Munn—accepted the fact that they would never be solved. Which, Wager had to admit, might turn out to be true; when you had a whole team assigned to an unsolved case, no single detective could be blamed.

Wager turned onto the bumpy and eroded Speer overpass; ahead of them and across the swirl of traffic filling the Valley Highway below, downtown Denver gave off a hollow glow from streetlamps and traffic lights that bounced across vacant sidewalks and office towers empty for the night.

"You wouldn't be headed over to Foxy Dick's?" Axton asked.

Angela Williams wasn't their case, but Foxy Dick's was in their jurisdiction. "Maybe we can help Lee out."

"I'm sure he'll be grateful."

Wager didn't give a damn what Lee thought. "It's a slow night. You got any better suggestions?"

Axton said mildly, "I'm with you, partner."

• • •

Foxy Dick's was farther out on Colfax and its marquee said *Girls Girls Girls.* It flashed on and off in a series of three short winks and then stayed on for a long count in case someone hadn't been able to read it the first time. Beneath that, a steadily glowing sign said LADIES NITE EVERY THURSDAY *Men Men Men,* and it was warming to see this small evidence of equality between the sexes. Like the Cinnamon Club, this entry was well lit, so a customer had to pause a moment before groping deeper into the darkness. Here, the bouncer was dressed casually in a dark turtleneck shirt and slacks and waited just inside the doorway, where a row of vending machines glowed coldly through their tiny windows. He smelled cop as soon as Wager and Axton stepped in.

"Can I help you men?"

Wager flashed his badge. "We'd like to talk to some of your people about Angela Williams."

"Again? I thought you got all you needed last time."

"We still need the killer," said Wager.

The bouncer frowned as he searched for any insult in Wager's words. "Oh." Then, "Come on. I'll take you back to the office."

He led them around the panel of opaque plastic sheets whose moving ripples of light teased passersby. The oval stage was at the far end of the main room and lit by the rapid flicker of a blue strobe light that froze the dancer into a series of still shots against the solid black background. Jammed all around was a crowd of chairs where a scattering of men and women sat and stared up at the girl. Wearing only cutoff designer jeans, she stood over one of the gaping men and bent from the waist, swaying her heavy breasts back and forth in time to the music's pulse. The man reached to slip a bill into her waistband and the girl swung a bit harder.

"Like putting a nickel in the slot," said Wager.

"What?" said the bouncer.

"He said you don't have a lot of people," said Axton.

"Yeah, well, it's Wednesday. It's not bad for a Wednesday."

The office cubicle was filled by a typewriter stand and an adding machine, a pair of filing cabinets and, in the middle, a small desk littered with celebrity magazines and newspapers. The magazines promised the true stories and asked penetrating questions. The newspapers were small in size and worn in print, and had mastheads like *The Singles' Trumpet* and *The Rocky Mountain Oyster.*

The man behind the desk was in his mid-thirties and had straight, sand-colored hair that was blow-dried into a shaggy cut. His baggy eyes lifted irritably toward them from an accounting sheet. "What?"

"Cops—ah—police, Charlie. It's about Angela again."

"Shit! We been through all this once. I told you everything I know."

"You told some other people," said Wager.

"So you can't talk to each other? You got to keep coming back here? Crapping business is bad enough without Angela getting herself killed and bringing you people around all the time!"

Axton closed the door behind the bouncer as he left. "Has business been that slow?"

"Everything's slow. Except the goddamn bills. They're quick enough."

"Are you the manager?" asked Wager.

"Owner. One thing I'm grateful for, I'm not the manager. Business doesn't get any better, he's the next to go."

"Where's he?"

"Working the music. We take turns."

"What's your name, please?" asked Max.

The man sighed with exaggerated patience and ran his fingers through his stiff hair, then patted it back in place over a high forehead. "Thomas. Charles Thomas. I've had this place for three years. I was here the last night Angela was. I saw her make her split with the bartender, and I didn't see her after that. She missed a few days, which is par for the course in this line of work. Next thing I hear from the cops, she's been killed. I don't know who did it." He flapped a hand at the music thumping against the closed door. "Somebody out there. That's my guess."

"Why?"

"Who else?"

"Maybe a boyfriend," said Wager. "Or her ex-husband."

"Maybe. That's your job to find out, right? All I know is, it wasn't me." Thomas leaned back and stared at the ceiling a moment. "I hear her husband—ex-husband—moved away. California or somewhere. Boyfriends . . . She had a couple, I guess. Nobody she met here," he added quickly. "No hustling the customers—that's a house rule. Some nights I got more Vice cops here than I do legitimate customers. And the cops," he added, "don't buy worth shit."

"But you know she had boyfriends?"

"Sometimes a guy might pick her up after work."

"Did you ever see him? His car?"

The man thought a moment. "Not him, no. I saw his car once. A Chevy, I think. Dark green, maybe. Or blue."

"License number?"

"Give me a break, man! This was a month, six weeks ago."

"Did you tell the other officers about it?" asked Max.

"I only just remembered it."

"Did you know Annette Sheldon?" asked Wager.

"Who?"

"Annette Sheldon. Shelly. She danced over at the Cinnamon Club."

"That dump?" Thomas frowned with thought. "No. But a lot of the girls move from club to club and some change their names. They're so bad they got to. You got a picture?"

Wager just happened to. He handed Thomas the copy of her publicity shot.

"No. . . . She's got nice boobs, but I don't recognize them." He looked up. "This is the other one that got killed, what, a couple weeks ago?"

"That's right. You never heard Angela mention her name?"

"No. Jesus, we got somebody killing the merchandise now. Business is that bad, and now we got this maniac."

"We'd like to talk to your girls."

"Shake them up a little more? That's what you want to do?"

"Right."

"That's what I figured." His hand waved over the stack of newspapers. "You know how hard it is to find a good dancer even when they're not scared?" Neither Wager nor Axton did, and Thomas sighed. "Come on."

He led them through the half-empty club to a tiny, filthy room. The smell was close with strong perfume riding on the odor of a stopped-up toilet half-glimpsed through a doorless frame. A lone girl sat at the smeared mirror and quickly pulled on her barmaid's costume. She was the same one who had been onstage when Axton and Wager came in.

"Silhouette, these guys are cops. They want to ask some more questions about poor Angela. I'll tell the other girls what they're after. Help them out, right? And then it's back on the floor as soon as you can—oh, yeah, you got an extra set tonight." He explained to Axton, "We're short. Two of the girls didn't show up." He left, shaking his head, "The help these days, Jesus!"

Silhouette looked better in the flashing lights; up close you noticed her face and the heavy flesh that was barely held taut by still young skin. She was, officially, twenty-one. But Wager suspected she was a couple years younger than that. This was her first dancing job; she never knew Angela Williams very well; she had never heard of Annette Sheldon; she was a little nervous at the idea of a murderer who specialized in exotic dancers.

"It sounds like, you know, Jack the Ripper or something. I wouldn't do it if it wasn't for the money. Some of those guys . . ." She gave a little shudder. "They're real creeps."

"Does anyone in particular bother you?"

"No. There's a rule: no touching the girls. It's just some of them, they say things . . . you know . . . like they want you to do kinky things."

"Do you?"

"No! But some of the girls do—if it's a big house and things are rolling, there's a couple who do those things. They laugh about it." She added, "They get the big tips, too."

"What's the owner, Thomas, say about that?"

"What the hell does he care? One of the first things he told me was that I'm a piece of meat to him. A 'marketable commodity' he called me, and as long as I bring in the cash I'm on the payroll." She shrugged. "But that's show biz, right?"

"And you make good money in tips?"

"Wages. We get hourly wages—six-fifty—and ten percent of the tips. We turn it over to the bartender every night."

The girls at the Cinnamon Club did a lot better. "But you still make good money?"

Her head went back with a little gesture of defiance. "A lot of times I make seventy, eighty dollars a night. I couldn't make that nowhere else—I quit high school. It was for creeps. Now I got a car and my own place and I do what I want with my life."

Which, if it was true, was what a lot of people hungered to say. Wager watched her go out to do her stint at the tables, and Axton gave a half-shake of his head, his blue eyes heavy with a vision of the girl's future. Wager, too, could guess what would happen to her in a couple years. But he didn't worry about it; he'd seen too much of it already, and he bet she had a good idea of what was coming herself. Like she said: it was her life and her choices, and that kind of freedom was worth a lot. And many times it was only found at the edge of the law.

Silhouette sent the next girl back from the floor; Sugar Plum was a tall girl with negroid features and pale yellow skin. She wore the tight shorts and thin blouse of the barmaid, and spoke aggressively. "They told me you wanted to ask some questions about Angela."

He did, and got the familiar answers. Then he asked what Lee had not: "Did you know Annette Sheldon? She danced over at the Cinnamon Club."

Sugar Plum looked at the photograph. "Yeah. I knew her. I used to work at that dump."

"How long ago was that?"

"Seven or eight months ago. But my agent got me a better deal here."

"Your 'agent'?" asked Wager.

Her face darkened slightly. "I'm in the entertainment business. I have an agent."

"That's a good idea," said Axton. "A lot of these girls don't and they get taken advantage of."

"It's their own fault, then. There's always a demand for good dancers. Like me."

"How well did you know Shelly?"

"Enough to say hello to and goodbye to." Her lips twisted slightly in one of those grins that shattered a pretty face and Wager understood why she smiled so seldom. "In show business, you don't make many friends."

"Why's that?"

"Everybody's after something, and nobody's in it for their health."

"Was Annette Sheldon—Shelly—after something?"

"Like a shark. She'd go after your regulars if you didn't watch her. She tried that shit on me once."

Axton asked, "What'd you do?"

"I told her to cut that shit out. I saw what she was doing —she kept her eye out for any big tipper, anybody's regular, and then she'd play up to him, you know. Thought she could dance!"

"But she did pretty well?" Wager asked.

Sugar Plum's smooth shoulders bobbed. "Everybody wants more, and she wanted more than most."

"Did she go after it off the dance floor maybe?"

"What's that mean? What're you trying to say?"

"Did she do any hustling?" Wager asked. "Did she peddle her tail to anybody after work?"

"She might have—I don't know. If there was money in it, I wouldn't put it past her."

"Did you ever see her with anyone in particular? Any favorite customer?"

"Sure, her regulars. Listen, a lot of men won't buy drinks from anybody but their favorite girl." She started to smile but caught it. "Real fans—they come in three or four times a week and order drinks from one girl."

"Is that all they want?" insisted Wager. "To buy drinks?"

"No. But most of them don't come on. Real gentlemen, right? I think they want you to give it to them for free—not just a screw, but real love, you know? Very polite and smooth when they're here, and then they go home and dream up all sorts of weirdo things they're doing to you."

This time the crooked smile broke through. "Go home and make love to old lady five fingers!"

"Did Angela have many steady customers like that?"

"Not so many she didn't want more."

"What about the same man?" asked Wager intently. "Did you ever see the same man talking to both Angela and Shelly?"

She shook her head. "Not that I remember. Maybe . . . I just don't remember. Unless they're tipping me, I don't even see them. I don't go after nobody else's regulars."

Axton handed her a business card. "If you do remember, miss—think it over carefully—if you do remember, please give us a call. Any time of day or night. It could be very important."

Her tongue, round and pink, slid across her lower lip. "You think the same john might have killed them both?"

"We don't know what to think. But it's a good possibility." Wager added, "If so, he might join another girl's fan club."

"Well, it's not like working in a church, that's for sure."

"Has anyone ever followed you or threatened you, miss?"

"I don't give them a chance." She ran a hand down the sides of the sheer blouse that revealed her nipples as dark, pert shadows. "A lot of men follow me, mister. But the only ones that catch me are the ones I want to."

"But you didn't see anyone following Angela or Shelly."

"No. But I know this much: it was their own fault if they let somebody rape them. A woman doesn't have to put up with that shit. In this business, you learn what to do."

Three other girls were called off the floor, one by one, and Axton and Wager went through the same questions with them, urging them to call the number on the business card if they remembered anything else. It didn't seem likely. Their answers all boiled down to the same familiar response: they did not know Angela well; they saw no one with her; they never heard of Annette Sheldon. And they weren't very eager to call the cops about anything. One other theme emerged—business was bad and getting worse, and four or five girls worked only on weekends now. Wager and Axton would have to come back if they wanted to interview them.

• • •

They sat for a few minutes in the unmarked car and watched the thinning traffic beneath the line of marquees. Even the radio transmissions from normally busy District Two were slow; scattered reports told of accidents, of domestic disturbances, of frightened women listening to a prowler snip at their window screens. Now and then an officer replied to the dispatcher, his microphone catching the pulsing wail of a siren, and a slight tightness in his voice the only indication that his car was hurtling down some dark street guided by one white-knuckled fist. But most of the radio traffic was the dispatcher's periodic status requests from the fleet of silent uniformed officers cruising the alleys and byways of the city.

"Do you want to go by the Cinnamon Club again?" asked Max.

Wager shook his head. "Angela never worked there."

"So what's the next step?"

"I think I'll talk to her mother in the morning. Maybe Lee missed something."

"It's a good thing you're not a union member." The union limited the uncompensated overtime a cop could do, whether he was willing or not.

"I don't think the killer is, either."

• • •

Angela Williams's mother was dark-complexioned. Her black hair, streaked with gray, was cropped short over a face whose brown eyes still showed the weariness of crying as well as a certain blank acceptance of one more heavy blow. She glanced at Wager's identification and then held open the screen door. "Come in, please," she said tiredly. "You want some coffee?"

"No, ma'am. Just some questions about Angela."

She led Wager into a small front room where a toy dump truck and a scattering of brightly colored plastic tools littered the worn carpet in front of a large television set. The TV flickered with a morning talk show, the audio a faint murmur, and a smiling emcee leaned back to exchange pleasantries with a wild-haired starlet who showed a lot of very white teeth. "He's still asleep." She saw Wager's glance. "I let him stay up and watch 'The Fall Guy.' He likes all the excitement. People getting blown up—people getting killed."

"How old is he?"

"Five. Six in November." Her shoulders lifted and fell in a sigh. "And just as sweet as the day is long."

"Is his father going to take him?"

The first spark of life came to her eyes. "His father! Ha! I wouldn't let that . . . that . . ."

"Yes, ma'am. Is his father still out in California?"

"Oregon. And he wouldn't even come for the funeral." Angrily lighting a cigarette, she gestured for Wager to sit on one of the chairs whose arms and back looked overstuffed and hot.

They were, and puffed out the faint aroma of stale dirt. "I understand Angela had a boyfriend. Brad Uhlan."

"Yes. I think they were going to get married, maybe. He's a nice boy. He's been good to Eddie since it happened."

"He was at work when it happened?"

"Yes."

"What kind of car does he drive, Mrs. Sanchez?"

"It ain't a car—it's a truck. A Dodge pickup with one of them camp shells on it."

Wager took a moment to leaf through the scribbled lines

in his small green notebook. "Did she have any other boyfriends? Anybody else she went out with?"

"Not for a long time. She didn't have no time. She worked nights and slept late. Afternoons, she liked to spend with Eddie. She was a good mother—and with no child support from that crud." The cigarette crackled as she drew fire into it. "She worked at that place because it paid real good money, but she was a good mother. She was a good girl, too."

"Did she ever go out with anyone who drove a dark blue or green Chevrolet—a late model?"

"I don't think so . . . not that I remember. That other policeman, he didn't ask that. Did you find out something more about who did it?"

"No, ma'am. It's just a possibility. Did Angela ever mention the name Annette Sheldon or Shelly?"

"She's a dancer?"

"Yes."

She thought back and then shook her head. "Not that I remember. She didn't really talk much about the other girls. Sometimes when they did something funny or when she was mad at one, like that one with the dumb name, what's her name . . . Sugar Plum. God, what these girls call themselves nowadays."

"What happened?"

"She's a hustler—a prostitute—she's always trying to pick up the big tippers, you know. Angela couldn't stand her. Nobody can."

"Did they fight?"

"Fight? You mean . . . ? No. Angela just talked about her sometimes. Mostly she wanted to forget work when she was home. I think she didn't want Eddie to know what she did." Mrs. Sanchez added quickly, "She wasn't ashamed of it! Nor me either—honest work is good work, and she had herself and that little boy to look after." Her voice dropped again. "My husband's dead. I'm on Social Security." She sighed and glanced at the toy truck. "Thank God she saved up some for Eddie. She didn't spend much—I couldn't of made it without her paying room and board, and I don't know what I'm going to do now. Food prices . . . everything . . ."

"Angela had a car?"

"Yes. One of them Caprices. Almost new and paid cash for it, and now the insurance company don't want to make good—they want to see if it turns up before they pay off. Maybe you can help me with that? They're quick enough to take your money, but when it comes time to pay . . . !"

"I don't know that I can help, Mrs. Sanchez. But there's an office for customer complaints in the state insurance division." He asked for a telephone book and looked it up in the blue pages. "Here it is—'consumer complaints.' Give them a call and see what they can do."

"Well, I guess that's better than nothing—I'm a consumer and I got a complaint. But I bet they're on the side of the big companies. Them agencies, they know what side their bread's buttered on." The corners of her mouth lifted and fell. "I appreciate your help, though, officer. God knows, that poor child will need what help he can get in this world."

"Yes, ma'am. About how much did Angela make, Mrs. Sanchez?"

The woman's eyes narrowed slightly and she stubbed out the cigarette in one of those ashtrays that was crusted in small hemispheres of glass. It looked to Wager like a wad of blisters. "Some weeks she'd do better than others."

"She was paid every week?"

The gray-streaked head bobbed.

"Seventy? Eighty a night? Some of the girls told me they made as much as four hundred a week."

"Yeah. Sometimes even better. And she didn't throw it away like the rest of those girls. Easy come, easy go, most of those girls."

"Eight hundred? A thousand a week?"

"I don't think that much. I don't know for sure. It was her money. She earned it. I'm her mother—she'd tell me sometimes if a week was good or bad. But it was her money and I didn't stick my nose into it."

"Did she have any debts?"

"She didn't owe nobody nothing. She paid cash for everything. That TV"—she pointed to the large set where, now, the talk-show host was singing and grinning at the same time—"she bought that for my birthday and counted out the bills right into the salesman's hand. Fifties and hundreds. You could have knocked him over with a feather."

"And you don't have any debts?"

"No—this house is mine. Food and heat and taxes, that's all."

"So Angela saved a lot. . . . In the bank?"

"Some." She did not like this direction.

"Where else?" Wager finally had to spell it out. "Look, Mrs. Sanchez, did your daughter ever lend money to anyone? Did anyone owe her enough money or want money from her badly enough to kill her?"

"That's what you think?"

"I don't know what to think. I'm going over possibilities. Is that a possibility?"

"Don't you bully me! I may be an old woman all alone with her only daughter dead and a poor little boy to raise, but you don't have to bully me!"

"Yes, ma'am. I'm sorry. I don't care how much Angela made. I just want to know what happened to the money in case it has something to do with her death."

"She was killed by some loco—one of them men, that's who killed her!" Then she said, "Certificates."

"What's that?"

"These—what do you call them—CDs. She'd save up five thousand and then go down and get a certificate. They pay good interest and they're safe."

"But she didn't lend money to anyone? Not even to her boyfriend?"

"Brad? He never asked. Not that I know. Sometimes she'd pay for the dates, sometimes he would. But lending money"— her head wagged—"that's business. She invested. 'Jesus saves but Moses invests,' we used to joke."

"She didn't invest in any business or real estate—nothing like that?"

"Certificates."

Wager thanked her and left his card and sat for a long time in his car trying to see down the avenues of possibility that his questions had opened up. He couldn't see very far, and there wasn't much there anyway. It was as if he had his hand deep in a hole, but through the blackness and beyond sight his groping fingers could sense a presence. Not touch; not that definite. Rather, a mere thickening of the air, and even that might not be real.

Starting the car, he listened for a moment to the deep, muffled rumble of the engine. That was something you could really touch: a good car, a heavy engine, the lunge of a steering wheel guiding a car fast down an open road. It was something a hell of a lot more concrete than a vague hunch. But hunches were better than nothing, and on the way back to his apartment, he stopped at a pay phone to dial a number from his notes. After a lot of rings, Brad Uhlan answered groggily and Wager identified himself and said what he wanted.

"She was picked up one night after work?" Uhlan repeated.

"By someone with a dark blue or green Chevrolet. Late model."

"How long ago?"

"Maybe a month. Did she go out with any other men, Mr. Uhlan?"

"I don't think so. She'd have told me if she did—we were pretty sure, you know, about getting married someday; we didn't have no secrets from each other. Maybe three weeks ago?"

"Could be. Why?"

"Well, I came by on my night off in my brother's car. It's a metallic green Caprice—'80. My truck was in the shop."

Wager thanked him and crossed off the item that had been sitting expectantly in its blank space on a leaf of his notebook. Another hunch, another try, another dead end.

• CHAPTER •

When Wager reported for duty twenty minutes early, as usual, the stale air of midnight was stirred by a flutter of excitement. Devereaux, shirt open at the neck and tie loose, mopped his forehead with a handkerchief and looked sheepish. Ross, his partner, sat frowning with his arms crossed.

"What's up?" Wager asked.

"Pepe the Pistol," said Devereaux. "I almost got the little fucker."

"Where is he now?"

"If we knew," said Ross, "we'd be doing the paperwork on him, wouldn't we?"

Devereaux dragged the handkerchief under his chin and down his neck. "Somebody called in, said he was over at his girlfriend's house. We went by and spotted him and he lit out as soon as he saw the car. Ross drove across the goddamn lawn with the kid in the headlights. So he cut between two buildings in the project. The car couldn't make it, so I went after him. I was that close!" He held his hands up a foot apart. "The little shit was climbing a fence and I got that close!"

"Armed?"

"He didn't flash any iron. He was too busy running." The handkerchief stopped under Devereaux's chin as he remembered something. "But the pissant's pistol hasn't been found yet, has it?"

"No." Wager grinned. "He probably had it in his hip

pocket, waiting for you to grab him. Then he'd pump six shots in you. What's his girlfriend say?"

"She wouldn't answer the door and we didn't have a warrant." Devereaux stood and folded his handkerchief. "Ross figures the kid was timing his visits for the change of shift, so we were in the neighborhood early. But we didn't know about the girlfriend's house until the call came in. That close!"

"That's real good thinking, Ross. Does the union demand extra pay for that?"

"Up yours, scab." The dark-haired detective strode to the board and flipped his name slide to Off Duty. "It don't take much to outthink a Mex."

Wager grinned at the back disappearing rigidly toward the elevators. "Have a good day, Ross!"

"Aw, Gabe. Why do you say things like that?"

"Because it makes me feel good, Dev. Ross is one of life's little pleasures."

Devereaux went out shaking his head. "Good night, Gabe."

Wager, starting his shift, half-listened to the radio sitting in its charger unit on his desk. The voices, alternating with the dispatcher's, were coming from the housing project where Ross had called in the alert for Pepe the Pistol. But they wouldn't have any luck tonight, Wager knew. The kid had found some hole in the tangle of dormitorylike buildings and was in it now, probably pissing one minute and laughing the next, trying to convince himself that he could outrun the cops forever. If the kid was smart, he'd head for LA or even Chicago. But he didn't seem that smart. Or hadn't been able to steal a car yet. Or maybe his mother just hadn't been able to borrow enough money to send him on his way. Pepe wasn't your triple-A credit risk. Still, it was unusually dumb to hang around like that, and Wager wondered idly why the kid did it.

At three minutes to midnight, Max came in with his handful of the day's mail and dealt Wager's out on the glass-topped desk.

"What's new?"

He told him about Devereaux and Pepe the Pistol. "I also set up a meet with Mike Moffett for around one."

"Moffett in Vice? What do we want with Vice?"

"Maybe he can tell us something we don't know about the skin shops."

Axton paused in his thumbing through the envelopes. "Annette's been bothering you, has she?"

"Yeah." Wager leaned back in the creaking swivel chair and tugged gently at a loose thread on a cuff button; the thread seemed to leap out and the button fell to the glass with a tiny click. "Damn." He fished in the drawer for a paper clip to hold his sleeve together. "I talked to Sheldon again."

Max looked up from a brightly colored sheet of paper that had pictures of Colorado mountain land for sale in Conejos County. A fisherman was smiling at a gigantic trout on his line, and the jumping fish was smiling back. Max could get a free gift if he would just drive over and look at the land. "And?"

"Sheldon's hiding something."

"You're sure of that?"

"I am."

"Is that why you went after Ross?"

Devereaux must have said something to Max when he came in. "What's that mean?"

"It means you get feisty when you can't nail something down. Which," he tossed the land offer into the trash, "is a hell of a lot of the time. No offense intended, partner."

• • •

They met the Vice detectives at a White Spot café on the corner of Pearl and Colfax, near the lower end of the strip.

Moffett and his partner, Nolan, sat in their unmarked cruiser in the restaurant's trash-littered parking lot. At the car window, half-bent with age and wearing what used to be a suit, an old black man grinned and pointed with his chin at something or someone across the crowded street under the lights of an adult-movie arcade. Moffett, behind the wheel, laughed back and the old man, his red-rimmed eyes slanting in Wager's direction as they walked up, murmured something and slid away into the clusters of mostly young men and women drifting past the café.

"Hello, Max—Wager."

He had noticed it before: most of the other officers called Axton by his first name and used only Wager's last. He liked it that way—it gave him a little extra distance from everyone. "Wasn't that Berry Juice Johnson?" Wager asked as they settled into the backseat. "I thought he was dead by now."

"He'll outlive all of us. He was telling me who he wants for his new main squeeze—LaBelle Brown. You know her?"

"I busted her once for dealing. She out again?"

"Out and working, but I don't think she's dealing. Not big, anyway." He wagged a thumb toward the arcade. The woman, watching the automobile traffic out of the corner of her eye, strolled along the curb to the end of the block, swung slowly about with her white purse over her dark shoulder, and began walking back.

"Say hello for me," said Wager. "I think she's got fond memories."

"You say hello," grunted Moffett. "Last time I popped her, she about tore my head off."

"It wasn't his head she wanted," laughed Nolan. "She was just too stoned to tell the difference."

"Did you get a make on that rolling drugstore?" asked Max. "The one we spotted a couple weeks ago?"

"The dark van? Hell, we've been trying to nail that son of a bitch for six months. He sets up his meets ahead of time only with people he knows, and it all goes down in ten minutes. He's pushing a lot of stuff, too. And getting bigger. If you see him again, use the telephone—he's got a police-band scanner mounted in that rig."

"Will do," said Wager. "What can you tell us about the Cinnamon Club or Foxy Dick's?"

Moffett turned his police radio down to a crackling mutter. "They're your basic skin shops. I think Foxy Dick's is a little harder place. The new guy at the Cinnamon Club—what's his name?"

"Berg," Axton said.

"Yeah, him. He thinks he's putting on a class act." Moffett spat out the window. "But they're all alike: scum traps."

"We had a victim out of the Cinnamon Club; she had a trace of cocaine."

"Not to be surprised. Most of the girls have habits. Half the pushers on this side of town make runs every night to supply the girls. That's why that guy in the black van's moved in—it's a good market." Moffett tilted back over the seat to explain. "A cop walks into one of those places, Gabe, and a red light goes on behind the bar. You see half-a-dozen dealers and waitresses head for the back like the place was on fire."

Nolan snorted a laugh. "When we want someone we stand outside the back door and send a couple uniforms in the front. It's like picking grapes."

"Do the girls push, too?"

"Some do. But it's not your usual thing. Most of them use everything they can get their hands on. They might steer a customer to a dealer for a fee or a free toot, but that's about it."

"True," added Nolan. "There's a large amount of coke on the scene now. Some of the girls dance four, five sets—coke keeps them going. It's a lot of exercise. That and alcohol. Drinks are free for the girls; it loosens them up onstage.

They can drink all they want as long as they can still dance, and, man, some of those girls can really sauce it away."

"What about whoring?" Wager asked. "Any of them make a little on the side?"

"On the side, on the back, on the front—you name it," grinned Nolan. "As long as they don't solicit customers in the club, they're safe. But who in hell can stop them from setting up dates after hours or on their days off?"

"They're not all whores," said Moffett. "Some of them; not all."

"Perhaps," said Nolan. "But if the rent's due and they're a little short, they'll pull a trick. A customer goes in and sees something he likes, he shows a couple hundred and tucks it back in his pocket." He grinned again. "She understands what it means."

"You ever bust any that way?"

"Used to. Can't anymore. Entrapment."

"Ever bust an Annette Sheldon—Shelly—or Angela Williams?"

Moffett said No. "I thought about that when I saw the Homicide reports come through. But I never had a contact on either one."

The men fell silent and watched the swarm of pedestrians and motor traffic pass the café's parking lot. Moffett, lighting a cigarette, glanced at Wager's sleeve. "Staples are better."

"What?"

"Your sleeve—the paper clip. Staple it next time."

"Right." Moffett, like Wager and so many other cops, was divorced; his ex-wife had custody of their two sons and most of his paycheck.

"Jesus," said Nolan. "Here's comes Raymondo."

He nodded toward a tall black jaywalking through the stop-and-go traffic. He wore something that looked like a white string-bead cape across his bare shoulders and down to his hips. Below that was a black jockstrap, and his legs were bare down to the high-heeled, white thong sandals that poised him on tiptoes. A voice from a passing car howled at him and he grinned and made kissing motions toward it and patted his nude buttocks.

Moffett yawned. "I got to admit, he is one of our brighter sights."

"Yes, indeed," Nolan said. "His real name's Raymond Green. We ran a make on him—nothing. Just your average Colfax citizen."

Wager had seen him before; it was hard not to. "How else might a girl make extra money at one of those skin houses?"

"She's got to have something to sell, I guess," said Moffett. "A lot of money?"

"Sometimes double the tips."

"That's a lot of money." The Vice detective's eyes covered the flowing crowd in a practiced scan while he thought. "Selling herself or selling dope. That's all I can think of."

Wager didn't think Annette Sheldon was selling herself—her free time seemed accounted for. But there was that cocaine trace in her corpse. And none of the other girls would mention Annette's or anybody else's habit—not to a cop.

Axton and Wager thanked the Vice team and sat in their own car a few minutes to watch the parade of cowboy hats with feathers, straw farmers' hats, afros brunette and blond, even a mohawk cut, which Wager had last seen in the late fifties when he was a kid.

"You think Annette was pushing on the side?" Max asked.

"Her husband says she brought home a lot of money—more than Berg says she made."

That little half-tune whistled between Max's teeth. "What about Williams? Did you talk to her mother?"

"She's closer to what she was supposed to bring home. If she was dealing, it wasn't much."

"So there's still no connection."

"Just the manner of death. The same m.o."

They watched the passing show. Across the street, LaBelle Brown smiled widely as a car slowed to a stop and she bent to talk to the driver before getting in. On the corner where the bright entry to a porno arcade lit the sidewalk, a pair of young men in cutoff denims kissed each other. A shirtless lad wearing bib overalls and barefoot said something to make them laugh, and a young white girl, seeing LaBelle away from her place, hoisted her hot pants and began strolling the curb.

"They're all playing at being something else," said Axton. "What is it, the television generation? Images become substance? Maybe they think they can flip a channel and be someone else with a different hat."

Here came Max's sociology bullshit again. "It's no different from any other uniform," Wager said. "Looking different is looking the same. And if I was born like some of that scum, I'd try to change my looks, too."

"Gabe, I think your milk of human kindness has curdled."

• • •

Wager didn't have a chance to find out what that meant; the radio popped its call for any Homicide detective, and the quiet spell of the last few tours was blown all to hell with a shotgun slaying. By the time Wager and Axton made their run across town and into the quiet neighborhood of small, neat homes that looked like Monopoly houses in a row, the medical examiner had come and gone, and the lab people were already sampling and photographing.

Axton, looming even larger in the shadow of red and blue lights flashing across the grassy yard, found the uniformed officer who first responded to the call. He began taking the man's report; Wager started to sketch and measure. In the background, beneath the various laconic voices of the radios, a steady moaning sob came from a woman who sat on the front step holding herself and rocking. Another woman had an arm across her rounded shoulders and said helplessly, "There, there," over and over.

"What's this one, officer?" The question came from a short, slender man dressed all in black: shoes, pants, and string tie with large loops. He wore a black nylon Eisenhower jacket with a white patch on the arm that said CRS. Behind him, a woman in black slacks and a similar uniform jacket peered over his shoulder.

"Domestic," said Wager. "Son shot his father." He stepped aside to let Lincoln Jones flash a series of photographs of the form lying on the lawn. It was curled from the impact of the round, but any pain had long since ebbed.

"Well, whenever you're ready, we're just over here. Okay?"

CRS stood for Cadaver Removal Service. Somebody on the city council figured they could save money by letting private enterprise haul the dead rather than dispatching a city-owned ambulance and crew. They must have figured right, because by now a half-dozen husband-and-wife teams had submitted bids to serve different areas of town. Max once guessed that there were fewer mom-and-pop groceries than there were mom-and-pop cadaver services.

Wager said "Fine" and stretched a tape measure from the corner of the porch to the head of the victim, whose lank iron-gray hair sprayed out in violent stillness. At the far end of the small wooden porch he could hear Axton talking to a young man who sat staring dully at the focus of Wager's measurements: "Tommy, I want to tell you what your rights are, and then I want you to tell me what happened. Tommy? You hear me?"

"Do you need some light, officer?" From just beyond the glow-pink tape roping the crime scene, a mobile television crew began setting up quickly to film the body as it was removed. A technician pointed to the light frame he balanced on his shoulder. "We got lights if you need them." Behind the crewman, the woman from CRS quickly checked her makeup with a small compact and patted her stiff blond hair into place.

Wager shook his head. The light might help, but it meant the delay of working around another pair of feet. And the paperwork, even on a smoking-gun murder like this, was going to take the rest of the night.

• • •

Modern police management worshiped quantification, and statistics were forever being updated and refined and compared. If homicides declined a percentage point or two, crime was being beaten. If they went up, the bad guys were winning. There were figures on the ratio between solved and unsolved cases in every category, and a red pencil marked a quantifiable line between the acceptable and unacceptable jobs done by departments. There was even an annual time study of the number of crime reports divided into the total man-hours available for each division and section. The result indicated the average amount of time that could be allotted to each crime. In Homicide, it was sixteen hours. Last night's domestic slaying had taken Wager and Axton only five hours each to wrap up a case for the DA's office, so Wager figured that left the remaining six free for Sheldon and Williams. At least that's what he'd tell the division chief, Doyle, if there were any union complaints about Wager putting in more unpaid overtime. Or maybe he'd just laugh at Doyle—there was genuine pleasure in seeing the Bulldog sweat, caught between a red-faced, fist-thumping Ross and Doyle's own knowledge that homicides weren't solved by time studies or union rules.

At any rate, Wager was on the street by nine that night, his Trans Am, with its goosed peacock on the hood, prowling the darker avenues that fed into the glare of East Colfax.

In the shadows, figures singly and in pairs drifted toward the light, drawn out of their efficiency apartments or from the tiny rooms carved from made-over mansions and paid for each day in advance. Even if, as with most of them, there was no business waiting on the strip, there was still the action. There was always something to see that was better than the close, stained walls of a rented room.

Wager was looking for some of those people who saw the most, those for whom knowing meant money. His list of CIs —Citizen Informants—went back years, to his long stint of duty on the Organized Crime Unit. Every cop had his list, and the names were on it for a variety of reasons: a kind of perverted friendship, sometimes fear, even the need to feel important. With some, an angle with the police became an ace in the hole in case of trouble elsewhere; with others, it was the hunger to know someone constant in a world where faces shifted and disappeared like sand in the wind. But however they got on the list, CIs were not team property —they were a cop's own, and you guarded the good ones like a kid guards candy.

When Wager finally spotted the glimmer of white moving steadily and massively through the gloom beneath the spread of ash trees, he flicked his high beams twice, pulled slowly past the man, and turned at the next corner into an even shadier street. A minute or two later the unhurried steps followed, and he heard the lurching gasp of the heavy man before the panama suit and hat leaned to the open window.

"As I live and breathe—the Spicky Piggy hisself."

"Hello, Fat Willy. I thought they'd have you buried in two graves by now."

"Two graves! Ain't two gonna be big enough for this man. What's this I hear you on Homicide now?" Willy liked to stress the black accent when he spoke to Wager. Wager heard the big man's telephone voice—his "white lips," he called it—when Willy was making a deal with some Anglo.

But the Chicano-black rivalry was still strong with Willy, and Wager sometimes wondered if the man expected him to sound like the Frito Bandito.

"That's right. And I keep expecting to run across you."

"Ha. It ain't 'cause some don't want it that way. How come you got off the Crime unit? They finally figure out you a crooked cop?"

"Naw. The city's cleaned up. Organized crime is no more, Willy, so they disbanded the unit and transferred me to Homicide. Pretty soon we'll have that cleaned up, too."

"Sure it is, and sure you will!" Willy tugged the brim of his hat closer across his face as the sound of steps passed in the dark behind him. "You cops ain't cleaned up nothing, and you never will, man."

"Faith, hope, and charity, Willy. Without these, a man is nothing."

"Well, I got faith you ain't never going to do it, and I hope you ain't looking at me for no favors, 'cause if you looking, it sure ain't gonna be for charity—ha!"

"I didn't expect it would be." Wager held up a bill and Willy slipped it from between his fingers and tilted it against the dim light of the street.

"Only a fifty? That's toilet paper, man!"

"You can always give it back."

But the bill, folded small, had already disappeared somewhere under the expanse of his linen coat. "What you trying to buy for that little tidbit? I hope it ain't much."

"A line on who's pushing at the Cinnamon Club and at Foxy Dick's."

"Half the telephone book, Wager! You want the names in alphabetical order or by the pound?"

"Tell me about it."

"It's no big secret—except from you cops. Fifteen, twenty dudes got regular runs to all them places. Just like the mailman. Keeps the girls happy, you dig?"

"All of them big?"

"Naw, man. They got too many for all of them to be big. But different girls got different contacts."

"Who has runs to both the Cinnamon Club and Foxy Dick's?"

"Now that I don't know right off. But it's got to be some of them. Them skin houses is one of the best markets around."

"I'd like to find out."

"You done overpaid me."

"And I'd like to know why they might want to snuff a couple dancers."

"You just underpaid me."

"If you find out something, I'll try to balance the account." He held out a card.

"Sho' you will. What's that?"

"A business card. It's got my home number on the back."

"I don't want that damn thing on my sweet body. Just tell me your new number, man. I got a memory for phone numbers—it's my business, you dig?"

Wager told him. The man's broad hand tipped lightly at his hat brim and, in the gloom, Willy's teeth shone briefly. "I will call you, Wager. Don't you call me."

He watched the pale suit fade into the darkness beneath the trees, then he pulled away from the curb to look for a telephone. His next contact had never been more than a voice over the wire or an envelope slipped under a door. As usual, the number was answered by a female.

"Is Doc there?"

"I'll see. Who wants him?"

"Gabe."

Then a man's voice, slightly raspy from cigarettes and nervously quick. "Say something, man."

"Hello, Doc."

"Jesus Christ, it is you! Hey, man, I couldn't believe it when the ginch said it was you. Hey, you back in Narcs, baby? It ain't been the same!"

"No, I'm still in Homicide. But maybe we can do a little business."

"Old times—I love 'em! Listen, I read about you and them, what was it, killer angels? I hope to hell you ain't got nothing like that going down."

"Avenging angels. No—this is something different. It's the killings on the strip. I want to know if they're tied to dopers or a pimp war or something like that."

"Oh, yeah—the two dancers. I read about them." The line was quiet for a breath or two. "I ain't heard of any pimp war going on. They don't like to kill off the merchandise anyway. They'll cut them where it don't show, but they don't like to kill them." Another breath. "Dope, huh?"

"It's a possibility, Doc."

"Yeah, it is. And if it is, it could be heavy. I mean, with two shootings, somebody must have a lot invested."

"I'll make it worth your while."

"Yeah, well, you always did—that ain't what worries me." In the past, Doc had proven reliable because he seldom promised more than he could deliver. But he always thought that what he did deliver was important enough to rival the Second Coming, and he figured that the importance of his information made him an equally important target. "Homicide's a tough rap. People don't talk much about it unless they're, you know, new in the business. Then they can't keep their mouths shut and you don't need me, you follow?"

"Nobody's talking on these, Doc."

"That's my drift. That means the guy ain't new at it. But I'd be new in those strip joints—somebody asking questions on new turf, he stands out."

"I need you, Doc. Really."

"Aw, yeah! Well, it never was just the money with us, right?"

"Right." Doc did it for love. Just like a whore.

"Okay—I'll keep an ear out. I don't like it, and I can't

promise nothing—it's not my usual line of contacts. But give me a few days."

"Thanks, Doc. I mean that."

"Like old times! Gabe—I love it."

There were a few other cryptic names and numbers penned in the back of his little green notebook; in the cold gleam of the telephone hood, he scanned the list of CIs left over from his days on the Narc squad of the Organized Crime Unit. One was dead and he crossed out that name. Another had been sent to prison. Wager had been meaning to visit him—someday he'd be out and be valuable again, and a prisoner always had a message or favor that someone on the outside could do for him. He tried another number, but a recording said it had been disconnected. That was a problem with Homicide: the cases very seldom involved what Axton called a subcommunity—not like the dope world or organized crime. So the tendency was to let the lesser names in your stable go unattended, and, like any other bunch of animals, they strayed. Now Wager was in need of them, and it was his own damned fault if they weren't around.

He dropped another couple dimes into the greasy metal slot and tried still another number. It turned out to belong to a person who had never heard of Lumpy Gallegos and who was very pissed to be woken up at ten-thirty at night by some goddamned drunk. Wager hung up and crossed off that number, too.

He had not tried the distaff side, mainly because he had no distaffs to lean on. But it never hurt to meet new and interesting people, provided you had a little leverage to make things go smoothly. He gathered up his unspent dimes and headed the Trans Am toward Colfax.

She was back again, the white of her plastic purse and the glow of her pink miniskirt competing with the other bright colors crowding the sidewalk. Wager cruised past once and slowed, catching her eye. He turned right and circled the block, pulling into the curb lane as she watched the car approach and ease to a stop.

His arm was on the steering wheel and his face half-hidden behind it. "Hop in, Mama—let's go for a ride."

She glanced into the backseat, found it empty, then opened the door. "Sure, honey. I been waiting for you." Getting in quickly, she told him, "Go around the block, honey, and let's talk business first."

Wager pulled away. "You're looking good, LaBelle."

He felt her squint toward him with sudden suspicion. The faint tang of marijuana puffed out of her clothes. "You know me? Who are you?"

"I'm a cop, LaBelle."

"Shit—lemme out. Right now, goddamn you!"

"Relax, baby. If I was looking to bust you, I'd give you the money before I gave you the word."

"Yeah? Now you want to shake me for a free sample? Stop over there in the light, pig, I want to see who you are."

He kept driving; she wouldn't jump from a moving car. "I'll tell you who I am: Gabe Wager."

"You son of a bitch."

"I put you away for three-to-five, LaBelle."

"You fucking greaser son of a fucking bitch."

"That's right, LaBelle—no hard feelings." From the corner of his eye he saw her gather herself for an attack. "But before you get busted for assaulting an officer, I got a deal for you."

"What kind of deal? I don't deal with pigs. You know that."

"Everybody knows that. Which is why I want to talk with you."

"You tried it before—it didn't work, piggy."

"And I respect you for it."

"Shit."

"Really, LaBelle. I asked you to fink on your friends, and you didn't do it. I respect that. But this is something different—you don't know the people, and it could be worth some real money to you."

"I know you. That's enough. You stop this thing and you let me out."

"I don't look for dopers now, LaBelle. I'm in Homicide."

"I ain't killed nobody. Not yet."

"Somebody's killing girls along the strip."

"What somebody?"

"That's part of the deal."

She looked at him and then out the window. Her hands began rustling in her purse and, under Wager's quick glance, came up with a handmade cigarette and lit it. The sharp odor drifted through the car and she watched for his reaction. "This here's an illegal substance, piggy. You want a hit?"

"I never smoke anything, LaBelle."

"You just blow smoke, that's all."

"I'm after a guy who blows off the backs of girls' skulls. Girls that work the strip."

"What's their names?"

He told her.

"I don't know them. They don't mean shit to me."

"You know the Cinnamon Club and Foxy Dick's."

"That who it is? Them amateurs? They can waste all of them, as far as I'm concerned." She drew deeply on the joint and held the smoke down a long time. "Cheap-assed amateurs, hustling johns!"

"I don't think either one of them was in the life. But I'd like to know for sure."

"That's what you want? Me to find out if they was hustling?"

"That, and anything else you can pick up about them or their clubs. Who they were seen with. Any deals they might have going. Anybody working out of the clubs in a regular way. Anything at all."

"Well, that's real sweet. What's in it for me?"

"Depends on what you get. I can go as high as a thousand if it gets me the right people."

"You want to make me a state employee, is that it?"

The money came out of his own pocket. Doyle had to authorize in advance any funds paid to informants, and Wager knew that none of this would be approved. But he didn't have much to spend it on anyway—certainly nothing that would bring him as much satisfaction as nailing a killer. "You don't get any retirement benefits, but it's tax-free."

She grinned, a sight verging on the ugly. "So I can still get my food stamps, right?"

"Right."

"I'll think it over." Pointing, she said, "Let me out over there where it's dark and I'll walk back. I don't want to be seen getting out of no Spickmobile."

• CHAPTER •

7

The next homicide victim on the strip was a male, and there was no indication that the murders were related. Wager and Axton had rotated to the day shift—eight-to-four—and now most of their time was spent in court, or following leads that the other shifts couldn't trace when offices and shops were closed, or finishing up the paperwork on bookings. If the team concept had any benefit, it was in areas like that; but, Wager knew, they had always covered for each other anyway, and had done so without having given up authority over their own cases.

Axton leafed quickly through the file left by Ross and Devereaux before he headed for the City-County Building and its long, echoing corridors of marble slabs and frosted glass doors. "Looks like a get-even hit," he said. "But give me a call if you need me—I'm in Wolford's court today." He handed Wager the file.

"Good luck," said Wager. Max would need it. Wolford was one of those judges whose sense of legal majesty outweighed his sense of the law. He liked an audience and insisted that every officer involved in a case be present throughout the entire hearing, whether the officer's role was material or not. Wager had tried to get Bulldog Doyle to run one of his time studies on the manpower wasted sitting in front of the pompous Wolford, but the division chief had only shoved out those lower teeth a little farther and said he knew damned well how much time was lost in that courtroom and it wasn't Wager's business to worry about it.

It was his business to worry about homicides, and Wager opened the manila folder of this, the latest, of the city's violent deaths. He warmed up his coffee and read of the killing of one Richard Goddard. Identified by his fingerprints and a slender information jacket in the police files, he had been found burned, carved on, and beaten to death late the preceding afternoon. The official crime report and the medical report were accompanied by unofficial notes that were far more interesting—speculations and street rumors picked up by the investigators. These indicated that the killing was a revenge slaying, which, of course, pointed toward the victim's good buddies and friendly associates, several of whom were listed on the contact cards in Goddard's jacket. That dossier also listed half-a-dozen contacts by Narcotics officers and two arrests for possession with intent. But no further action—no arraignments, no trials, no convictions. It was a pattern inferring that someone had used the arrests to turn Goddard into an informant, and Wager telephoned the man who might know.

"Sergeant Politzky, Vice and Narcotics."

"Hello, Ski—Wager in Homicide. We have the remains of one Richard Goddard. Was he somebody's snitch over there?"

"Goddard. . . . I can't place him. Let me ask around." He couldn't resist adding, "He won't be going anywhere, right?"

Politzky watched a lot of sitcoms on TV. It was one of the hazards of talking with the man. "He'll stay put, Ski."

"If he doesn't, I want to know what vitamins he uses—ha!"

"Just call me if you get anything, Ski." He hung up as the man was asking what Wager wanted him to call him. Spreading the papers across his desk, he read through a statement by Goddard's parents taken early this morning by Devereaux and Ross. Several names they mentioned as friends of their son also appeared on the contact cards. Some of those were marked as having jackets of their own down in Records, and—given the probabilities—those were the people to start with. Ross and Devereaux had gotten as far as listing the addresses of the most promising before going off duty this morning. With Max in court, the legwork was left to Wager, and he drained his coffee and got going.

Judging from their record of arrests and rumors, two names looked good: James, AKA Jimmy, King; and Charles, AKA Lizard, Plummer. Plummer was still on parole; his address would be current. Wager started with him.

. . .

The man who answered the apartment door tried to pretend that Wager wasn't a cop. "I don't want to buy nothing."

He had his badge case in hand. "Police. Are you Charles Plummer?"

He had high cheekbones and tiny black eyes in puffy, wrinkled lids that accounted for his nickname. His black hair, brushed back and slicked over to hide a balding spot on his crown, ran far down his neck and ended in a little shaggy fringe that curled up in what used to be called a duck's ass. "I'm him. What do you want?" When he spoke, his lips scarcely opened, and his voice verged on a husky, private whisper.

"I want to know about Richard Goddard. Do you want to talk here in the hall, down at headquarters, or inside your apartment?"

Plummer blinked once or twice, then stepped aside and held open the door. "Come in." He closed the door behind him. "You with Homicide?"

"That's right. Detective Wager."

The man lit a cigarette and wagged the match out; a little swirl of smoke hung in the air for a moment and caught the light in a pearly question mark. "I heard of you. People say you're a hard-ass."

"I'm one of the nicest guys you'll ever meet, Lizard. Warm and affectionate. Do you have an alibi for yesterday morning?"

"That's when Rick bought it?"

"More or less. The fun and games lasted awhile."

He sucked on the cigarette and cupped the butt under his palm, prison style. "I read about it this morning. Too bad." He drew again. "I was here. Home." His glance went around the box of a room. In an alcove, a small refrigerator was tucked under a hot plate. The cold-water sink served both people and dishes.

"Anybody see you?"

He shrugged. "I don't know. The mailman, maybe. I sleep late. I get off work between eleven and midnight and sleep late."

"What do you do for a living, Lizard?"

"I'm a dishwasher. Holiday Inn." For the first time since answering the door, he looked straight at Wager. "I don't have nothing to do with it. I swear."

"You did some time for dealing. We figure Ricky either ripped somebody off or was nailed for a snitch. And you're a known associate."

"I'm clean. I did my time and I been clean since."

"You're still on parole, Lizard. It doesn't take a trial to put you back in the can for consorting with a known felon."

"Hey, I didn't know Goddard was a felon. He never said nothing to me about being busted."

"He's got a jacket. That's a public record."

"Man, all we did was drink beer and talk! I always have a few beers after work and I'd run into him now and then. And that's all it was: talk!"

"What about?"

"Things—everything. Hell, I don't know. What do you talk about when you drink beer with a guy?"

"You might talk contacts. You might talk buying and selling. You might talk about the profit margin in an ounce of pure."

"I'm out of the action, Wager. I told you—I'm clean now. And I don't know nothing about Rick dealing, either. He never said nothing about that to me."

"I'm just telling it the way a parole officer might see it, Plummer. One who doesn't want any black marks on his record."

The man sucked again on the cigarette and then pinched out the fire between his fingers. He stripped the paper from the butt and dumped the remaining tobacco in an ashtray that held a little pile of earlier remains. The pellet of paper shot into the trash. "I had nothing to do with it, Wager." He looked up, black eyes two glittering specks. "You're trying to turn me, aren't you? You want me in your stable, don't you?"

"I can always use the help of a concerned citizen."

He shook his head. "I'm clean. You got nothing on me. Nothing!"

"Consorting, Lizard. Suspicion of homicide. Failure to cooperate in a police investigation. Violating the fire code with a dirty ashtray. I've got all I need, because it doesn't take much for a parolee."

"I didn't know the guy had a record!"

"That makes no difference and you know it, Plummer. Your name came up in the contact cards as a known associate of a murdered dealer. All I have to do is whisper that to your PO. What do you have left, four years? One whisper, and you're doing them inside."

The man turned and walked the three steps to a narrow window that looked across two feet of air at a grimy brick wall. From somewhere came the muffled thump of a stereo, like a manic hammer against the ceiling. Plummer glared up at the sound. "Fucking kid and his fucking record player!"

Wager shifted his weight to his other leg and waited.

"What is it you want?" Plummer spoke to the glass and the wall beyond.

"If you were in on it, I want you to turn state's evidence against whoever helped you out." Wager continued as the man turned angrily. "Or, if you had no part of it, I want you to find out who did."

"That's all? You just want me to walk down the street asking, 'Hey, who rubbed Goddard?' "

"I want you to go out and listen, Lizard. Just tell me what you hear."

"Sure—just like Goddard. You say he got it for being a snitch and now you want me to stick my neck out." A thought struck him. "Was he one of yours? Is that what you're doing—putting me in his place?"

"I don't know if he was a snitch. Maybe he shorted somebody on a deal."

"Which is what you want me to find out."

"That's part of it."

"Part? What the hell more?"

"Let me know what you hear about these two." He tore a leaf of paper from his little notebook and wrote down the names of Sheldon and Williams. "They worked at the Cinnamon Club and at Foxy Dick's. I want to know if they were dealing."

Plummer frowned as he read the names. "Pussy palaces—that's not my turf. That kind of crap just turns me off. It's too damn depressing."

Wager lifted some twenties out of his wallet and set them on the arm of the worn sofa. "Expand your horizons. As my guest."

Plummer looked at the bills and then at him. "You're not really after the guy who snuffed Ricky, are you? You want the one who did for these broads, don't you?"

"I want them both. But Ricky will be easier—it took more than one person to beat him to death, and they did it that way for a message. Sooner or later somebody's going to spill. But those two . . . I can't even come up with a motive on them."

"The paper said they were raped—a sex crime."

"That's one theory. Maybe the guy's still around. Maybe you can buy him a drink and he'll tell you all about it."

"Great." The man's eyes swiveled back to the small stack of twenties; finally, he told Wager where he spent his time drinking and where he'd met Goddard: a hole-in-the-wall bar called the Everready Lounge. It was halfway down the Colfax strip and there might have been a little dealing going on. "I mean, who can tell, you know? It's small, it's quiet, there's a few girls work there steady, and a lot of regulars, so you know who's around. If I was in the action —which I am not—it's the kind of place I'd like."

"Does Jimmy King hang out there?"

"King? You know about him?" Plummer spat a shred of tobacco. "Yeah. He likes to think he's big-time. A punk like that! He wouldn't last twenty minutes in Canon City. His asshole'd be as big as Eisenhower Tunnel in twenty minutes."

"Is that where he met Ricky?"

"Once in awhile. Him and somebody name of Clinton. I don't know him too good. A few other dudes once in awhile."

"Any names?"

He shook his head. "Wasn't my business to ask."

"What did they look like?"

"People. They didn't look like hoods or street scum, if that's what you mean. Just people. Straights." He thought back. "One guy had a big mustache and glasses. Another looked like an albino—you know: white hair and pink skin. There was one big guy—not too tall, but heavy, you know, with his hair brushed up like a brush. Just people."

"But King had business with them?"

"I guess. Him and Clinton, anyway. The punk's got his own booth in the back. Thinks he's a real godfather, you know? He sits back there and these people come in and talk with him. But I don't know what about, Wager. I never asked."

"What's Clinton look like?"

The cigarette crackled faintly as Plummer thought. "About forty-five. White guy. Not too tall, not too short. Likes to wear suits all the time like he's a salesman or something. Brown eyes. He's got brown eyes."

"Color of hair?"

"Dark, I guess. It's got a lot of gray in it."

"And Ricky had some business going with him and King?"

"Yeah. He did."

"What do you think it was?"

"I guess maybe Ricky was dealing a little. It wasn't big-time, but he wanted to be big-time. I guess he thought King was something hot with his own booth and all. But, shit, I seen bigger in the Boy Scouts."

"Where does Clinton fit in?"

"I'm not sure. He may be the supplier. He's bigger than King, that's for sure."

"Why?"

"Well, you can tell—Clinton comes in once in awhile and goes back to King's booth and that kid's sucking right up to him. Waving his fucking hand at the bartender for a drink for his asshole buddy Clinton, and all. But it's Clinton does the talking and King listens. King's stooging for him, that's what it is."

"Do you have a line on Clinton? Do you know him from anywhere else?"

Plummer shook his head. "That's the only place I ever seen him. Like I told you, Wager, I'm out of it. I go to work, I go there for a few beers, I go home—that's it."

Wager paused at the door before opening it. "Who do you think killed Ricky?"

Plummer groped in his shirt pocket for a pack of Camels, shook one to his lips, and then shrugged. "Clinton finished him off."

"Why?"

"Him and Ricky and King were pretty thick there for a while and then something happened. King was pissed off at Ricky about something—really pissed. A couple nights ago, Clinton came in and said something that scared the shit out of Ricky. He came over to my table like he was a goddamned zombie and drank, I don't know, six or seven gins. Didn't touch him, he was that scared. He cut out, and I never seen him again." Plummer lit his cigarette. "Clinton done it. King don't have the balls."

Wager laid another twenty on the pile to pay the man for losing his virginity as a snitch. "Okay, Lizard—you get more for me, there's more of this for you."

"Don't call me that," the man said. "It's not my fault I had this skin condition when I was a kid."

Wager studied the scaly, swollen flesh around the man's eyes and then shrugged. "I thought it was because you ate flies."

"You fucker," said Plummer as he closed the door.

In his car, Wager radioed to Records for anything on a Clinton who matched the description Plummer had given him. By the time he reached Colfax and the Everready Lounge, Records came back with two possibles: Henry Albert Clinton and William Frank Clinton. Henry was a burglar currently doing time in Canon City. William had an old jacket with four counts of assault or armed robbery and two falls; no arrests since being paroled in 1965.

"Send a copy to me in Homicide, please."

"Ten-four."

He found a parking slot along the curb near the Eveready Lounge and backed the car into it. The bar sat between a check-cashing service and a shoe shop whose dusty gray window display was all that was left of a string of small stores which, at one time, sold hardware or greeting cards or appliances to a quiet neighborhood. Now they sold anything that a whisper and the rustle of money could buy in the dark. The lounge didn't have a parking lot of its own, and that explained why it had a regular trade: people living nearby walked over each evening knowing there wouldn't be too many tourists; that kind didn't usually like to get too far from their cars.

Along one wall of the bar was a line of booths whose high backs gave a little privacy for head jobs. The center was open for dancing, and a long bar served the johns who hadn't yet drunk enough courage to go to a booth with one of the girls. This early in the day—eleven—the place was almost empty and had that cool, stale smell of waking up in damp sheets. From somewhere behind the bar came the domestic aroma of coffee. In one booth, two girls pushed food around their plates with the drowsy look of eating at their own kitchen table.

Wager did not try to hide who he was; it wouldn't have worked anyway. The bartender, bald head bent over a stock list, looked up, and his face went blank as he nodded good morning.

"I'm looking for James King," said Wager. He strolled down the row of booths and peered in each one. The sound of the girls' forks stopped.

"I don't know anybody named that."

"Sure you do." He strolled back toward the bartender. "He lives here. I want him for questioning about a homicide. Anybody that knows him and doesn't tell me becomes an accessory after the fact."

The bartender, his round face cut in thirds by heavy

eyebrows and a narrow mustache, said, "What was that name again?"

"King. James King. He uses that back booth all the time."

"There's a kid named Jimmy sits there a lot. I don't know his last name."

"Any idea where he is now?"

"No. You might ask the girls. They talk to him sometimes."

Wager turned to the two women, who looked at him across a cop-hating distance.

"Do either of you know James King?"

Neither answered. They sat with the stillness of trained animals that suffer the touch of men's hands but don't like it.

"He's wanted for a murder investigation," said Wager. "That's a heavy charge."

"You ain't with Vice?" The younger one was maybe sixteen years old. Her pale hair, dark at the roots, was cut in bangs across her forehead and hung straight to frame a snub-nosed face. Her wide brown eyes were made even larger with thick eye shadow, and pink makeup almost hid the deepening wrinkles below the corners of her mouth.

"No, miss. Homicide."

On the scale of crimes, murder was more serious than either girl had been involved in yet, and you had to draw a line somewhere. Even if you might be pushed across it—as so often happened—you drew still another line farther down and then you held out for as long as you could before you crossed that one, too.

"You going to tell him where you found out?" asked the older one. She wore a powder-blue cashmere sweater and a wide skirt; she, too, had bangs, but her dark hair swept over her ears into a long fifties-style ponytail. Wager guess she specialized in middle-aged businessmen.

"No. And he'll be too worried to ask." Behind him, the

bartender turned on a radio just loud enough to keep their words from reaching him. A female voice mashed flat to the sound of country-and-western wailed, "I used to be your steady flame but now I'm just your ash."

The girls glanced at each other—you go first, no you—and finally the older one shrugged and said, "He's got a place on Fillmore, just off Colfax. 1485. Apartment 4."

• • •

The building was made of brick and designed like a brick, too. It was two stories high with a central corridor leading straight back. Pairs of doors marched down the hall. Number 4 was the second on the right. Jimmy King was too scared to act tough.

"I never heard of Richard Goddard. I don't know the guy."

"Bullshit. His mother says you came over to his house two or three times. You're not going to call his poor old grieving mother a liar, are you, Jimmy?"

King was thin and had a downy mustache that curved around the corners of his mouth. A small rash of pimples reddened each side of his pointed chin. Now, as he stared at Wager, he picked nervously at one, drawing a tiny smear of blood.

"Think about it, Jimmy. I found out you and Goddard were buddies. I found out where you live. I found out how you get your pocket change. I found out about Clinton, and I know you and Goddard and Clinton had a deal going. Now you should start telling me what I don't know. Like what your part in it was."

"Nothing! I know him, yeah, but I swear I had nothing to do with killing him!"

"If you did the beating and killed him," Wager went on, "your ass is peanut butter and it's going to be spread all over the landscape. But if Clinton did the heavy stuff, and if you didn't mean to kill Goddard—and if you tell me what you know—then maybe we can work a deal."

• • •

Some were like that—they made you wonder how dumb a man could be to help kill somebody he knew for a reason that anyone could figure out. Maybe dumb had nothing to do with it. At least not in the usual meaning. But dumb in the dull and unimaginative way that led some people to surrender themselves to the will of another person and become their tool. It was early afternoon now, and Wager stood in a corner of the brightly lit and silent interrogation cubicle. Max, back from his court appearance, was having his turn at King. The suspect's thin face glistened with sweat and his worried eyes kept shifting from Axton to Wager and back. His fingers scratched at cuticles until shreds of dry flesh lay on the gray table like bloodless scabs.

"I'll bet Goddard screamed, didn't he, Mr. King?" Axton's low voice gently nudged the silence made heavier by the buzz of fluorescent lights. Max's style wasn't Wager's. Wager preferred to attack the bastards with his knowledge of their guilt, and he got his share of results. But Max had a way to make a suspect feel that the hulking, sad-eyed man across the table shared the suspect's guilt and his fear of what was going to happen; that nothing the suspect admitted could shock or make an enemy of those forgiving eyes that had seen everything. And the soft voice implied the relief that would come if the suspect only told all about those terrible things he never really meant to do.

"And I'll bet something else, Jimmy. I'll bet you didn't want to be there. I'll bet you wanted to close your eyes and stop your ears and then open them up and find that the whole thing was just a nightmare." His quiet voice grew even softer. "That your friend, your buddy whose mother fed you, wasn't being beaten to death. That you weren't really there, watching."

A row of glistening drops oozed from a crease over King's knotted eyebrows, and even from his corner Wager could see the quiver at the awkwardly tilted collar point of the man's sweat-stained shirt.

"It's your tail, King," said Wager in a bored voice. "You help us out, we'll help you. You don't help us," he shrugged, "screw you."

"You're not going to get off free, Mr. King," said Max. "But if you didn't kill him, there's no reason to pay for that. I don't think you really wanted him dead, Jimmy. Dead is a long time. I think you just wanted to scare him. What was it, he bought some dope on credit and didn't come up with the payment? You bought from Clinton and sold to Goddard, and Clinton wanted to show you how to get your money back?"

King's mouth worked like he was chewing a ball of cotton and he closed his eyes tightly before opening them with an almost sightless stare. "I wasn't there."

"Then where were you? Tell us where you were and we'll check it out, Jimmy."

Another sliver of flesh came off his cuticle, and then the fingers went to his blotched chin. "I was at the lounge. The Everready Lounge. All night long."

"Unh uh," said Wager. "You weren't. You left about midnight. Clinton left around eleven-thirty and you and Goddard left later. You're the last one to see him alive, King. Clinton planned it that way. You've got no alibi, and I bet Clinton does. Think about it."

It was so quiet they could hear the man swallow. When he finally spoke, his voice was hoarse and flat with resignation. "I want a lawyer. I got nothing to say without a lawyer. I want a lawyer."

"Sure, Jimmy," said Wager. "It's your life you're throwing away." He opened the door and called a sheriff's officer to the interview room. "Keep him segregated," he told the thick-bodied man who idly jingled his ring of keys. King would have to wait awhile for his lawyer—he was theirs to have and to hold for seventy-two hours before filing a charge. Seventy-two hours of sitting alone, and thinking, and worrying.

• • •

Axton sat on the edge of his desk, his thigh in the taut trouser leg spreading across a foot of the glass-topped surface. "I thought he was going to crack. I really thought he'd buy state's evidence."

Wager thought so, too. "He wanted it. He was tempted."

Axton whistled quietly. "He was afraid to, wasn't he?" Whistle. "Clinton?"

"That's my guess. He watched Clinton or somebody Clinton hired work Goddard over and he doesn't want that to happen to him."

Axton picked up the telephone and dialed Records; before he could ask, Wager thumbed through the afternoon mail and drew out a Xerox of Clinton's rap sheet. Axton, hanging up, grinned at Wager. "I should have known you'd run his record." He glanced down the sheet. "This one's been around . . . and learned a few things."

Wager agreed. "He's smart enough to hide behind King."

"And he's mean. Assault . . . assault with . . . King's probably right to be afraid of the guy. Still," Axton tossed the sheet back onto the small pile of mail, "eight-to-ten years minimum, that's a pretty high price." The whistle. "I'll talk to him again in the morning—promise to keep Clinton away from him."

"It's worth a try." According to Lizard, King had thought he was a tough guy. Now the kid's play-acting had become real. More real than King wanted. Yet he still didn't take the way out that Max had offered. And Wager didn't think it was because of any pride King might have—scum like that had no pride. It was Clinton. They'd have to run Clinton down, question him, discover what Wager already knew: that he would have an alibi in his mouth and a leer in his eyes. Clinton was one of the leviathans.

The pop of his GE radio interrupted his thoughts. "Any Homicide detective."

"X-89. Go ahead," said Wager.

"We have a probable suicide at 5002 Elizabeth Place. Officers at the scene."

"On our way."

One in the morning, one in the afternoon; a steady pace made the shift go quickly. Wager grabbed his coat and followed Axton down the cushioned hall toward the wide elevators and the streets below.

· CHAPTER ·

The day shift, like the others, slipped into routines more or less designed to give time for the scheduled paperwork, to leave a little space for the unscheduled homicides, and to let the long-unsolved cases do as they always did: wait. Because of the effort to have an officer's court appearances coincide with his day shift, Wager and Axton spent a lot of weary hours sitting on the blond wooden benches in the City-County Building, where they listened to the shuffle and drone of the law in action. More hours passed knocking on doors to follow up requests from the night shift, and some time was even spent on routine patrol, more to let the wind and motion blow away that cramped feeling that came from hours at a desk than to serve and protect.

For Wager, there developed another routine as well, one of groping and dead ends, of itching for whatever it was that never seemed to arrive. King had stuck with his story despite Max's best efforts, and was now out on bond. Munn and Golding had found Clinton and questioned him; he had a friend who swore they were playing cards when Goddard was beaten to death, so he, too, strolled the streets like any other honest citizen. Annette Sheldon and Angela Williams moved farther back in the Open drawer, to sit there until a lucky break or the Resurrection, whichever came first. Even Pepe the Pistol seemed to drop out of sight despite occasional tips called in anonymously by friends and relatives of the slain.

Axton, reading a memo from Bulldog Doyle that ordered officers to cease and desist from driving patrol cars across lawns, did not deny that King was lying or even that Kenneth Sheldon could be hiding something. But he did believe that King would talk and Clinton would be nailed, and that the exotic dancer cases would stay unsolved until someone was arrested in some other city for a similar homicide and confessed to these as well.

"You think the killer skipped?"

"The two murders came within a week of each other, Gabe. It's been over a month, now. If the guy was around, I think he'd have hit again."

"It doesn't explain Sheldon's act."

"That's only your feeling." He spread both large hands before Wager could answer. "I know, I know; you've been right on things like that before. But what's the connection between the Sheldons and Angela Williams? None—not a thing, right? It all points to a stranger-to-stranger. Somebody watched them dance and then killed them, and that somebody has moved on."

"I don't see how Sheldon makes a living in that shop of his."

"I don't follow."

"He doesn't have any business. One time I saw a delivery truck drop off a couple vending machines. The rest of the time, nothing. And he has no employees."

Max did not bother to ask his partner why or when he kept an eye on Sheldon. "So?"

"So how many machines can one man fix? What's he charge, fifty bucks an hour? He's got overhead, taxes, insurance, and he still has to make a living out of it. He hasn't moved out of that expensive apartment; he hasn't changed his style at all, as far as I can find out. I think he even took another vacation in Vegas."

"Maybe it was a sentimental journey."

"Maybe. But he's not bringing any money in from that business of his."

Axton thought it over. "You're saying it's a cover for something."

"Unless the guy is just a lousy businessman. Which is possible." Then he added, because he knew Axton was thinking it, "Even so, there's not a damned thing connecting his business to the two murders."

"Right," said Max.

Which meant that Wager, like everyone else, had to wait. Not that he was bored: in the slack between old paperwork and new court appearances, there were the occasional shots fired by officers which required detailed reports from Homicide detectives, patrolmen who requested help with legal niceties in search and arrest or with juvenile suspects, queries and alerts from neighboring departments and states, and even occasional VIPs to be shown through the still-new headquarters building. Wager was never assigned to that detail. The Sheldon and Williams cases, in short, had been given the team's sixteen hours each and were now dead ends. No matter how much Wager might believe that his finger was on something, there was no way he could get his hand around anything solid—not officially. Maybe unofficially there was something he could do, but even that had to wait, too, until one of his CIs came up with a halfway decent lead.

• • •

The wheezing voice pulled Wager out of sleep. Even with his eyes still closed, he knew who was on the telephone. But it took him longer than it should to anchor Fat Willy's words to a case. For a moment, he thought it was something to do with a narcotics buy—Willy had set somebody up for a buy-and-bust—but that wasn't quite right: he couldn't come up with the target's name. And he wasn't in the Organized Crime Unit anymore—he wasn't working undercover. He was in Homicide, and Willy was talking about the Sheldon and Williams murders.

"You hear me, Wager? You there, man?"

"I'm not awake yet, Willy. What's their names?"

"Shit, how many times I got to tell you? You wanted dudes who deal regular at the Cinnamon Club and Foxy Dick's, right? Well, I got them: Curtis Evans, Sugar Watney, and Little Ray McAfee. They work other places, too, but you didn't pay none for that."

Wager blinked at the digital clock whose dull red numbers glowed 1:08; he recognized the first two names, and they would recognize him. "Who's Little Ray?"

"Somebody new. I don't have no line on him yet. He's a sawed-off little honky runs around wearing them bib overalls, you know, like a farmer. But I bet he don't know which end of a horse the oats goes into and which end they come out of."

"Anything on Sheldon or Williams dealing?"

"Naw. But, hell, they been dead for a month or so. Nobody's talking about them anymore. And since there ain't but one reason to ask about them, I am not."

"Don't hang up yet, Willy—this McAfee, can you set me up with him?"

"What?"

"I want to talk to him."

"Well, he sure as hell don't want to talk to no cop, Wager. Can't you figure that out all by yourself?"

"Don't tell him I'm a cop."

"You look like a cop. You talk like a cop. You smell like a cop. Sometimes, man, I am downright ashamed to be seen in your presence."

"Go through a cutout, Willy."

"How's that?"

"You introduce me to somebody else; he sets me up with McAfee. You're in the clear."

"You even think like a cop."

"Set me up with him. It's important, Willy."

"Uh huh—and how important's 'important'?"

What the hell, payday was only a couple weeks off. "A hundred."

"We got different ideas of important." The wheezing breath held the line open. "There's this other little item I picked up on. You better know about it."

"What's that, Willy?"

"Somebody is mentioning your name."

"What are they saying?"

"It ain't all that clear. Just somebody been asking around about you—personal stuff, you know. Where you hang out. Where you live. Family."

"Who?"

"That ain't clear either. Somebody asked somebody who asked somebody—on down the line. You know how it is."

He knew how. The why was something else. "Anything to do with a man named Clinton?"

"Wager, it could be one of a thousand of your admirers. People don't like cops, and a lot of people don't like you especial. You don't have a warm personality, my man. But because somebody is asking about you especial, I ain't eager to be the one who leads you to McAfee, you dig?"

Willy was right; there were a lot of people who would lean back and smile widely if something happened to him, and not all of them were outside the law. But you didn't lose sleep over it; start doing that, and you'd end up like Munn, sucking on chalky tablets and trying to live long enough to die a civilian. "I'm not afraid if you're not, Willy. And I never figured you for chickenshit."

"Aw, man, come off that crap! I'm talking business. Somebody's asking about you—you know what that means for my line of business. And now you want to tie yourself to me? Bullshit!"

"It's either that or I walk up to McAfee and tell him you sent me."

The slow voice said incredulously, "The shit you would! You would, wouldn't you?"

"I would. It's that important, Willy. Now how soon can you do it?"

"I'll call you."

Two nights later, Wager met the big man in the glow that spilled from Colfax down the windowless ripple of brick wall that was one side of the Aladdin Theater. Fat Willy sat in his white Cadillac drumming thick fingers on a steering wheel padded with a tiger-skin wrap. When Wager tapped on the car roof, Willy peered haughtily a moment and then his jaw dropped.

"Holy Jesus! Is that you?"

"It's me."

"Holy Jesus. You could walk right by and I'd never know you. Hey, you better not let the Immigration people see you."

Wager stood there in stained and faded Levi's, a sweat shirt with the sleeves cut off at the shoulders, a tassled Mexican vest of rough wool flung over that. He wore a leather cowboy hat with a flat crown, and huaraches. He had not shaved since early this morning and had darkened his stubble with a coat of mascara. "It's my ethnic heritage. I wear this, you wear a plantation suit."

"That's panama suit, Wager. Not plantation. And I wear it because it's cool!"

"Right." Wager got into the car and sniffed at the smell of new leather. "Aim me at him, Willy. The night is young and I'm so beautiful."

The car pulled away from the curb with only the slightest whisper from the engine, and a pensive Fat Willy steering lightly. Finally, he said, "You even make jokes. Not very goddamn good ones, but it is a Wager I don't recognize. Which," he added, "is fine with me."

He hoped a lot of other people would have the same response. "Who do we meet first?"

"This here 'cutout.' A kid name of Meldon. He sometimes buys from McAfee, but I own him."

"Does he know me?"

"She-it, Wager. Just because somebody been asking about you, you think you're a picture in *People* magazine or something. You got a press agent, too? There's a hell of a lot of people don't know who you are, and a lot more don't care!"

"What'd you tell him?"

"I just told him you had business with McAfee and told him to set it up."

That would do. McAfee would suspect that Wager was a narc and go through a series of wriggles and twists to get Wager to spill it. But since he wasn't trying to build a case against McAfee, Wager had a lot more latitude to convince him that he wasn't a cop. Ironically, the tight spots in this little maneuver would come from his fellow policemen; the legitimate undercover people would scream all the way to the department chief if they caught Wager on their turf, and there would be no way Max or Doyle or even the Little Lord Jesus could protect him if that happened.

Willy let Wager out of the car at a quiet residential corner just down from a half-block of neighborhood stores. Lights here and there behind pulled shades glowed yellow, and in someone's backyard a dog brayed once—deep, eager, and hungry. "Wait here," he said, and the long car slid away like an ocean liner. The only sound was the hiss of its fat tires. When it glimmered out of sight, a slender black youth sauntered down the steps from a shadowy front porch.

"Come on."

Wordless, Wager followed Meldon toward the stores and their little island of light.

"Little Ray, he wasn't too eager to meet you, man. I had to tell him it was something really important."

"I appreciate it."

"That's nice. But if Fat Willy hadn't asked me as a special favor . . ."

"Fat Willy's a good man to do favors for."

"Yeah, well, neither one of us is a good man to cross. You get my meaning?"

Wager did not answer and Meldon was content to take that for agreement.

"He's in here." Meldon turned into one of the stores. A white false front rose squarely against the night sky and on it large, black script, painted by a wavering hand, read ALLEN'S RIBS. A screen door opened to a small restaurant, brightly lit and filled with Formica tables whose chrome legs had long since been scratched to rust. A short line of blacks stood in front of the order counter and looked curiously at Wager. From one or two of the small tables where people sat chewing on sauce-smothered ribs came flat, hostile glances. Meldon led him through a small arch into an adjoining room, this one half-filled with customers in secondhand booths of assorted styles. In the last one, facing the room and looking out of place among the glistening black faces, sat a lone white. Meldon stood aside to let Wager slip into the booth first, then he perched on the edge of the unpadded bench.

"This here's him. He ain't said much."

Little Ray stayed busy with his food. He wore denim overalls and a military green T-shirt. He had a red bandanna tied above his ears that clutched his curly dark hair into a tall spray. When he moved his head, it swayed like something crawling through grass. "Okay, Meldon. Business is business, right?"

Meldon's eyes flicked from Little Ray to Wager and back, then he shrugged and slid out of the booth. Little Ray nipped the meat off a dripping bone and chewed slowly, his gaze anchored on something over Wager's shoulder.

"Hottest fucking ribs in Denver," he said to the seat back. He set down a slender white bone and picked up another, with its meat vague under the dark red sauce. This time he looked over Wager's other shoulder.

Wager watched him gnaw through half-a-dozen. The waitress, a smiling girl with cornrowed hair, brought him coffee. Little Ray wiped his mouth and fingers on the oversized paper napkin and sipped at the plastic glass of Sprite. Then he finally looked at Wager. "So what's your business with me?"

"It's not mine. It's the people I represent."

The man's face stayed still, but something changed in his eyes. "Like who?"

"Some people from out of town. They asked me to look around for somebody they could invest in."

Little Ray smiled and swirled his glass and watched the bubbles stick to its sides. "You don't look like a broker to me."

"That's the way my associates want it."

"Uh huh. And maybe I'm not interested in what your associates want. Maybe I like things the way they are."

"Nothing stays the same, right? And everybody wants more," said Wager. "I'm talking a very profitable arrangement for the right person."

"Sure. That's why you come to somebody like me. I'm so important you can't do without me."

"The people I represent want somebody who's not already tied to the action in Denver. An independent." The girl came to clear the plates and ask Wager if he wanted more coffee. He shook his head and when she was out of hearing, said, "These people want to set up operations here. It's a growth area. The whole Sun Belt's a growth area, and Denver's hot now." Wager gazed steadily at the man's flat eyes. "I've been looking around for somebody the cops aren't on to yet—somebody able to handle his own organization and still hungry enough to hustle."

"And you think I'm that somebody. And all I got to do to prove it is sell you an ounce or two and then you flash your badge and say 'Guess who.' Come on, this horseshit went out with *Little Caesar.*"

"I looked at a lot of people," Wager went on, as if the man hadn't spoken. "I like the way you operate and I like your market—the clubs and skin houses. I think you could expand that real quick with the right support."

A hint of unsureness crossed Little Ray's eyes. Wager wasn't talking of buying from him—which was the usual narc trip—but of selling to him. "I got all I need right now."

"I checked out Curtis and Sugar, but I don't think they can handle the kind of volume my associates have in mind."

"Volume? That much volume?"

"In a month, maybe six weeks, we can push prices to the bottom. When people like Curtis and Sugar see their profit squeezed out, they'll move on. Or they can work for us. Us and whoever's in with us."

Little Ray gazed at the vision of a price war that would wipe out the small independents. "That would take a shit pot full of money."

"My associates look at it as a short-term investment. Right now, the market around here is unorganized. We want to bring in a little stability. And we want to do it with the right people. You do it right from the ground up, you save yourself a hell of a lot of headaches later on."

The man reached a finger to scratch delicately beneath the headband. "I still think you're shitting me. You come in here and hand me this line and expect me to roll over." His hair wagged when he shook his head. "If you've got any associates—which I doubt—you tell them words ain't enough. I didn't get into this business to be suckered, my Chicano friend."

"I'm not Chicano, Little Ray. I'm Cuban. And I'll spell out the deal." Wager counted the points, starting with his little finger. "One, a steady supply of quality goods—a full range, once you got your market set up. Two, an exclusive franchise to the territory. No competition, and that's guaranteed. Three, the district manager doesn't go on the street; he supervises, but he puts distance between him and the street." Wager smiled. "That's for our protection as well as yours. Four, if you ever need it, the best political and legal assistance money can buy." He let that soak in and then held up a thumb. "There's a fifth point: you get asked once to join us. If you do, you're with us. If you don't—no problem. Nothing's going to happen to you. We'll just find somebody else who wants more money than he knows what to do with, and after awhile you'll move on."

"You're full of horseshit. If you were that big, you'd bring your own people in."

"We've started that. From Miami and LA. I'm one of them. But what we need is a district manager who knows the local territory and personnel. It saves a lot of time and makes for a nice, quiet transition."

"Horseshit." But he said it less certainly.

"Take some time to think it over. Ask around. Find out what's going down in LA now." He smiled again. "Ask about the Cubans—the Flotilla people—the ones Castro sent to the Land of Opportunity. Don't make a hasty decision one way or the other. Anybody comes in with us, we want them to be sure. It's what you might call a lifetime commitment."

Little Ray did not answer Wager's smile or nod goodbye. He sat there trying to be absolutely certain that this scruffy-looking Hispano was so full of crap that his eyes had turned brown. But Wager could see the man's doubt. Latinos . . . Cubans, Colombians—they were all over the drug scene now. Miami, Los Angeles, New York . . . And they were organized. And very rich. And very mean . . . There were so many stories murmured on the street, so many whispered rumors. . . .

Wager closed the shop's screen door behind him and took a deep breath of cool night air. It had been, he thought, a good exit line. And now how in the hell was he going to get home?

• • •

His first call after work the following evening was to Doc.

"I ain't heard nothing, Gabe. Not one thing. Whoever wasted those girls, if they're still around, they're not saying nothing. Amateurs, they'd be bragging; no talk, they must be pros."

"You're right, Doc." Wager interrupted the man's nervous, cryptic speech. "But stay with it. And I'd like you to put something out. I want you to say you've heard organized crime is moving into the area."

"Jesus, it's already here—the Scorvellis."

"This is a new bunch from LA; say they're Colombians, Puerto Ricans, whatever. They want to organize the dope sales along the strip. You don't know their names and you don't know who's in it; all you hear is they're big. Can you do that for me?"

"Sure. No sweat. Something like that, you whisper it once, and it spreads faster than the clap." He asked, "Is it true?"

"It might be."

"Jesus. I guess it was only a matter of time, right?"

"Right—Denver's growing up. One more thing: I hear someone's asking around about me. If you hear who it is, let me know."

"Jesus! That don't sound good, Gabe. In fact, it makes me nervous."

"It happens all the time. I just want to know who the players are."

"You're pretty goddamn cool about it." The line was silent as Doc tried to figure what it might mean for him. "Well, I don't like getting near something like that. I'm kind of out on a limb, you know? But if something comes my way, I'll tell you. For old times' sake."

"Thanks, Doc."

Wager's second call was to Vice and Narcotics. He requested that officers Moffett or Nolan telephone him. Very important. When, in about twenty minutes, Moffett called, Wager set up a meet on the south side of town well away from Colfax.

"Is this about the van?" asked Nolan. The two Vice detectives sat in their conspicuously unmarked car with the police band turned to a low crackle. Moffett smoked a filter cigarette that filled the cab with a musty odor.

"No. Do you know a couple small-time pushers named Curtis Evans and Sugar Watney?"

"Oh, sure. We've popped them a couple times. But what's the use? They're out again faster than we can finish the paperwork on them. At least this way, we know who's doing what."

"Any chance of you hassling them for me?"

There was a meditative silence before Nolan finally said, "I suppose we could. For what reason?"

Wager had noticed that about Nolan: some people said "Why?" He said "For what reason?" Some said "Because"; Nolan said "Due to the fact that." Wager figured it gave the man an extra moment or two to think before he had to commit himself to a verb. But in this case, he could understand Nolan's caution; Wager was asking the two detectives to upset that precarious balance between the scuttling figures that make up the action and the watching eyes of the law hanging over them. "I'm trying to flush out some information on a couple homicides. If I can make my man think he's being squeezed, then maybe he'll want to cover himself on the heavier rap." That was close enough to the truth, and it omitted nicely the figure in the flat leather hat who was entrapping Little Ray.

"How much hassling you want?" asked Moffett.

That question meant "How much paperwork?" and Wager had to admit that he was asking for a lot. "If you can hold them on a seventy-two, I'd appreciate it."

Moffett stubbed out his cigarette and tossed the filter through the window. "I guess. They're known dealers, so that's no problem. As long as we don't have to file on them. What the hell, we might need a favor someday."

Which was how a lot of police work got done.

• • •

The move was set for Friday night. Wager wanted it done a certain way, and the Vice dicks had a pretty good picture of the suspects' routines. Besides, Friday night gave Evans and Watney a holiday weekend on ice—their lawyers couldn't get a friendly judge to sign a writ before the key finished turning behind them.

Wager's wide-brimmed hat shaded his face under the rows of white bulbs in the Cinnamon Club's marquee. He studied the photographs tacked on the red velvet of the display case, especially Annette in her feathered publicity pose. Maybe Sheldon hadn't seen that the picture was still up; or maybe he thought of it as another shrine. Most likely the picture hung there forgotten, like her file in the Open drawer.

"Mister, can I have your loose change? God, I'm hungry, mister. Mister?" A whining voice hung at his elbow and Wager turned to see the resident wino, his grimy hand upturned in a frayed and oversized coat sleeve. "Please, mister? Just your loose change?"

Wager took it as a good sign that the panhandler didn't smell cop; he dropped a couple quarters into the gray hand as a voice from inside the doorway called, "Hey—leave the gemmn alone!" The hunched figure shuffled away quickly, and Cal, frowning after the curved back, said, "Winos! I chase them off every ten minutes. Come on in, sir, and look around."

In the crowded room, pulsating cigarette smoke passed for air. Wager stood beside a line of vending machines to let his eyes adjust to the dull red light as he peered among the second and third rows of silhouettes for the clustered hair of Little Ray. Beside him, two tourists held drinks up to their lips and kept their eyes on the girl onstage. "Mobridge was never like this," giggled one nervously; the other shook his head. "South Dakota—I'm never coming back!"

"You want a drink, sir?" One of the girls he had interviewed—Clarissa?—hung in the gloom like ectoplasm and didn't recognize him. He ordered a beer and let her lead him to one of the few empty tables well back from the dancing ramp. Onstage, flesh glinting in the hot red light, a girl Wager did not know lifted her slender leg high in a chorus kick and then spun sharply. Her body turned smoothly as her head snapped quickly around to face the muted spotlight in a crimson grin. It was the first dance of her set; she wore a sleeveless dress slit high up the side and tight enough to show her lively nipples.

"Here you are, sir. That'll be three dollars."

Wager handed her a five and waved away the change. "Is Little Ray around yet? He told me to meet him here."

There was only a slight pause. Then she folded the bill and said confidentially, "He's over there—the corner table. My name's Clarissa when you're ready for a refill." She smiled and posed. "I'm on in two more sets," and was gone into the smoke.

Wager, shielding his glass from the crowded shoulders, worked his way around the wall to Little Ray's table. It was near the closed end of the dancing ramp but far enough back so the light didn't fall too heavily on him. It was also conveniently near the girls' locker room, and as Wager sidled close he saw a quick exchange between Little Ray and one of the waitresses—money for something that fit neatly into her curved palm.

"Hello, Little Ray." Wager crowded a chair up to the small table and sat.

The bushy-headed figure leaned back nervously but tried to act calm. Wager would be nervous, too, if he was carrying that much junk. "You think you're going to set me up, Mr. Narc?"

"I'm not a narc," he said truthfully. "But I am here on business."

They both watched while the dancer ended her first number. She unzipped the dress with her back to them and then spun with arms high and breasts taut and bouncing and plastic-smooth in the dull light. Wager stood and reached a bill into her sandal and she smiled widely just for him. Above, the disc jockey swung into the next number, a slower rhythm that gave her time to catch her breath and to play with the tight panties that looked pink in the glow.

"A good dancer," said Wager. "A real artist."

"Yeah. Right. Look, man, I don't have any business with you. I don't even know your name."

"Don't get your blood pressure in an uproar." Wager smiled. "You have business you don't know about yet. It will entertain you and it won't cost you a thing."

"What the hell's that mean? Look—I got to go. I got places to be."

"Your customers'll wait. It's good business to make them wait for the candy man once in a while."

"Horseshit—you can't—"

"Enjoy." He nodded toward the girl who pranced up the ramp to pause and dance with hips and shoulders in front of an arm that reached out a bill. "This one's new, right?"

Little Ray glanced at the girl sullenly. "Yeah."

"What's her name?"

"Viva."

"Did she work anywhere else before she came here?"

"You're sounding like a cop."

"Just making conversation. We got a few minutes yet."

"For what? What's this few minutes? I'm going, man!"

"Hey, hey—I told you; it's going to cost you nothing to watch. It's a demonstration just for you. Free."

"Horseshit! I'm getting—"

"Sit down." Wager's voice was low but sharp. "They just lit up the bar."

Little Ray's eyes, pink and wide in the shadows, darted to the spot of gleam high above the cash register that blinked like a scarlet Christmas light. Wordless, three or four waitresses slipped quickly toward the back. The music rose to a throbbing roll as the dancer teased first one and then the other smooth hip from the tight grip of her underwear.

"You son of a bitch."

"Cool it, Little Ray. If I was a narc, I'd have to make a buy from you to get evidence. You know that." Wager leaned forward against the noise of the music and the shouts and applause of the room. "Listen, you remember those five points I told you about?"

"I remember."

"Good. You're about to see two of them: an exclusive franchise and the best protection money can buy." He jabbed his chin toward the door where Moffett and Nolan, their ties and sport coats looking like uniforms, moved purposefully through the tables with the bouncer a hulking worry behind them. "You know those guys?"

"Jesus Christ!"

"Keep your cool. They're not after you."

In silence, Little Ray and Wager watched the two shadowy Vice detectives hover at a table across the crowded room. Then, a moment later, a third figure stood in the dim light and the three formed a little parade, Nolan in front, Moffett at the back, Curtis Evans between them, his familiar plumed baseball hat a beacon in the haze. They reached the brighter light of the entry and changed formation, a detective on each side of Evans as they went out briskly. The small red bulb stopped flashing.

Little Ray stared at Wager. "How'd you know they were coming for him?"

Wager smiled.

"How'd you know, man!"

"I told my associates you wanted a demonstration."

Little Ray hovered between doubt and belief, a note of awe in his voice. "You telling me your people bought those narcs?"

"I don't know. That's something I don't ask about. My associates deliver—that's all I know." He leaned across the table and dropped his voice so that it was blurred under the quick pulse of the dancer's final number. "Sugar's been picked up, too. They're going to be eating county food for the whole weekend." He tapped the table with a finger to underline his words. "That means their routes are yours for the next three days. A little demonstration of the exclusive franchise that my associates offer."

The man leaned back and gazed at Wager.

"I told you, Little Ray: exclusive franchise, and protection. Now you got a chance to pick up on their customers. If you can get enough stuff to service them."

"I can get it. My contacts are good, man. I can get however much I need."

"That's cool," said Wager, relieved. He didn't have any idea what he would do if his bluff had been called on supply. "Now let's find a quiet place to talk."

"What about?"

"You wanted a demonstration. We gave it to you. Now you're going to pick up a fistful of change, compliments of my associates. But they would feel hurt if you took all that without even talking to me. Very hurt."

"You want to watch me sell something, is that it?"

"No. I told you—and I'm getting damned tired of telling you—I'm not a narc. What I want is a picture of your market. If this thing goes the way I think it can, we're talking megabucks."

"You just want to know about my setup?"

Wager nodded. "And how we can make it a lot bigger and better. Let's get some fresh air."

They drifted through the milling elbows and eyes of the strip; Wager pulled his hat brim low over his face while Little Ray gave guarded nods and murmurs to the occasional quick greeting that passed. He steered the man into the recessed doorway of a low office building where the shadows concealed their faces and the display windows let them survey the flow of people. "How many dealers do you have working for you?"

"Four, sometimes five. Kids, you know? Three of them are real good. The best one's a girl—thirteen, fourteen. But smart, and nobody but her customers has spotted her." He added with a slight grin, "Fucks like a bunny, too."

"You're going to be moving a lot of stuff. You're going to need an army, not a bunch of kids. What about the dancers? Do the girls ever push for you?"

"Not for me. I think Sugar works a couple, but I don't like to use them. Listen, kids are better than those broads. They got boyfriends, and most of them have habits, too. You get a street merchant trying to support her old man and her habit, you're asking for trouble. Kids have loyalty—I'm a big brother, like."

"What happened to those two dancers who got shot a month or so back? Did they cross a dealer?"

"Maybe. I don't know. I didn't know either one of them very much."

"You never sold anything to—what's her name, Shelly?"

"No. She might take a toot every now and then. I'd line one out for her as a tip, you know? But that's it. The other one—Angela—she didn't even toot." He pulled away slightly. "Why all the questions about them?"

"They were murdered. Murders bring cops. I want to know you didn't have anything to do with them."

"I didn't! I really don't think they were dealing for anybody." He thought back. "I heard it was a sex killing; you know—somebody raped them and shot them."

Wager nodded and shifted to the hopes and dreams of a mid-level dealer who was beginning to scent the truly big time. "Tell me how you might expand your operation."

"I got to admit I've been thinking about that. Ever since that first meet, I've kind of been thinking about it. I thought, okay—so what if he's for real? How would I handle it?"

"That's fine," said Wager. "That's just what my associates want to know." He listened as Little Ray's voice grew more animated in the description of teams of five dealers each, geographically spread along the miles of the Colfax strip. Each would be under the direction of a leader. He nodded as the man talked, but underneath the smile of interest, Wager felt the letdown of another dead end. Little Ray's answers about Annette and Angela felt like the truth, and all Wager's careful work was for nothing.

"I'll run it like sales teams, you see? The leader buys for his people and takes a percentage—the more they sell, the more he gets. I've even been thinking about bonuses, too—sales competitions and maybe a free trip to Hawaii for the winner, that kind of thing. And you can't beat the security. None of them—none of the team leaders—knows any of the others. I make sure their territories don't overlap, so they don't run into each other or compete with each other. That way, if a narc gets onto one team, that's all he gets."

"That's good," smiled Wager. "Distribution, control, and security."

"Yeah, right! I didn't put it in those words, but that's right. Just good sound business practices."

"What about supply? Where do you get your stuff now?"

Little Ray's hesitancy was a reflex. Wager explained, "My associates plan on organizing this thing all the way up. That includes supply. Your supplier may fit into the organization or he may be competition. When the time comes, we want to check him out."

"Well—okay, it's a guy named Lazlo. He comes by once a week—Wednesday, Thursday, or Friday. So we can stock up for the weekend."

"How do you arrange your meets?"

Little Ray frowned.

"Come on, come on—you're with us or you're not!"

He decided. "He tells us where and what day the meet is. What time to be there. The same six or eight of us make the buys, and it all goes down in about ten minutes. We put in orders for next time, and he drives off. It's always the same people and never the same time or place. We make damn sure nobody's tailing us when we go to the meet. Very secure; he works out of his car." A sly note came into his voice. "You want to know where the next one is?"

Wager moved away from the bait. "No. But can your man resupply you for this weekend? Is he big enough to have stock on hand when you need it?"

"I got enough. I'm gonna make a killing this weekend."

"Fine. You don't want to miss out on that new business." Wager asked, "What kind of car's this Lazlo drive?"

"A dark blue van."

· CHAPTER ·

Wager's apartment, high above Downing Street, was dimly lit by the city glow that spilled through the balcony doors and bounced off the white ceiling. In the half-light, the alert bulb on his telephone answering machine made a tiny, hard gleam; Wager pressed the Rewind button as he wandered through the rooms, flipping on lights and stripping off his Mexican vest and the huaraches that always dug into the backs of his heels. Yawning widely, he pressed Play and heard the rushed quack of a voice speak from the machine: "Gabe, this is Doc. I'm on to something really hot. I'll have more for you later—be sure and give me a call later." The tape clicked and went into the carefully modulated tones of a telephone recording telling his recorder to hang up and try again. Several clicks and buzzes indicated calls and no messages, and then Doc's voice in a more urgent plea: "Gabe, man, where are you? I need to talk to you, man!" Well into the tape came the last message from Doc, and then the hiss of unused time: "Gabe, this is Doc. I got a very important item of information for you but I can't say anything now. It could be what you wanted. Give me a call later —it's important."

Doc's items of information were always very important to him, and only sometimes so to Wager. Still, it was part of the care and feeding of this particular CI that he pump up enthusiasm for everything the man dragged in, no matter how hard he was yawning and wanted only to shower away the clinging odor of cigarette smoke and drop heavily onto his hard mattress. It was almost one A.M., and chances were that Doc wasn't home yet. Not on a Friday night. He wasn't sure what Doc did with his time, or where; but in the past, the weekends were poor times to call him. Nonetheless, after grabbing a cool bottle of Killian's from his otherwise empty refrigerator, Wager dialed Doc's number and drank deeply while it rang. A breathless female voice answered quickly, "Hello?"

"This is Gabe. Doc wanted me to call him."

The voice sounded disappointed. "He ain't here now." Then, as it had apparently been told to do, "Is there a message?"

"Just tell him I called."

"Sure. What was the name?"

Wager spelled it for her and then hung up, yawning again widely enough to crack his jaws. All this extra fun was beginning to catch up with him, but there was no rest for the wicked: he'd pulled the weekend roster and in six hours would be on duty again. He'd try Doc then.

. . .

Even if he had remembered, he wouldn't have had the chance. At nine-thirty, a call came in for Homicide to report to the alley in the south 1800 block between Washington and Clarkson. A body had been found in a trash dumpster. When Wager and Axton arrived, the usual cluster of cruisers and uniforms filled the narrow concrete way, and the medical examiner was striding quickly back to his car.

"Finished certifying already?" Axton asked him.

"Not very damn difficult. Bullet in the back of the head."

A horn tooted once behind them and Wager looked over his shoulder to see a glistening black van trimmed in silver nose cautiously through the small crowd of civilians. A stereo boomed loudly for a moment before it was turned off, then the van eased into a wide spot in the alley, and the black-clad husband and wife got out. He waved familiarly at Wager and the woman smiled, too. Then they leaned against the shady side of the van to wait until they were needed.

"Man, when I go, I do not want them people toting my carcass. Definitely." Officer Blainey, shaking his head, met Axton and Wager. "One time I saw them drive up with their kid—about eleven years old. They'd been to a drive-in movie in that thing and got called out. This kid's still eating popcorn out of a box and he's dressed all in black, too!"

"Maybe he thought it was just another movie," said Wager.

"I bet they even do their grocery shopping in it." Blainey swabbed a handkerchief across his face. "Here's all we got so far." His pen ticked off the items concerning the victim: white male, about forty-five, one shot to the back of the head with a small-caliber weapon. No ID yet, and they didn't want to look for one until the Homicide detectives came or the scene was recorded by the police photographer, who hadn't yet arrived. The victim had been discovered a half-hour ago by a man collecting aluminum in the various dumpsters and garbage cans lining the alleys.

"That him?" Wager nodded toward a shabby figure in a stained military overcoat standing by himself at the fender of a police car.

"Yeah. He keeps trying to wander off. I told him to stay right in that spot or I'd park the car on his goddamned foot."

The man wagged a skinny hand at a fly circling his head.

Max said, "I did the interviews last time."

Lifting his notebook, Wager went over to him. Axton went to peer into the dumpster.

"You're the one who found the victim?" Wager showed his badge.

"Yeah. Listen, officer, how much longer you going to

keep me here?" He had the seamed and puffy face of a wino, but his bristly jaw showed little gray yet—somewhere in his thirties, Wager guessed, though he looked closer to fifty. He kept his coat buttoned despite the heat, and, from the odor, Wager figured he suffered from the chill that came with filth.

"What's your name, please?"

"Polk. Jerry Polk. I mean it, officer. I really got to get going."

"What's your big hurry, Jerry?"

He gave a shake to the gunnysack at his knee. "Cans. If I don't get them, the trash collecters will. It don't do them no good—I'm the one needs them. And I only got half a sack yet. They'll be here soon!"

"You make this route often?"

"Every Saturday. Every one I'm not in the tank, leastways."

"What's your address, Jerry?"

"Larimer Street."

"Anyplace in particular on Larimer?"

"No."

"Where do you get your mail?"

The man shook his head. "I don't." He frowned with thought. "I like the Juarez Bar a lot. Just ask for Jerry."

Wager wrote that down. "Tell me what happened."

"Not much. I opened it up to look for cans and there he was. I didn't even know it at first. I mean, I saw it and all, but I didn't even think it was somebody for a couple seconds. I almost touched him before I knew it was somebody."

"You knew he was dead?"

"I saw his head."

Wager asked a couple more questions, but Polk had seen no one leave the area, had seen no suspicious vehicles, had no idea who might have done it or even who it was. "I don't know, officer. I never saw him before."

He let the man go, watching briefly as he hustled past the

first half-dozen garbage cans to put in distance before the cops could change their minds. Then Polk veered toward the rust-colored dumpster at the end of the alley and hauled himself up to its lip, the gunnysack clinking against its side. Wager turned toward Axton, who stood noting something down.

"Archie Douglas is on his way over from the lab—Jones is off today," said Max.

"Any identification?"

Axton showed a wallet, one of those nylon kinds with a Velcro lip that snarled when you opened it. "It was empty—possible robbery. Driver's license says it's Lewis Rowe, 1258 Pearl."

"That's not far away." Wager peered in at the body, which looked oddly comfortable on its bed of stuffed trash bags, miscellaneous household scrap, newspapers and cardboard boxes, discarded clothes, and ripped-up letters. The dumpster had one sign warning against playing on it, and another to scare away people who did not live in the Emerson Arms Apartments. The sign hadn't worked for the murderer. Wager turned from the sticky tangle at the back of the man's head and the sound of busy flies that had found something tastier than grapefruit rinds. On each side of the alley, rows of apartment windows overlooked the dumpster. Here and there, faces peered down at all the excitement.

"There's a hell of a lot of doors," sighed Max.

They would have to knock on every one, asking the routine questions: Did you see anything? Did you hear anything? The autopsy would tell them for sure whether the man had been shot here or elsewhere, but only knocking on doors would tell them whether anyone had witnessed something. "A hell of a lot," agreed Wager.

"Here comes Archie. He said he'd bring the warrant." The dumpster was private property. Any evidence found on private property had to be covered by a warrant.

The stocky man lugged a large red tool kit in one hand and a Speed Graflex in the other. He was sweating in the morning sun and when he saw the dumpster, he shook his head. "You want me to dust this thing? Oil—rust—dirt: why bother?"

Wager knew what Archie was saying: it was a hell of a lot harder to get scientific evidence in real life than it was on television. "Do what you can." He watched as the lab man took a light reading before starting his photographic record of the approach to the scene.

"No television today?" asked Max.

"The cameraman's not in on Saturday, and I don't trust myself with that thing. We'll televise the autopsy, though—you can take that home for your Beta, Max. Ha."

Wager hadn't thought it was funny the first time he heard it, but Max laughed politely. Douglas said, "Oh, here," and handed Max the warrant in a narrow brown envelope. Then he took stills of the alley approaching the dumpster, writing down the details of each picture: location, compass heading, time, distances. Then he moved to the dumpster, taking a series showing the approach, and finally the interior with the body. When he pulled back out of the open door, his face was red and he seemed to be clenching his mouth to hold back a spurt of saliva. "Okay—call the disposal people."

Max went to deliver the warrant to the apartment manager; Wager beckoned to the black-clad team. They pulled the gleaming van past the police tape and down beside the dumpster. The man hopped out of the truck and briskly opened the back. The wife was ready inside to slide a gurney out the rear. When it was unfolded, the man and woman paused to put on disposable rubber gloves and white industrial masks. Then the man crawled into the dumpster and the woman handed him a black rubber bag. After a few minutes of rustling and occasional resonant thumps against the steel walls, Wager heard the zipper wrestled shut. Then the man's head, slightly disheveled, popped up. "Ready, Wanda?"

"All ready."

The small end of the bag slid over the metal lip like an eyeless slug. The woman, sprayed blond hair catching the sunlight, guided it onto the gurney. With a stifled grunt, the torso flipped out, Wanda expertly bracing it against her forearms and bouncing it heavily to the pad. A moment later the man clambered out to hold his pants crease in one hand and slap the clinging garbage off with the other. Wanda strapped down the bag. The industrial masks dangled at their necks like stethoscopes.

"Ready, Wanda?"

"All ready."

They unlocked the gurney wheels and pushed it quickly to the van, collapsing its stand as they slid it in. The man peeled off his rubber gloves, took Wanda's, and tossed both pairs back into the dumpster. Then the van glided away, a sudden burst of stereo music hanging in the hot air behind it.

"Definitely," said Blainey, "them body snatchers will not haul my ashes."

Douglas went back for final photographs of the site after the body's removal. Max returned, followed by a worried-looking apartment manager clutching the brown envelope. He grinned at Wager. "I'm too big to get through that door."

It wasn't much different from interviewing the witness. Wager, breathing lightly against the fetid smell, clambered onto the spongy mess and probed and dug with a stick for anything that might have fallen out of the pockets of victim or assailant. The only thing he came up with was a pale green slime over his shoe and a lingering odor in his sinuses.

"Well," said Max as Wager wiped at the slime with a wad of newspaper, "it had to be done. I'm just glad it was you and not me. You ready for the next of kin?"

"Let's stop by a gas station first. I want to wash my hands."

Behind Max, Blainey was rolling up the fluorescent tape that guarded the area; at the end of the alley, a patrol car flicked off its bubble lights and swung back toward the busy morning traffic. The civilians began to drift off. From somewhere down the alley came the hiss and roar of an advancing garbage truck.

• • •

The victim's address was in a block that, a couple decades ago, had started converting to large apartment complexes that had not quite taken over. Some of the multistoried buildings looked like old motels that had changed purpose. Others were newer, their floor plans angled to give each balcony a little privacy and as much of a view of the mountains as possible. Pinched between the blank walls of two tall complexes, the victim's address was one of the few single residences left. Wager and Axton went up three steps to the small, shadowed front porch, their feet crackling on its concrete slab.

The heavy-set woman who answered their knock seemed to be in her mid-twenties. Her long hair was tucked behind her ears and hung straight down her back. She wore a thin cotton blouse that swung freely when she moved, and her skirt was one of those loose, pleated kinds that the Flower generation used to wear. She was barefoot and looked warily at the badge Wager showed her.

"Does Lewis Rowe live here?" he asked.

"Yes. But he's not here right now."

"Are you Mrs. Rowe?"

"No. There's no Mrs. Rowe."

"Are you a relative?"

"I live here," she said. "He's my old man."

Axton glanced at Wager and then at the woman whose pale blue eyes were troubled now. "What's your name, please?"

"Rosalyn Shiddel."

"May we come in, Miss Shiddel?" Max asked.

The worry deepened into a frightened premonition—which, of course, was the purpose of the question. You prepared them a little for the bad news just by showing up. Then you hinted a little more by asking to come in. Most of them knew before you finally had to say it.

She stood back from the door, hands clasped in front of her hips. "What's wrong? Something's wrong, isn't it?"

Axton told her, his deep voice a murmur.

"Oh God, no!"

"Does he have any relatives living here?"

"No—just me. I mean, I'm not a relative, but . . . Oh God, no!"

"We'll need someone to identify him, miss. It won't take long."

She was numbly silent on the ride to the morgue that filled a basement wing of Denver General Hospital. Neither Wager nor Axton said much either. They pulled into a No Parking area; Axton flipped the visor to show its ID. Then they led the woman, now wearing straw sandals, into the cooler air of the identification room. The sheeted figure lay in the harsh medicinal light, a baggage tag looped to one toe. As usual, Wager went to the covered head while Axton quietly moved behind the woman to grab her in case she collapsed. He lifted the sheet to reveal the profile and was pleased to see that some orderly had thought to surround the seeping skull with a rolled towel that hid the blood.

"Can you identify the victim as Lewis Rowe of 1258 Pearl Street, Denver?"

"Oh God—Doc! Oh God, God!"

Wager stared at her. "Doc? Did you call him Doc?"

She nodded, wide eyes still fixed on the gray profile. Inside the open mouth, the teeth were the same color as the drained flesh.

Wager let the coarse sheet settle back and took out his little green notebook. In the back was a list of telephone numbers with cryptic initials beside them. He asked the woman, "What's the phone number at your house, Miss Shiddel?"

Too much in shock to wonder why he had asked, she told him, each figure confirming what he already knew.

• • •

They interviewed the woman at Homicide. It wasn't a good place during the workday, even on a Saturday: telephones rang, Assault or Burglary detectives wandered past with professional curiosity, the chatter of a dozen radios made a crackling background of restless noise, and someone was always coming through asking for someone else. But the surroundings served to stifle grief, if there was any, and to make a victim's friends and relatives believe a little more in the importance of the questions the detectives had to ask.

"He was one of your snitches?" Axton muttered as they stood at the coffee machine and poured cups for the three of them.

"He called yesterday to tell me he had something important. I think it was about Sheldon and Williams." He did not like to think it was about himself.

Rosalyn Shiddel took cream and sugar in her coffee and Axton measured it out. "And he was shot in the back of the head with a small-caliber weapon."

"And then dumped."

"Yeah. The autopsy'll tell us for sure—but, yeah, I'll bet he was."

Wager followed Axton back to the desk where the woman sat wadding a Kleenex in one hand and tugging at a strand of lank hair with the other. She smiled briefly when Axton set her coffee on the glass top, then she looked down at her Kleenex again.

"Can you tell us about last night, Miss Shiddel? About where you were and where Doc went and anything he might have said?"

She couldn't give them much information. She was home all evening watching television, and Doc went out about ten. He never told her much about what he did. That was part of the arrangement, and it was okay with her because Doc had always been good to her. Some of the men she'd been with were either wimps or real bastards, you know? They either hung onto you like a wet dishcloth so you couldn't even take a—go to the bathroom—by yourself, or they'd treat you like dirt, like you were a servant or a dog or something. But not Doc. So she never asked.

"Did he tell you anything at all?"

"No. He said he was going out on business. He said he'd see me later."

"But he didn't hint what kind of business or where?"

No. Doc did that a lot—went out on business, and she believed him. He never came back stinking of other women, and she could tell when the business, whatever it was, went well, because he'd get sort of hyperexcited. He was that way anyhow, excited, but when it went well, he really got off.

"Was he hyper last night?"

"Kind of, before he left. He tried half-a-dozen times to call this guy Gabe, but there was never any answer." She looked up, remembering. "He called."

"Who?" asked Max.

"This guy Gabe. He called, I don't know, maybe midnight or one o'clock, and wanted to talk to him."

Axton glanced at Wager, who nodded slightly. "Did Doc ever have any friends or acquaintances over to the house?" asked Max.

He did have a few, but she remembered only their first names. The last time they had visitors was a couple weeks ago. "Doc liked to stay private—he used the phone a lot for his business calls, but we didn't see many people." Yes, she answered to another question, he did have some favorite places to go. He liked Sandy's, that place over on Kalamath near Colfax. They went there a lot, and sometimes had dinner at the Ravioli Palace on Gaylord. Doc really liked Italian food. And movies. They went all the time. They'd spend maybe an hour looking at the ads in the paper and drink some wine and talk it over, maybe share a joint because it mellowed him out; they really didn't get high, you know, just a little buzz-on. That's what Doc used to call it, "a buzz-on." The phrase broke her down in whining sobs and Wager and Axton stepped back to give her time to herself.

"What the hell were you doing calling him at one in the morning, Gabe?"

"I'll tell you about it later."

Axton, watching the woman, said, "Can't beat that for an alibi, I guess." Then, "Are you maybe up to a little extracurricular activity?"

"Maybe."

"Well, I've been your partner long enough to know I can't talk you out of it."

That went without saying, so Wager said nothing.

"If you get in a squeeze, call me."

"I can handle it."

It was Max's turn to say "Maybe."

They questioned Rosalyn Shiddel for another hour, including times out for spasms of tears. The worst came when they asked for a photograph of Doc. She didn't have one, she said. She'd wanted one, but Doc didn't like pictures, and now she never would have one, and that's what broke her up.

Then they drove her back to the small house that sat like

a knickknack between the tall apartment buildings. She told them that Doc never mentioned any relatives, and the only property he had was the furniture. He always had enough money for rent and food, but she didn't think he had a bank account. There were a lot of things she didn't know, including what would happen to her now. Neither Wager nor Axton could advise her on that, beyond telling her to get a lawyer—maybe the common-law statutes covered her. They left her standing on the other side of the rusty screen door, barefoot again and with a fresh Kleenex wadded in her hand. Neither man wanted to look back as they left. When they reached the car, Wager said, "How about some lunch?"

"Italian food?"

"Right."

She was still staring through the screen as they pulled away.

• • •

The Ravioli Palace had a glass awning that hung brightly like half an umbrella on the blank face of a yellow stucco building. The long, well-lit room was half-filled already, and from the noisy kitchen floated the aroma and heat of sauces and baking meats. A smiling waitress in a black nylon dress with a white ruffle down the front led them to a table and pulled a pencil from her graying hair.

"You want a drink before you order?"

Wager had a coffee; Axton a 7-Up. The menu, a mimeographed sheet clipped inside a plastic folder, said at the top, *If You Don't Like Garlic, Go Home,* and the food, when it came, lived up to the warning.

It finally occurred to Max. "You didn't even know what he looked like!"

"We only talked on the phone."

"How long was he in your stable?"

"Six years."

"And you never met the guy? That's really something."

It was nothing. People that you'd never met died every day. And having met someone never kept them from dying. And nobody you ever met would keep you from dying either, when the time came. Life was made up of goodbyes, his mother used to say, so you should act kindly toward others, as if you expected to say goodbye. She'd believed that last part, and tried to live up to it. But the meaning had changed a bit for Wager: you expected goodbyes, and when they came, you accepted them and went about your business. And Doc knew the risks. Even if Wager had sort of talked him into it.

When the waitress began clearing the dishes, Wager showed her Doc's driver's license with its small color photograph and asked her if she knew the man.

"Sure, I know him. Him and"—she dredged up the name—"Rosalyn! They always have a pizza half-and-half: anchovies and pepperoni."

"Were they here last night?"

She hesitated. "Are you friends of his?" She smiled nervously. "I mean, it's not my business; I don't really know him except he comes in here all the time. Anchovies and pepperoni, every time."

Axton showed his badge. "He was shot last night and we're trying to trace his movements."

"Oh, my! Shot!"

"Was he here?"

"No. Oh, my, isn't that too bad!"

"Did he ever come here with anyone else?" Wager asked.

She fiddled with the pencil sticking out of her hair. "Before Rosalyn, he had another girl. I can't remember her name, though."

"How long ago was this?"

"Oh, my—a year and a half? A long time, anyway. Was Doc hurt bad?"

"He was killed."

"Oh, my. Poor Rosalyn." She studied her order book for a few moments as if looking for words. Finally she asked, "Do you folks want dessert?"

Axton drove across the sun-softened tar streets toward Kalamath and Sandy's. It was one of those August afternoons when the clouds were already piling up over the mountains west of town and promised to boil into towering thunderheads that would sail east across the prairies toward Kansas and Nebraska and, eventually, the sprawling green land of tree-lined farms that was the Mississippi valley. Later in the day, toward evening, you would see the clouds disappear over the eastern horizon, their tops glimmering white like distant sails, their feet under the curve of the earth, and a blue haze where rain and hail and wind pounded down. Then the radio would broadcast warnings about severe thunderstorms and tornado sightings, and, here and there on the gullied prairies, small streams would explode with yellow boiling water and the foamy debris that jammed culverts and washed out bridges and sent slices of Colorado clay roiling eastward toward the giant rivers. But here in Denver, just inside the formation of the storms, the streets were scorched and dusty and the odor of an occasional lawn sprinkler steamed off the glittering surface with the smell of summer. It was, Wager thought, like one of the old sayings vaguely remembered from childhood, one of the many he'd half-forgotten—something about the rain falling on some, while the sun shone on others, and only El Buen Dios could say why.

Doc was about Wager's age, maybe a little older. Maybe, like Wager, he had hopped barefoot and yelping across the summer heat of dirt streets before they were tarred and paved. Maybe, like Wager, he had sought the relief of some neighbor's cool sprinkler winking diamonds of water in the sun.

Max slowed and turned onto Kalamath, the shade of the

remaining trees forming a tunnel of coolness down which bicyclists weaved past parked cars, and kids on skateboards thumped noisily over the concrete slabs of sidewalk. Here and there, joggers sprinted past, running as if all eyes were on them. Wager looked at the lean, tanned legs of a girl running through the mottled shade and half-wondered if Doc had found pleasure in such a sight. There were a lot of things about Doc he would never know, and he had no reason at all to get maudlin over the man's death. Snitches died every day in every way, and sooner or later everyone joined them. There was no reason for Wager to feel diminished. But he did.

The heavy sun came back as they reached a block where the sheltering trees had been sliced down to make the street wider. Ahead, the glittering swirl of windshields and hot metal marked busy Colfax, and now the homes were mixed with old-fashioned small apartment buildings and occasional two- and three-unit businesses. Max turned the car into a narrow drive leading past a chipped corner that bore a scarred sign, PARKING IN REAR.

"Ever been here?" he asked as they walked to the entry of the small tavern. The two large windows in front were half-blanked out, and above the blue enamel a painter had scrolled in long-faded gold, *Sandy's Bar.*

"No." But he knew what to expect—one of the few remaining neighborhood taverns. There were a few booths and a lot of tables, and a long, dark bar whose carved pillars rose up to the ceiling, holding a mirror and surrounded by shelves of bottles, most so high out of reach that they were probably never used. Wager suspected that a lot of the brightly labeled containers were empty, anyway. At arm's level were the bourbons and scotches and ryes that most of the single men ordered when they spent the evenings watching the television set mounted up in the corner. The ladies tended to drink gin and vodka, and customers of both sexes believed they had a true friend in the bartender.

Maybe they did; he looked like everybody's friend, a round face with a quiet smile and a fringe of white hair over his ears. He moved placidly behind the counter, chatting with a middle-aged man and woman who nursed a couple bottles of Miller's. There was no jukebox, the television set was off, and not one fern sprouted anywhere. The only sound was of quiet voices and the hum of two large fans on the ceiling. Wager understood why Doc liked the place.

"Help you gents?"

Wager opened his badge case. "We're investigating a homicide, a man who came in here a lot."

"Oh?"

"Lewis Rowe. Also known as Doc."

The man's scraggly eyebrows lifted. "Thin guy? Kind of nervous? Always telling jokes?"

Wager showed the bartender Doc's driver's license. "Is this him?"

The bartender settled a pair of bifocals across his fleshy nose and tipped his head back to peer through the lower half. "That's Doc. Well, I'll be darned." He called to the couple sitting at the cool end of the bar, glancing their way. "Fella here says Doc's been killed."

"Killed?" The woman wagged her head. "Isn't that just awful!"

"How'd it happen?" asked the man.

That's what they were trying to find out. Wager asked, "Was he in here last night?"

The bartender tugged thoughtfully at an earlobe. He had gray hairs sprouting there, too, as if the baldness on top had forced the hair out in other directions. "Yeah—I believe he was." He called down the bar again. "Doc was in here last night, wasn't he?"

"Sure was." The woman had one of those quacking voices that seemed to be pressed flat somewhere in her throat. "Sat right there at that table. Talked about going to the greyhound races tomorrow with Rosalyn. Poor woman."

"Was he with anyone?"

"No," said the bartender. "Doc usually came in just with his wife or by himself. He was a real nice fella, real friendly. It sure is a shame."

"What time did he leave?"

"Oh, gosh, let's see—Friday night's a busy night—let's see . . ."

"It was a little after eleven," came the quacking voice. "You just turned on 'Benny Hill' and Doc said he wanted to watch it but he couldn't. He had to meet somebody, he said."

Axton was standing closer to the woman. "Did he say who?"

She shook her head.

"Or where?" Wager asked.

"Yes, he did say where—we joked about that. He said he had to meet this man, and I said it wasn't a man, not at that place, and that's why he came in without his wife. We always joked like that, you know."

"What place?"

"The Cinnamon Club. That topless-bottomless place over on Colfax. Doc had to be at the Cinnamon Club to meet this man about something, but he didn't say what."

• • •

They sat in the car in the small parking lot behind the tavern and did more thinking than talking. You looked for patterns. In a series of possibly related crimes, you always looked for a pattern. That's what the idea of a modus operandi was all about. If something worked once for a criminal—burglary, rape, even murder—chances were he'd do it the same way again. A learned technique could be polished with repetition, leaving more time to guard against witnesses or evidence. It was the same thing that led animals down familiar paths at the same time every day: they knew what to look for each time, had an idea how a victim would behave, were more aware of any threatening change in the pattern or the menace of a larger predator. And now Wager was a predator, looking for the worn path, the warm spoor, the gently rising blade of grass.

"All he told you was that he had something important about Sheldon and Williams. You think he was going to find out more?"

"My guess is it was about Sheldon and Williams—he didn't say for sure. And I guess he asked one question too many."

Axton sighed and started the car. He eased out into the busy traffic on Kalamath. "Have you come up with any ideas at all?"

"Nothing." About his contacts and moves, Doc was as silent with Wager as he was with everyone else. Now he was as silent as the grave. "I've found out that Annette Sheldon was making a lot of money. I think it was a lot more than she made as a dancer, and I think it has something to do with dope. But none of my leads corroborate that." He added, "Angela Williams apparently brought home only what she made as a dancer. Other than the way they were killed, there's no tie at all between them that I can find. Can you make something of that?"

Axton grunted a negative sound. "But it keeps coming back to that, doesn't it? That all three were killed the same way."

"Well, the murderer didn't make Doc look raped."

The big man snorted. "Right. He was robbed instead. Or made to look that way." He sighed again and swung the cruiser back toward the block where Doc's body had been found. It was time to start knocking on all those apartment doors.

• CHAPTER •

10

By the time the shift ended, Wager was wincing when an apartment had neither bell nor knocker. He could buzz from the lobby and identify himself so they'd open the security door; but once in the building and going down the long halls a door at a time, he had to use his knuckles, and after four hours of it they were sore. All to no profit—so far no one in the surrounding apartment towers had seen or heard anything when Doc's body was tossed on the trash heap. When they returned to Homicide, Max scribbled a note for the oncoming shift, telling them where he and Wager had quit canvassing. Stretching mightily so that his fingers brushed the ceiling of the office, he asked casually what Wager had planned for his Saturday evening.

"A night on the town."

"Look, Gabe, what you're doing . . . It's tough enough when somebody goes under legitimately—when they have the proper backup and authorization. . . ."

"I know."

"Yeah, well, just make sure you're covered, okay? And I'm not talking about the bad guys. More than one career's been flushed because somebody went out on a limb by himself." He led the way to the elevator and pushed the button for the underground parking garage. "Have you thought about telling Doyle what you're doing?"

He had, and decided against it. "I'm just drinking a few beers and talking to some people. On my own time." And he didn't want to take the chance that Doyle, with an administrator's reflexive No, would tell him that the Homicide Division was a team, and that, by God, cases would be dealt with according to the operations manual or he—Detective Sergeant Wager—could get his butt out of his—Chief Bartholomew Doyle's—Homicide section and into the Traffic Division.

The garage doors opened to the cool odor of stale automobile exhaust and a scattering of concrete pillars holding up the gloom between distant lights. The two men paused for a moment, groping for something that would not let the shift end on an argument.

"Munn thinks he spotted Pepe the Pistol again."

"Where?"

"Over in the projects near his girlfriend's house. The word is she's knocked up and that's why he's still around."

"His buddies are dead but chivalry's not, is that it?"

"Just young love, I guess." Max's large shoe scraped the gritty concrete floor. "If you need help, Gabe, will you give me a call? Don't try and do it all by yourself, okay?"

"Sure."

"I mean it, partner."

"Right—will do."

He watched the big man thread his way between the silent cars, and a few moments later heard the slam of a door. Max was all right—Max was his partner. But he had a wife and kids to worry about. He was the kind of guy who had a lot more fear for them than he had for himself, and so sometimes he wouldn't take chances that he thought might hurt them. Not the physical threats and dangers—those came with the job, and Max, like every other cop and most of their families, accepted those chances. It was the paperwork dangers that worried the big man, those ill-defined risks that lay outside the boundaries of authorization. But Wager liked to believe that if you let that happen, then pretty soon you might not act at all—you only reacted.

You hid behind what the team thought, and you let rules govern how you moved and where you headed. For Wager, that was no way to go after murderers.

• • •

He slept heavily until the alarm went off at nine and then took a long, steamy shower after a series of push-ups and squats and sit-ups that worked the stiffness out of muscles and put a feeling of alertness back in his mind. Sound mind, sound body—everything but a sound plan. He was still groping for a coherent pattern that would lead to a motive, but doing something was always better than doing nothing. "Do something, lieutenant!" He could still hear the terrified voice of an ashen corporal shrieking at their new platoon commander, a kid who, by the calendar, was Wager's own age. They hunkered, drenched by the urine-smelling spray of a rice paddy, while the earth shuddered and the goggle-eyed corporal screamed, "Do something—even if it's wrong—do something!" He did; he stood up and caught one right in the head—*thoonk!* That's just how it sounded, like a stick hitting a ripe watermelon: *thoonk.*

But right or wrong, do something. And that led Wager back to the strip, his Trans Am surging and slowing with the heavy Saturday night traffic that crammed the four lanes. He passed LaBelle's corner but she wasn't there; half-a-dozen blocks down, he swung out of the stream of cars to look for a parking place along one of the crowded side streets. Across from a small neighborhood grocery store that lit up the corner of a large apartment building, he found a telephone hood with a machine that still worked. The Everready Lounge was a block and a half away, and he dialed its number.

"Is Charley Plummer there?"

"I'll ask." A hand muffled the receiver and Wager could

picture the bartender calling over the crowd. A cautious voice finally answered, "Yeah?"

"This is Gabe. I want to talk to you."

"Now?"

"That's right. Meet me on the corner of Colfax and Washington—south side. Ten minutes."

" . . . All right."

Wager saw the thin figure hunched like a half-closed hand before the Lizard noticed him. The man walked slowly, close to the storefronts, his glance restless but elusive with that kind of guarded awareness that prison taught. And which served on the street as well. When their eyes met across Washington Street, Wager tilted his head down the darker sidewalk leading away from the strip. Without a reply, Plummer turned that way.

He waited in the shadow of a tall hedge halfway down the block. "What have you got for me, Plummer?"

"Not much." His lips scarcely moved and Wager had to lean close to hear the hoarse murmur. "I hung around Foxy Dick's like you wanted me to. I asked about that one—Angela. I said I was just back in town and wanted to see her again. Hell, most of them don't remember her name by now." He hesitated. "That other place, the Cinnamon Club, that was a little different."

"Different how?"

"I can't put my finger on it. I asked about that one—where she was."

"So?"

"So the bartender—what's he, Vietnamese? Anyway, he calls the bouncer and says, 'He's asking about Shelly.' It was like it was some big deal, you know?"

"Any threats?"

"No, nothing like that. But this big sumbitch, seven feet high and a face like a gumball, he comes over and says, 'What for?' 'I been out of town,' I says. 'I want to say hello.' 'She ain't here no more,' he says. 'She got shot.' And then he stands there like I'm supposed to say something. Hell, what am I supposed to say? 'Sorry to hear that,' I says. 'How'd it happen?' 'Why do you want to know,' he says. 'Hey, man, I'm just asking,' I says. 'Ask somewhere else,' he says, and he looks at me like he don't really believe what I'm telling him. Looks at me all the way out the goddamn door like he wants to remember me. I didn't even get a chance to buy a drink."

Wager weighed the Lizard's story, turning it over. Then he showed the wizened man a sketch of Doc that the police artist had put together from the driver's license and the corpse. "Did this guy show up while you were there?"

He bent to peer at the drawing. "I don't think so. It's darker in there than it is here, and I didn't get to see many people. I mean, he sort of ran me out, you know?"

"He was killed last night. The last place we trace him to is the Cinnamon Club. He was asking about Shelly, too."

The puffy eyes swiveled up. "Holy shit, Wager, what are you getting me into?"

It would be nice to be able to say "Nothing." Like it would be nice to be able to say that Doc was still alive. "That's why I'm telling you. Better stay away from there for a while."

"Hell yes, I will! And more than a while, man. I told you before, I don't like them places anyway." He added, "And I'll tell you something else—I'm not working for you no more!"

"Why's that?"

"Clinton!" The whisper hissed. "He's laughing at you fuckers—he helped beat that kid—Goddard—to death, and he knows you can't lay a thing against him."

"That's because Jimmy King won't name him. I figure he's afraid to."

"He's too smart to. He gets out of the can, he's still alive; he fingers Clinton, he's dead."

"Has Clinton said anything to you?"

"Not to me, no. But he's making noises like he thinks somebody spilled on both him and King. He could think I'm one of them somebodies."

"Has he asked anything about me?"

"About you? Goddamn, man, he better not even think I know your name! I don't even want to know your name!"

"Somebody's been asking around about me. I thought it was him."

"What the hell's he got to ask? He knows you're a cop. And besides, Wager, he's laughing at you. I hope to Christ he don't know I'm finking for you—he won't be laughing no more, and neither will I."

"Just stay cool. King could have shot off his mouth to anybody and probably did. Clinton won't do a thing—there's still too much heat."

"I hope to hell so. But for any more stooling, go find yourself another pigeon. My insurance premium's getting too high, Wager."

He remained in the shadows as Plummer, a small roll of new bills in his hip pocket, turned back toward the noisy lights of Colfax; his elbows angled out and his walk waddled slightly, like—Wager thought—a lizard.

The Cinnamon Club.

It wasn't Rome, but all of a sudden most of the roads seemed to lead there. The trouble was, they were more like trails than roads, and twisted and dim ones at that. And none of them showed how Angela or Foxy Dick's fit in. Or who was asking questions about him.

Wager, his mind going over the facts and guesses that the Lizard had stirred up, drove down Colfax to LaBelle's roadside stand. Do something, lieutenant.

• • •

Even among the extra crowds and flurries of a Saturday night, Wager could make out the regulars on the strip as he slowly drove by. They formed a pattern of reference points like boulders under a frothy mountain stream. At first glance, the swirls and splashes of laughter and music seemed chaotic, but, when looked at long enough, the chaos revealed a pattern: that bulge in the flow of pedestrians was around Hey You Jones, the half-crazy beggar who every night stationed himself as close to the movie theater as the management would allow. That dimmer section, where pedestrians hurried their pace because there was nothing to lure them, was the wall around a fancy French restaurant; and that long-haired kid sitting on it and swinging his feet was the restaurant's rent-a-cop, watching over the customers' cars parked behind the partial safety of that wall. Across the street, a burst of loud, welcoming laughter, where one of the steerers for the Nude Review Disco greeted a pair of cowboys like they were descending gods. Up there, where the traffic of a major artery cut across the strip, a frizzy-haired blond in short-shorts and high, shiny boots posed on her corner. Periodically, like a figure in a cuckoo clock, her black pimp, Emery Reeves, AKA The Spook, emerged at the doorway of Pert's Place to check on her. Wager didn't know this girl's name yet, but he would in time. Ahead, turning into the line of stop-and-go traffic, an unmarked police cruiser stood out as if it had flashers: Moffett and Nolan making one of their routine patrols, another part of the subsurface permanency.

Down past the shill for the Varieties, the half-naked Raymondo in his black jockstrap waved toward someone dealing something on a corner; and beyond that, back at her regular place now, stood LaBelle. Wager blinked his lights as he neared, and her dark face stilled. Then she shrugged. He paused at the curb and leaned across to open the door.

"You getting to be a regular, honey." Her pink dress had a network of fresh wrinkles and she smelled of a bath of strong perfume. "Once around the block, piggy—it's a busy night."

"Saturday night crowd?" He eased back into traffic.

"That and payday, honey—down at Fort Carson. Most of the other girls gone down there this weekend."

"What have you got for me, LaBelle?"

"I got what every man wants, honey." She giggled slightly and he saw the large, black circles of her pupils.

"Are you on hard stuff again?"

"You go to hell." The giggle changed abruptly to a sneer. "What I'm on—what I ain't on—that's my business. Not yours, not nobody's. Mine!"

"Sure, LaBelle. All I want is some information. Do you remember what I wanted you to find out?"

"I remember. You think I'm a monkey-woman. Maybe I am, piggy, but I remember you."

Wager wasn't very good at dealing with drunks or people who were stoned. Even in uniform, he'd had his problems trying to mask the repugnance he felt for their lack of control and the ease with which they fell into self-pity. And he never quite erased the suspicion that most of them were not nearly as blanked out as they pretended to be. But he tried to stifle his reaction—LaBelle was touchy enough when she was sober; she was twice as volatile when high. And he needed any information she could give him. "Anything on Annette Sheldon?"

"Never heard of her. I asked around, but them dancers, they not real professionals, so they don't have no regular customers, you know? I heard of maybe a dozen that's in the life regular. 'Call girls'—sit on their tails and wait for a man to call them, you know? Shit, amateurs!"

"But not Annette?"

"No. Nobody out of that Cinnamon Club that I heard of."

"What about Foxy Dick's?"

"Not the one you wanted—that Angela. What's she, another Spick?"

"Anywhere else?"

"Well, yeah! A lot of places got girls that does what their

pimp tells them. But not me, piggy. I don't have no pimp and I don't need no pimp. LaBelle Brown is her own woman, and I don't work for no man." She added, "I heard most about a dump way out east on Colfax—the Turkish Delights."

That one used to be the Arabian Nights before the Iranian embassy thing. It was past the city limits and beyond Wager's official territory. "Did you hear anything about either girl dealing dope?"

"I told you I ain't." Her hand flapped toward the approaching corner. "But these days, who ain't dealing? Let me out here, piggy. I got to use the little girls' room. And that'll be twenty dollars for my time, honey."

He watched her sashay into the porno arcade, a familiar word and cackle of laughter for the doorman who paced his three or four steps back and forth in front of the entry. Then Wager pulled an illegal U-turn away from the avenue and looked for another telephone. He might as well make the full round like the busy little bee he was, flitting from one bright blossom to the next. Almost, he thought wryly, like LaBelle.

Fat Willy's office was a bar phone, and he did not like Wager to call him there. But sometimes the big man needed a little goading, and the frustrations Wager felt about these cases gave him a touch of satisfaction in needling Willy.

"I told you I would call you, Wager." The muttered words barely carried over his labored breathing.

"Do you want to talk now or meet me somewhere?"

"Man, you cannot take a hint, can you?"

"What have you picked up on, Willy?"

"Nothing more on you, since you're so worried. That meatball, Little Ray, he's running around like Sherman marching through Georgia. I hear tell he's going to be the main man for the whole strip—or so he says."

"Just rewards for honest labor. Did you ever hear of a guy named Doc?"

"I heard the name."

"He got killed last night."

"I heard that, too. It's my business to hear things."

"Anything on it?"

"Just that he got it in the back of the head. It sounds a lot like them two girls, Wager. Pretty soon people going to ask what you're doing to protect the citizenry."

"What have you heard about the Cinnamon Club?"

"Word I get is they're worried about going under. Them and Foxy Dick's, too. But, hell, a lot of people's worried about that nowadays."

Wager remembered both Berg and Thomas complaining about bad business. But he thought that was just the usual poor-mouthing that managers handed out. "They look busy tonight."

"Sure—but one weekend ain't a whole week. My sources tell me that both them people borrowed big to get going, and times, they are hard. They are also a-changing, and that has people worried."

"What's that mean?"

"They got a law against bottomless dancing where liquor's served—the one they been appealing. It's coming up for decision soon. The state supreme court."

That had been pending for years, since the legislature passed the law and the clubs had joined together to dump it into the judicial mill with a challenge. First amendment. Artistic expression. Wager, like everyone else, had almost forgotten about it. "It won't hurt business that much."

"Any much is too much right now. And my sources tell me that if they go to a federal appeal, they're going to have a big overhead item with lawyers' fees. Man, the lawyers end up with it all, don't they? Sometimes I think I'm in the wrong business."

"Annette Sheldon was bringing in extra money, Willy. A lot of it, and it doesn't look like she was whoring for it."

The line was silent for a lurching breath or two. "She dealing?"

"Little Ray couldn't tie her to the action. I can't find anybody who can."

"Uh huh. But that don't mean she wasn't. It only means she wasn't big at it."

"It was steady income. Long-term and steady and out of the club. If she was a competitor for Little Ray, he'd know her."

"Uh huh, yeah, you right. Well, now you got my curiosity up. Man my size got a lot of curiosity in him. Maybe I'll mosey over to that Cinnamon Club and look at some white pussy."

"Just before he was killed, Doc visited that place."

"No shit?" In the background someone started a jukebox with some hard, tuneless pulse. "Was he one of your people?"

It couldn't hurt Doc now. "Yes."

"And now you telling me to be careful, Wager? You worried about ol' Willy?"

"I'm just telling you what happened."

"Haw—next thing you'll want to tuck me in bed. Give ol' Willy a good-night kiss and tuck me safe in beddy-bye! That what you want to do, Wager?"

"I don't give a damn if they slice you into pork chops, Willy. All I want is the information."

"Mr. Hard-Ass hisself, worried about his poor little Willy-Boy." The voice went falsetto. " 'Y'all take care of yourself, y'hear'—ha!"

Wager half-grinned at the buzzing telephone. It served him right for hinting at any tie other than money or leverage between him and Willy. They'd known each other for ten years or more, longer than he'd known Doc. But this relationship was one where score was kept by a hazy kind of coup-counting; the money was always paid, the information was usually straight, but the manner of trade required triumphant laughter over some discovered weakness in the other. Score one for Fat Willy; Wager half-wondered, and not for the first time lately, if he was getting too old and kindly for this type of work. He'd have to tone himself up —bayonet a few babies, maybe. Or visit the Cinnamon Club again.

• • •

He reached it a little before midnight, the same time, perhaps, that Doc would have been leaving last night. The bouncer recognized him as he crossed the glare beneath the marquee, and it wasn't just Wager's suspicious nature that detected a nervous scurry among some of the girls working the crowded floor.

"Something you need?"

Wager held out the police sketch of Doc. "Was this man in last night? Say, from eleven to around twelve or one?"

The bouncer tilted the paper against the glow falling in from the marquee. "I already told those other two cops: I don't know." A thundering crescendo of drums forced him to half-shout. "It was real crowded last night."

"Witnesses say he came here about eleven, to meet a man. Later on, he was found shot."

"I don't know if he was here or not. I didn't see him."

"All right," said Wager. "Let's start with the bartender."

The bouncer tugged at his lower lip, then turned. Wager followed the man's wide back to the bar. The counter light glowed faintly up against the tiers of bottles, each with its bright chrome spout like a curving finger. Berg, the manager, was already there; Wager figured that he, too, had a little red light that blinked Cop.

"What's the problem, Cal?"

"He's looking for somebody. Says he was in here last

night." He handed the drawing to Berg. "I don't remember the guy."

Berg peered at the drawing in the dim light. Overhead, like heat lightning, the steady flicker of strobes from the dance ramp sent red pulses across the glitter-spray of the ceiling.

Berg shook his head. "It was crowded last night. For a change. You're not going to want to question all the girls again, are you?"

"Why not?" Wager handed the drawing to Nguyen, the bartender, who held it in the light beneath the bar. As he expected, the Vietnamese shook his head, gold teeth glinting.

"Because we're busy tonight! Goddamn, look—the house is full. Best night all week, and you show up to hassle my waitresses!"

"It shouldn't take long, Mr. Berg. Just call them to the office one at a time. Yes, they've seen him; no, they haven't. And they're back on the floor."

"I'm a taxpayer, goddamn it! I run a legitimate entertainment business, and I don't have to put up with this kind of harassment!"

"And I'm running a police investigation of a homicide. I'm trying to do it without issuing warrants or calling all your employees down to headquarters to answer questions there."

"Is that a threat?"

"Yes."

"You're threatening me? Goddamn it, what's your badge number!"

Wager held it up and waited until Berg had made a show of copying it on a bar napkin that he poked angrily into his trouser pocket. Then he said pleasantly, "Now, Mr. Berg, I'm going to give you one minute to make up your mind: either call in the girls or you're under arrest for accessory to a crime."

"Accessory!"

He nodded. "Colorado Criminal Code, article 8, section 105, paragraph 2(d), 'the obstruction of anyone in the performance of any act which might aid in the discovery, detection, apprehension, prosecution, conviction or punishment of a suspect.' You will also be charged under section 106, 'refusal to permit inspections,' and section 108, paragraph 1(b), 'refraining from reporting to law enforcement authorities the commission or suspected commission of any crime or information relating to a crime.' " It was a section of the criminal code that had served Wager well in the past, and he had long ago memorized this little speech. "Sections 106 and 108 are misdemeanors. But 'Accessory' is a class-four felony and punishable by up to ten years in prison and a thirty-thousand-dollar fine or both."

"Thirty—!"

"And ten years in Canon City." He smiled.

"Shit. Come on." Berg stamped his way through the crowd toward the office. Wager, behind him, could feel the presence of the bouncer at his back. In the office, with the closed door muffling the noise of the dance floor, Berg took a moment to light a cigar and blow a stream of thin brown smoke across his littered desk. Then, "Cal, start bringing them in. Quietly, you hear?"

"Okay, Mr. B."

He waited until he heard the door close behind Cal before telling Berg, "I hear you're worried about the business folding."

The man's face jerked up in the small circle of light that covered the desk top. The glare accentuated dark rings under his eyes. "Who says? I'm worried about profits. Who the hell's not worried about profits? But the business is good —it's sound!"

"Happy to hear it." Wager tried another angle. "One of the girls told me that Shelly brought in maybe a thousand in a good week. Does that sound about right to you?"

"Yeah. For a good week. We ain't had many like that in a long time, but, yeah, Shelly did all right."

"Her husband says she averaged fifteen hundred in a poor week."

Berg slowly took the cigar off his lip. "He said what?"

Wager repeated it as the man leaned back out of the light.

"She might have done that good once or twice," said Berg. "Maybe that's what he meant."

"Do any of the girls ever skim?"

He shrugged. "A little, maybe. But Cal and Nguyen keep a good eye on the cash flow. And so do I. It's not exact, but you get a rough idea how many bills a girl gets stuck in her G-string each night. Where's she going to hide it?" He chewed his cigar slowly. "If Shelly was skimming that much, she'd have been spotted; she'd have been out on her sweet ass long ago."

"Maybe she had some business on the side."

"She wasn't laying the customers, if that's what you mean. You can tell if a girl organizes a little business on the side. It's my license to tell, right?" His eyes half-closed, he looked somewhere into the darkness beyond Wager, then he ran a restless hand across his pink scalp. "She could have been screwing around outside. Maybe she was. I can't watch them when they're not here. But she wasn't pulling any extra money out of this place, that's for sure. Not one damn dollar. Her husband's not telling you right, Wager." He poked the cigar through the air with a burst of fresh anger. "And you can charge me with every goddamn section you want to, it won't do you no good. I know nothing about anything she did, except dance and serve drinks!"

"The man whose picture I showed you, he was asking about Shelly the night he was killed. He came here to meet somebody."

"Well, he didn't meet me. I didn't see him."

"He was a snitch, Mr. Berg. He said he was onto something big, and he came here to check it out."

Even in the soft, yellow light of the desk lamp, Berg's face looked as gray as the ash on his cigar. He stared at Wager for a breath or two and finally said, "If he was a snitch, anybody could have hammered him. If he was a fucking snitch, he deserved to be hammered!" The cigar plugged his tight mouth.

The girls, ushered in by a stiff-faced Cal, took turns looking at the drawing. None of them recognized the man until Carmen, one of the new dancers, said she might have served him. "He sat away from the ramp. A beer drinker," she said.

"Was he with anyone?"

"Not that I saw. I went up for a set, and he didn't even tip me." She shrugged. "Screw him—I let him suck his one beer all night."

"No one came to his table to talk?"

"Well . . ." she tugged at the gold earring glittering down the side of her neck, ". . . there was maybe one guy who did, but he didn't order anything. I don't remember much about him."

"Could you see his clothes? Did he have a hat? Has he been here before?"

"Well, I'm new here—I don't know if he's a regular. He didn't have a hat, though. . . . He had a lot of gray hair. In that light, it's hard to tell, but I think it had a lot of gray. I remember thinking he'd be a winner or a loser." She explained, "Old guys, they either tip real good or real bad."

Wager led her through it a couple more times, but she came up with nothing more. In fact, she began to wonder if it really was Doc she saw in the first place.

"Did you see either man leave?"

"No. It was a busy night and we don't run up tabs anymore. Too many men go out the door without paying for their drinks, so I spend a lot of time making change."

Wager thanked her and gave her a business card and asked her to call him if the man came in again—it could be very important. She smiled and left, the rear of her shorts riding up to show little crescents of pale, soft flesh.

"Okay—you happy now? Is that it?" Berg shoved back from his desk to let Wager out.

"Do you know who the man might have been?"

"A guy with gray hair? Do you know how many guys with gray hair come in here?"

"I had the feeling you might know. I had the feeling you wanted the girl to shut up."

"You got the feeling of indigestion or something. I didn't see either one of them. I don't know either one of them. Now can I get on with running my business that pays the taxes that pay your salary?"

• • •

He made one more stop, this one in the parking lot of the White Castle where Moffett and Nolan liked to survey the scene at this, the busiest end of the strip. Their unadorned sedan sat nosed toward the street and, as he went past, Wager caught their eyes. He parked his car behind the grimy stucco building and walked over to the two Vice detectives; there was no percentage in having his Trans Am sit fender to fender with a police car that everyone on Colfax recognized.

"Quiet night?" asked Nolan. Moffett, wordless, settled a Styrofoam cup of coffee on the dash and fumbled for a cigarette.

"So far." Wager unfolded the drawing of Doc and handed it to the two men in the front seat. "You were on last night?"

"Ain't we always," said Nolan. He looked at the sketch with practiced eyes.

"He's a homicide victim," Wager explained. "Lewis Rowe—Doc."

Moffett took his turn, then handed it back without a word

and stared moodily at the passing crowd. Nolan asked, "Was this the one you pulled out of a dumpster?"

"Right."

Nolan shook his head, then glanced at Wager. "Could it be somebody special?"

"Why?"

"Ross and Devereaux, they've already inquired."

"He was one of my snitches."

Wager wanted to let it go at that, but Nolan didn't. "Was he involved in something?" Meaning: something the Vice detectives should have a hand in, something that crossed lines into their territory.

"No," lied Wager. "But he was pretty good. And I knew him a long time."

Nolan shook his head again. "You can't let it get to you. It happens, that's all."

Moffett suddenly jabbed out the long cigarette butt. "The shit it does! And the shit it can't get to you!"

Wager raised his eyebrows.

Nolan gave a little shake of his head and he, too, gazed out at the traffic that was growing heavier as closing time neared. It gave his partner a private moment to stifle the unprofessional burst of anger. "We just had a really crummy one," Nolan explained to Wager. "This juvenile—a kid ten years old—prostituting down on Sod Circle. It took us half-a-dozen tries before we could arrest him. You know why?"

Wager did not know why.

"Because every time he got out of one car, another one would pick him up before we could make contact. Ten seconds—twenty seconds, and another faggot was already grabbing him."

Moffett, his voice now sounding bored and flat, added, "Faggots—they put out all this crap about the rights of consenting adults. About how they're not chicken hawks.

All that crap. Pure crap." He spat out the window. "Ten years old. It was like feeding time at the zoo."

"We transported the juvenile over to Denver Gen," said Nolan. "He was bleeding from the anus. It took sixteen stitches to close up his anus." He, too, spat out the window.

"It happens," repeated Wager. It was the cop's litany for all that humanity could think of doing to itself.

"It certainly does."

"You're on your own time right now?" asked Moffett. He lit a fresh cigarette.

"That's right." He knew what that question meant, too.

"Okay. We'll ask around about Doc."

"Thanks." And though Wager did not ask them to funnel the information to him alone, he knew they would; the reason cops so often told each other that it didn't pay to get personally involved in a case was that they did so anyway. And a lot of cops stretched the limits of procedure a little bit to help somebody who had enough personal interest to work a case on his own time.

• CHAPTER •
11

It seemed to Wager that his real work took place in his time off, while those hours he spent earning his pay were eaten away by various routines. He did not like the day shift. Not for the same reason Max disliked it; his partner preferred the midnight-to-eight because it gave him the afternoon and evening with his family. He often got home in time to see the kids off to school and then woke up for supper with his family and a few hours together before it was their bedtime. But Wager liked the night shift because that was when most of the action took place. With sundown, the streets came alive, especially on the long summer days when the light lingered until nine, and the cooling sidewalks sucked people out of their stuffy apartments and homes to small front porches or grimy steps, to tiny strips of lawn, to littered sidewalks and curbs where they stood and talked or gazed and were gazed at. In a way, Wager thought, the street was his family. Max spent time with his kids, Wager spent time on the street; and they both found that it gave them a reason to get through the other stuff—the paperwork and routine garbage of the day shift.

Now, conspicuous in the tie and jacket he had worn to the funeral home, Wager strolled through the swirls and eddies of the crowd drifting along Colfax. His clothes, his assured walk, his aura of casual purpose screamed Cop to those around him, but he was not uncomfortable. He knew what was in the minds behind eyes that always seemed to be looking away and faces closed in expressionless innocence. A bit of fear, a bit of hatred, a lot of unease. Just like, Wager smiled to himself, a real family. It was the same family Doc had, though none of them would go to Doc's funeral. Or to Wager's.

The viewing of Doc's body had begun at six, and it probably ended at six-fifteen, when Wager left Rosalyn Shiddel sitting alone among the row of chairs and the brown couch arranged with muted lamps and coffee tables to look like a living room that just happened to have a corpse in it.

"I didn't think nobody would come," she said. A Kleenex lost bits and pieces on the soft beige carpet, and the air conditioner, turned up high and placed strategically near the casket stand, made a soft, rushing sound that cushioned the silence.

"I read the announcement in the paper."

She nodded. "I didn't know what else to do. I don't know the names of any of his friends." Her puffy eyes wandered back to the figure who lay looking stranger in a suit than he did in death. His head was turned slightly toward the room to seem more natural and to hide the hole at the back of his skull; the mortician had managed a slight smile on the dyed lips but the pale silk casket lining glimmered oddly among the stiff back hair. "He looks so peaceful, don't he?"

"Yes." It crossed Wager's mind that more people might have paid respects if the funeral home had installed a telephone. "Do you need any help? Is there something I can do?"

She shook her head. "I called the legal aid people like you said. They gave me a list of lawyers, but I don't think I'll bother. The rent's paid through the month, and after that I think I'll go out to California. That's where my family is," she explained. "They won't be happy to see me, but family's still family, ain't it?"

"I suppose so." There wasn't much to say after that. Wager sat for a few more minutes in the cool, hushed room, breathing the faint odor of chrysanthemums drifting from the wicker stands at each end of the casket. It wasn't Doc anymore, and that feeling of something lost wasn't for the corpse lying there, but for himself, Wager realized. And if he wasn't going to feel sorry for Doc, he could spend his time better than feeling sorry for himself. After a silence, he said, "I'd better be going, Miss Shiddel."

"Yes—thanks for coming by. Doc would appreciate it." She stood, too. "The funeral's at nine in the morning."

"I'll be on duty," he said.

"Oh, sure. Well, thanks for everything." A plump and moist hand shook his.

"You're welcome."

. . .

In the low, hard sunlight of late afternoon, the brightly painted sign for the Cinnamon Club turned faded and uneven. The early show had started—the music was carried to the doorway through a small speaker that was supposed to tantalize passersby, but no one was passing by yet. The resident winos who usually hung around the doorway like a brace of flies hovered alone and edgy just across the property line and pretended to inspect the window of a secondhand bookstore. Astrology. Wager headed for them.

The taller of the two caught his outline reflected in the glass; he turned and started to shove an upturned palm at him, then quickly changed his mind, giving the other a quick elbow. They began to ease away.

"I'd like to ask you two gentlemen a couple questions." Wager held out his badge case.

The tall one, white bristles in all directions over the seams in a lean face, gazed around the empty sidewalk. "Us?"

Wager nodded and showed them the drawing of Doc. "Two nights ago, about midnight. Did you see this man come out of the Cinnamon Club?" Before they could say no, he added, "He's a homicide victim. He might have left here with someone."

The short one had black hair that lankly covered a sun-darkened pate; he, too, needed a shave, but his whiskers were patchier, like an unhealthy animal's, and darkened only his jowls. Whenever he spoke, he lifted his chin to stretch his neck and gargle slightly. "We maybe did. Two nights ago, though, that's a long time."

The tall one gave a sheepish grin. "Long time without a drink, anyway."

Wager had a five-dollar bill ready. He rolled it over the fingers of his other hand. Two pairs of eyes followed it. "Five bucks is yours either way. Just tell me the truth. Did you see this man?"

The short one gargled. "Yeah. He gave us five dollars, too."

"This man did? Five dollars?"

"Yeah." Both men leaned slightly toward the bill, but Wager kept it tightly folded in his fingers.

"What time was that?"

"Maybe twelve-thirty, one. We get here maybe an hour or two before the place closes. Then until closing's the best time if that son of a bitch don't run you off."

"Who? The bouncer?"

"Yeah. That son of a bitch."

"Was this man with anyone? Did he come out with anyone?"

They glanced at each other and then at the bill. Then the short one gargled again. "It looked like it. They didn't say nothing, but it looked like they was together."

"What did the other one look like?"

"Not too tall. Big, but not too tall."

"Did he have gray hair?"

The older one shook his head. "Blond. Almost white, you know, like an albino. But he wasn't one—just real blond."

"Have you ever seen him before? Do you know him?"

"I've seen him around, yeah. But I don't know him."

"Does he come to this club a lot?"

"Not much. Some."

"Has he been around again?"

"No."

"Which way did they go when they came out?"

"That way. Around the corner."

"Would you know the blond man if you saw him again?"

The tall one licked his lips. "Mister, we're awful thirsty. All this talking—"

"Would you know him again?"

"I don't know—maybe. I just don't know."

Wager handed the bill to the tall one, whose blue eyes, pale and wet-looking, widened happily. Without another word, the two lurched down the sidewalk toward the liquor store in the next block.

Doc had given the two panhandlers five dollars. He had tipped the waitress nothing, but he had come out and given those two enough money that they remembered him. Doc had been with the blond man; he had been worried and frightened, and rightfully so. He had given those bums a big tip in case somebody had to come asking for him. Doc's last tip. If he weren't so cynical, Wager might almost believe another of his mother's favorite sayings: Everything happens for the best. But somehow he didn't think Doc would go along with that.

The inside of the Cinnamon Club seemed even darker after the lingering sunlight; despite the faint echoing sound that told his ears the room was almost empty, the cooled air was no less thick with cigarette smoke. On the runway, a thin brunette smiled and twisted through a slow number. The routine was made up of her hands sliding up and down her wiry body and occasionally patting out the music's rhythm with tiny slaps. The bouncer wasn't on duty yet, and

Wager guessed that Berg had not arrived either, because the Vietnamese bartender, looking at him, shuffled first one way and then another, like a chicken seeking a place to hide.

"Hello, Nguyen," Wager smiled.

The man's gold-streaked teeth answered automatically and his head bobbed. "Drink? On the house?" It was a kowtow Wager had seen in the villages and along the country roads of Vietnam—the recognition of police authority, a placating of those who carried life and death in the pistol on their hip.

"No thanks," he said, then repeated it in Vietnamese: *"Khong."*

Nguyen's glittering smile stayed wide, but his eyes did not. "You were in Vietnam?"

"Up near Hue. Third Marine Division."

"Ah—marines." A minor note of respect. "I am from Saigon. Much army and air force. Not too much marines in the south." The head bobbed again. "The marines were good fighters, yes?" He shrugged, "But . . ."

Wager nodded. The thing to remember was that you fought well. And that it was over. He put the drawing on the bar. "Two nights ago, this man was in here."

Without glancing at it, Nguyen smiled and shrugged. "Maybe yes, maybe no. Very busy, not like now. So I don't see."

"He walked out of here between twelve-thirty and one. Right here. Right past the bar. There was a man with him. Do you remember?"

The smile disappeared.

"The man had white hair—blond. Hard to miss, even in this light. And he's been here before." Wager leaned across the bar toward the Vietnamese and caught the faint smell of garlic on his breath. "Do you remember?"

"No!" The bartender's head wagged. "No—I don't see him!"

"The police, Nguyen. Sooner or later, the police find things out. And I'll find out if you're lying to me."

"No! It's true—I don't see him!"

"If you lie to me," Wager folded the sketch away, "I'll remember you. You and every one of your family, Nguyen."

He gave the man another moment to say something, but the Vietnamese, mouth puckered with worry, only stared at him like a bird at a snake. Wager handed him a business card with his home telephone number penciled on the back. "If your memory gets better, give me a call."

The man stood mute and rigid, and the business card lay untouched on the bar, a smudge of white.

• • •

It was still early, but Wager called anyway. Fat Willy's answering service, a bartender whose voice was now familiar, said the usual, "I see if he's here." A couple minutes later Fat Willy's lurching breath sounded at Wager's ear.

"We got to stop meeting like this, Wager. And I mean it, man."

"How'd things go last night? What'd you find out?"

"You know," he sighed, "some of the bro's swear you ain't a man until you had some white pussy. But it don't do a thing for me. Funny, a foxy mama—now that turns me on. But that white meat, it's just like looking at a dog or a horse, you know? Nothing."

"Did you hear anything about Annette Sheldon? Or Doc?"

"They's some deals going down. Shit, where ain't they? Your good friend Little Ray was twitching around worse than them honky asses on stage. But I didn't get a whisper about that Doc."

"What about a blond-haired man—almost an albino. He left the club with Doc the night he was killed."

"A real whitey?" From behind Willy came the clack of a cue ball breaking rack, followed by a squeal of high-pitched laughter.

"Have you run across him?"

"No. . . . I ain't seen him."

"But you've heard something about him? Come on, Willy!"

"I hear about a lot of people, Wager. My business is hearing." In the silence between the big man's slow, heavy breathing, a background voice wailed, "Shit, man, you call that a shot?"

"If you're thinking price, Willy, this isn't the time. I want that man."

The figure on the other end of the line made up his mind about something, and it wasn't in Wager's favor. "I'll let you know if I run across him."

Sure he would—after whatever deal he was thinking about went down. "I want that man, Willy. No shuckin', no jivin'—I want him."

Heartiness came back to the rumbling voice. "Whoo! You talking like a real bro'! Everybody got their want, and some people even get their gets—I'll tell you if I see him."

• • •

Wager cruised the Trans Am in that almost peaceful time that comes just before dusk, even along the strip. He went all the way out beyond the city-county line and past used-car lots, furniture stores, gas stations, quick-print shops—the increasing number of businesses that had nothing to do with nightlife or sex. Dotted farther apart and growing brighter as the sky darkened over Colfax, the signs for bars and discos and clubs kept the strip alive. But this far out, the johns had to drive from one beckoning glow to the next, and this early the empty curbs and gravel parking lots at the buildings' sides were marked only by occasional cars left like driftwood from last night's flood.

He was looking for the blond man, Wager explained to himself. But he knew that his chances of spotting the suspect were worse than bad. The real truth was, he just wanted to drive, to feel his mind sink into the comfortable mental cushion that steady driving offered. There was not one thing he could do, but it felt better just to be in motion. Not a very different feeling, he smiled, from his fourteenth year, when the older kids in his gang began to get their driver's licenses. Then, the world's possibilities suddenly expanded as far beyond the barrio as two dollars' worth of gas could take them. Looking not for trouble, just for the new horizon, for the excitement that always lay just beyond it. And with that expansion came a loss of detail. When you were a kid and you had to walk everywhere, you couldn't go as far, but you saw a lot of things up close. Like this low sunlight that made telephone poles look almost furry with their brown color. It was an image that brought back that long-dead time and place of the barrio: a telephone pole tan and splintered by the spikes of pole-climbers, and Wager, maybe nine or ten, throwing dirt clods at it in the quiet of an evening. The hollow pop of a hit was pleasing, and he liked the way a freckle of clay clung to the dark wood after the dusty explosion. You knew the fences and the yards and the names of dogs, and where paths cut into the high weeds of empty lots and where somebody had started digging a fort. You knew it all, so that by the time you were in your teens you hungered to see something new, to shake off that familiar dust, not caring that it would be blown away forever. He wondered if Doc had felt that kind of nostalgia for things so lightly held and so easily given up. Yes—everybody felt it at one time or another. Doc, like Wager, wouldn't admit it aloud; but he had felt it because he, too, had been a child and somehow had become the man he was, and then had been killed. By someone else who had once been a child, too.

A car swung past him, its exhaust a loud rip of sound through the light traffic. A few minutes later, Wager saw it in the parking lot beside a small nondescript tavern, the dust of its sudden stop still hanging in the fading sunlight. A handful of young men, laughing and shoving at each other's shoulders, spilled out of the car toward the building.

A few drinks, a round or two of quick jokes and loud laughter, and they'd be back in the car, feeling the motion pull them toward new adventures. Things weren't that different, and that knowledge added to Wager's melancholy, a feeling that seemed to seep from the trash-littered curbs and empty sidewalks, the vacant concrete, and the almost-empty shops turning mauve and purple with the fading heat of another summer day.

All the people who made the strip work—the pimps, the whores, the pushers and dancers, the hustlers and hustled—had once been children. They had gotten their first car, and spun their wheels in idle, joyous motion. What had happened? How had their motion led them here, while others—their friends, kids who shared the same cars and aimless drives—were now in expensive houses, had their own businesses, were lawyers, maybe, or teachers? Was it that, like Wager, these people had never stopped moving on? Was their taste for excitement always stronger than the appeal of settling down to a constructive if boring life? Had they swung in orbit until their chance to anchor themselves had blown away like the dust they stirred? The strip brought that type of life: a kind of weightlessness that was guided in one direction after another by the whisper of promise—for some, money; for others, friendship or love; for many, just continual change. It was an appeal Wager could understand because he shared it; and especially on quiet evenings like this, when movement seemed both empty and fulfilling, an odd feeling of yearning mixed with satisfaction, and, amid all the motion, a softening of one's sharp edges of suspicion and awareness.

He angled the Trans Am to the curb just across from the Turkish Delights and sat, motor idling, to gaze at the fretwork that formed a mock-oriental entry to the bar. The rest of the building was black cinderblock that faded to charcoal gray, but the onion-shaped basket stood out like a giant red-and-gold wart at the corner. It had to look better at night; with the right lights and the throb of drums and laughter wafting out the door, the entry made promises to men who came seeking. For a fee—always for a fee. Because there was no sense fooling himself, Wager knew. The people who worked the strip were no longer children, no matter what their age. There was freedom perhaps, but even that was found only by a few. The other part of that life, maybe the biggest part, was the unending struggle to find the dollar that would buy that freedom. Money flowed like a river down this strip, and if you were in the right spot at the right time, you could siphon off enough to keep you warm and happy for the rest of your life. Annette Sheldon had found one of those spots. But if the current shifted? If you became one of those who were fed upon rather than feeding? Then your value was your use to someone else—in whatever way they chose to use you. And if you were more valuable dead than alive, that, too, could be arranged. It wasn't that life was necessarily cheap along the strip—it was just relative to the cost of other things, and you had to keep struggling to stop somebody else from putting a price on your life.

Waiting for a break in the increasing traffic, Wager dropped his car into gear and swung around to head back toward downtown. The lights now outshone the darkening sky and the street took on its tunnel effect, as if the glare was both walls and ceiling that could keep out not just the rain and wind, but tomorrow's pitiless sun as well. Moffett and Nolan should be on duty by now, and maybe they could dig up something about the blond-haired man.

• • •

The telephone bell was felt before it was heard, a pecking in the brain that sent a spasm through sleep and then blended with the clattering sound to pull his gummy eyelids into slowly blinking awareness. He dragged himself, boneless as a wet towel, across the bed and groped for the phone, knocking it off the nightstand but able to hang onto the receiver long enough to flop back and press it to his ear. "Yeah?"

"Is this Detective Wager?" The female voice sounded hushed and nervous.

"Who's this?"

"I know about the blond man. The one who was with Doc."

"Who is this?" His vision cleared. In the dark, the red figures of the digital clock said 1:42.

"Can you meet me in forty-five minutes?"

"Why don't you tell me now?"

"I can't. Meet me—please!"

"Where?"

"Twenty-third and Blake. Under the viaduct."

That should be private all right—and dark as an outhouse at midnight. "At two-thirty?"

"Yes." The line clicked into a buzz.

• • •

The taste of a hurried cup of coffee was still tart on the back of his tongue as he eased the Trans Am across the eroded railroad tracks and lumpy tar of the streets that formed old downtown. Here and there a streetlight glowed dully, its glare fading before it struck the pavement, and the shadows of the warehouses loomed as thick and vague as bales of wool. He was twenty minutes early. Two blocks from the viaduct, he turned onto that section of Wazee which ran parallel to Blake, and flicked off his headlights as he came within a block of the viaduct. Coasting to the curb, he closed the door softly, moved across the empty street in the hollow light of the city's glow, and paused at the corner to study the viaduct and the area around it. Like much of lower downtown, many of the brick buildings were designed as factories and warehouses. They had tall, windowless walls that boxed the broken sidewalks, and here and there worn spur lines from the nearby railroad yards glinted like narrow puddles in the black streets. The viaduct's ramp lifted somewhere down the block so that by the time it crossed Blake it was high on its square metal legs. A band of concrete overhead, it rumbled dully from an occasional set of wheels. In the shadows between the piers, old Twenty-third Street was still surfaced with paving blocks—large, slightly rounded stones polished by heavy tires and showing as dim streaks that rippled from the occasional distant light. Wager saw nothing move—not a human figure, not an unlit car, not even a warehouse cat. And in the total deadness of the place, he felt the back of his neck tickle as the hairs rose: it was a trap.

Slowly, keeping to the darker shadow of the building walls, he worked his way in a circle around the unlit corner. Once, lights wagged stiffly over the bumpy pavement as an automobile cruised toward him, tires loud in the quiet night. He slipped into the deep recess of a delivery entrance and watched the vehicle's outline hiss past. The box of emergency lights on the car's roof showed it was a police cruiser, and it moved with the steady pace of a routine patrol on a dull night. The ruby taillights bounced down the block, flashed once, and then turned out of sight toward the Denargo area.

Waiting for his night vision to return, he checked the time and began to angle toward the pool of shadow that was the viaduct. He was still ten minutes early. If it was a trap —if his spasm of fear was right and, for some reason, he was being set up, then he still seemed ahead of whoever it was. The whoever that knew he was looking for the white-haired man. The whoever that got his telephone number from the card he left in front of Nguyen.

Wager paused at the shadowed corner one last time and strained to see into a dark that thickened as the viaduct pinched toward the pavement below. Still nothing moved. Not a sound. No vague darker shape that could be an automobile or a figure waiting against the paler gray of a pier.

Unconsciously, like a man entering icy water, he took a deep breath and started walking across the intersection toward the viaduct. The pavement's grit was loud under his shoes and he could picture the clear silhouette he made in the open street. He crossed the midpoint of the intersection, where a manhole cover caught a steely gleam from the sky; then he was into the shadow and squinting down the row of piers whose grayness receded into a blur. The oddly bright numbers on his watch said 2:28, and he paused, stilling his breath to listen for a whisper of movement or the far-off whine of an approaching car. Nothing. He walked slowly toward the next pier, eyes shifting from one point to another to use the off-center night vision that had been part of his life in Vietnam. Then he heard it, the flat rustle of tires moving slowly, and a moment later the muffled sound of a car engine almost at idle as it quietly approached.

The faint noise echoed from the surrounding brick walls and the concrete sky above, blurring its direction. Wager stepped close against a pier, turning his head this way and that, but it came before he could spot it: a dark sedan in the narrow lane beside the rising bed of the viaduct. Lightless, it turned between the steel legs, then suddenly flashed on its high beams, pinning him in their glare. The headlights bobbed with a jerk of brakes and, as his watering eyes strained past the barrier of light, he heard a door quickly open. He spun around and found narrow shelter behind one of the thin piers whose stark shadow leaned sharply away from the lights. His own twisting shadow was split by the beam as he heard the first shot, a muffled, soft thump that said Silencer, and saw a flash struck from a steel piling in the dark to his left. Pulling his pistol as he sprinted wildly for the next pier, he dodged, keeping the row of steel beams flickering between him and the killer. He may have heard a second shot; he definitely had heard the engine rev sharply. The black shadows of the steel legs began to sway back and forth and whip across his running form as he desperately tried to keep the killer off balance behind him. To each side of the viaduct, the street widened into one-way avenues, and down the center, between the steel pilings, stretched an endless alley of open space. Behind him, he heard the fat tires squeal rhythmically on the stones; now the shadows hung momentarily still on one side as the motor raced and Wager, seeing them slip past faster, reached a hand to the cold, gritty flange of a pier and flung himself in a tight arc as the glinting fender lurched for him, brushed his hip, and threw him heavily against the steel. Behind the speeding glare of the headlights a rapid flicker of orange sparks sprayed toward him, a hot breath across his wincing face. He felt the punch and smell as bullets, muffled by the silencer, sizzled into the night, and then the car was gone. Its taillights swerved from under the viaduct in a squeal of melting rubber as it sped beyond a building's solid black corner.

Wager, still clinging to the thin steel of the viaduct's leg, stared numbly into the silent street. Slowly, he reholstered his unfired pistol and felt his breath settle into something like normal gasps. And the almost irrelevant thought crossed his mind, that it was good he had not had time to fire a round—that there was a lot of paperwork every time a cop fired a bullet. That the Bulldog would want to know exactly what Wager was doing all by himself on this case and why he was idiot enough to walk into an obvious trap. Wager would not have been able to answer him.

• • •

He seated himself at the far end of the counter in an all-night restaurant and let his eyes study the fake cowboy decor. He had been in here a hundred times, but now it was as if he saw it all anew. It did not make it any more attractive—just new. Like the pressure of the counter stool under him, and the almost sweet smell of brewing coffee, and the quiet murmur of voices from the room crowded with night people. All that was new, too. The wallpaper was tan with brand markings scattered over it, and the menus had happy cowgirls twitching buckskin fringes beneath the restaurant's name: Howdy from Cowboy Bob's 24-Hour Chuck Wagons. The round stools and the seats in the filled booths were covered in imitation piebald calfskin; the waitress, her face expressing her weary feet, wore a green uniform that was out of place, but which Wager had never noticed before. Her baggy eyes, from across a new distance, frowned at something on Wager's face, and her hand went to her own cheek.

"You been in a fight?"

"Why?" His voice, too, sounded new and distant in his own ears.

"You got a cut or a burn or something. Right there."

Wager's fingers touched a numbed welt. It seemed to grow as he brushed his fingertips along it, and, under their pressure, a stinging ache began. "Bring me some coffee—black. I'll be back in a minute."

The bathroom mirror showed a hot, red welt angling up across his cheekbone. It didn't look as big as his fingers had told him, but it was big enough—and far closer than he wanted to come to any bullet. He stared at the mark for a long, meditative minute before soaking a paper towel in cold water and pressing it to his flesh. He wasn't scared; maybe fright would come later. He still had nightmares about the first time he had been shot at, so long ago, but the later times had faded into half-comic war stories and now they seemed as if they had happened to someone else. Right now the someone else seemed to be staring back at him out of the mirror, and he felt the same numb distance from that self-image that he had felt from the waitress.

He lifted the towel and looked for a trace of blood, but saw none. There was a little luck in that. The big luck was that the killer had missed. All those bullets—it must have been a semi-automatic—and this close, and the guy had missed. The silencer. The clumsy weight and balance of an extra couple inches of steel on the end of the barrel.

He pressed another wet towel to the welt, satisfied that it did not seem to grow any bigger as he watched. Nor any smaller. He'd have to come up with some story for the people at work. Cut himself shaving . . . A night of passion . . .

Strange how a cop could develop a curiously mixed sense of his own vulnerability. How, sometimes, he could, as the little brass sign on Sergeant Brozki's desk boasted, walk through the valley of the shadow and fear no evil because he was the meanest son of a bitch in the valley. And at other times, feel as if the cross hairs of a rifle were centered on his back, and a finger was pulling the trigger. . . .

Earlier, as he'd driven out east on Colfax, he had felt curiously invulnerable, cushioned by his nostalgia from the awareness of what might happen to any cop at any time. When he thought back, he could recognize that divided consciousness when he'd answered the telephone, one part of him agreeing with sleepy carelessness to meet the voice, the other trying to wake him to the possibility of real danger. But he had been in his invulnerable phase; he had happily bullied a Vietnamese bartender; he knew that nothing would happen to him and not just because he was a cop but because he was Gabriel Villanueva Wager, who could take chances and pay no price.

"You all right? You cold?"

He blinked and focused on the waitress, whose baggy eyes looked at him with concern.

"You're shaking," she said. "You got a fever?"

"No." He looked down at the coffee cup in his hand, uncertain how he got back to the counter and to his seat. "Nerves," he said. "Too much coffee."

"Well, here," she lifted the saucer and wiped the counter with a sponge. "Let me get you some decaf. You drink that much coffee and you're gonna get sick."

Wager shook his head. "That's okay—I don't want anymore." He set the cup down as cautiously as he could, clattering it briefly before his cramped fingers could clear the handle. Sucking in a deep breath, he forced his shoulders down and forward, stretching the clenched muscles at the base of his neck and feeling them drain of tautness and strain. Golding had shown him that trick, taken from one of the earlier fads the man had followed in his journey to spiritual oneness with whatever. But even a stopped clock was right twice a day, and Golding's little exercise worked. Stretching again, Wager felt the muscles slack, felt his breath and pulse slow, his trembling flesh settle into relaxed suppleness.

He had been terrified. When the car swung in to nail him, he had been too startled and frightened to fight back against the surprise of those searing headlights. And when his feet, ungoverned by his mind, had fled, terror had gripped his soul as deeply as any time in Vietnam, when he had huddled helpless and totally isolated beneath the quivering timbers and leaking sandbags, the churning thunder of rockets and mortars that had made living only a matter of luck and death only a matter of time. Only twenty minutes ago, he, Gabriel Villanueva Wager, had been so mindlessly terrified that he had run. It was something you could —after a while—admit. Maybe it was something you could even live with. But he had to wonder if it was something he could work with. He had to wonder if the next time—and there was bound to be a next time—he would suffer the paralysis of terror. Or would he explode mindlessly, in fear of that paralysis? He had to wonder if he could still govern his own flesh.

Wager covered the chit with a bill and went into the cool, welcome darkness where his familiar Trans Am waited. He wasn't immune; he wasn't chosen; he wasn't special. He was blind to danger, or sleepy, or just careless. That happened, but it couldn't happen too often. He was not immune, and he'd better not be careless, because the slayer of three people was now after him. All because he was looking for a man with white hair. *Thoonk.*

· CHAPTER ·
12

Maybe it was the bags under his eyes; maybe it was the taut and growing anger that had replaced last night's shock and the preceding inexplicable depression over Doc's death. Maybe it was just the smell of a long, bad night on his breath; but no one at work—not even Max—asked about the streak of raised and burned flesh along his cheek. He caught his partner eyeing it a couple times, and once he seemed ready to say something. But Wager, carefully setting the pile of reports and court depositions squarely on his desk, looked flatly into the man's blue eyes and said, "Nice day, isn't it?" Max could take a hint.

Now, after a solid sleep that spanned the late afternoon and early evening and left the hinges of his jaw aching from the weight of his motionless head against the hard mattress, Wager steamed his flesh awake in a hot shower. By the time he finished dressing, the red numbers of his clock said 11:42. He squared the wide-brimmed hat low over his eyes and checked himself one last time in the mirror. The Taco Kid rides again. The scruffy, unshaven figure looked back with a tight smile that never made it to the eyes—so much for that day's ration of humor.

Fifteen minutes later, he swam among the crowds of the midnight streets.

"Pssst—want a hit?" The mutter came from a shiny-eyed blond girl who may have been sixteen; her bangs and straight hair framed her face to make it look younger, and she smiled widely at him and glided past in a haze of cloudy excitement. She disappeared beyond the shoulders of a pair of homosexuals walking with their hands in each other's hip pockets. They whispered something and giggled. A shirtless kid in ragged, filthy jeans asked him for his change, snarling "Fuck you" when Wager shoved past his upturned palm. A young couple pushed a baby stroller and held hands and smiled vacantly at the motion and noise. They paused to deal for a joint held up by a bearded man who leaned with one thin leg cocked back against the photograph-covered wall of an adult-movie arcade. He grinned down at the baby. "Aw, that's a cute kid—I had a kid like that once. Can he have a sip of my beer? Kids love beer." On the corner, his sequined shirt sparking light from the passing headlights, a pimp talked to two girls with worn backpacks and wide eyes. He smiled whitely and laughed, then shook his head and pointed toward a coffee shop, his arm snaking around the taller one's waist. "Hey, man, you looking?" A boy caught Wager's attention and gave his bleached hair a carefree toss; but his eyes held anxious hunger as they tried to read him. "You want it, I got it. If I don't have it, I know who does. You looking, man?" A light hand rested on his arm, "Come on, honey, you're too macho for boys," said the unseen voice, while a tired youth with a beatific gaze and gunnysack robe handed out ink-smeared fliers which promised that Jesus would forgive anything and save anyone. The crowd, like a school of minnows, suddenly parted as two policemen strolled down the middle of the sidewalk in their own little capsule of space and eyed Wager suspiciously.

He swung wide around the span of sidewalk claimed by LaBelle Brown and saw her, white purse swinging saucily against her pink dress, as she paced the curb, eyes challenging the slowly passing cars. Making his way through the crowds, he reached the light-filled entry of the Cinnamon Club and paused a moment in the haze of cigarette smoke that rolled like a pale fog out of the doorway.

"Hi, there's a seat over here." A girl whose dark curls cupped her breasts smiled and started to lead him to a corner.

"I'm looking for Little Ray. Is he here tonight?"

"I don't know him. My name's Emma. You ready for a drink?"

She put him at one of the tiny tables almost against the back wall. On the ramp, glistening in the red lights as if her flesh were oiled, a girl finished her third number. She had tightly curled blond hair down to her shoulders and an amazingly round and active rear end. The music roared to a pulsating climax and on the last note the girl froze, pressing her fingertips against the ceiling and sucking in her stomach to accentuate her pointed breasts and arcing posterior as the disc jockey, voice hoarse in the microphone, yelled enthusiastically, "All right—let's hear it for Fanny Hill!" The girl smiled at the shouts and applause and modestly knelt to pick up the bills on the runway as the music shifted to a slower tempo. Wager searched the silhouettes for Little Ray's clutch of hair.

With his third beer, Wager's head began to throb from the stuffy air and the ceaseless impact of noise. Finally, close to one, the man came in, and Wager didn't let him get as far as a table.

"Let's step out back, Little Ray—I got some questions."

"Hey, man, where the hell you been? I thought we had a deal going."

"Maybe we do, maybe we don't—maybe somebody screwed something up."

"What's that mean?"

"Let's go out back and talk."

"I got some business first, man. This is my office call, you know?"

"They'll wait. It won't take long."

The hardness in Wager's voice worried the man. "What's the problem?"

"Somebody set me up," said Wager. "I want to know who and why."

"Hey, now—I don't know nothing about any setup!"

Wager nudged the man's arm toward the rear exit. "That's what I want you to tell me, Little Ray: how much you don't know about it."

They stood in the cool air and pale glow of the parking lot behind the club. Every slot was filled with late-model cars and Wager counted four Datson ZXs, each with a slightly different flash of racing stripes. Some salesman had offered the girls a group discount.

"What kind of setup, man? What are you laying on me?"

"Somebody tried to waste me. I figure it's somebody who heard you shooting off your mouth about our deal."

Little Ray's eyes gave him away. "No, man—I ain't said nothing to nobody!"

"Bullshit. It's all over the street. You're claiming you're the next capo di capo or some shit."

"No—now, listen—"

"You listen, asshole; my associates, they don't like people talking about their business. 'Discretion'—you know what that means? It means you keep your mouth shut when you do business with me or anybody I speak for. You got that?"

"Yeah, sure, but I—"

"I heard you been shooting off your mouth. I heard it from people I respect. And something else, Little Ray; somebody you talked to tied it to me. And they went after me. It was very close, Little Ray." Wager shoved the barrel of his Star PD under the man's chin and hooked a roll of pale, trembling flesh over the muzzle. "And if I get even a hint that you had a part of it, you are a dead man, Little Ray."

"I didn't! I mean, I might have said something to a friend or something about a big deal coming down. I mean, who wouldn't—it's really big, you know? But, man, I did not—I did not!—set you up or finger you to nobody!"

Wager stared into the man's eyes and let the silence and the barrel of the gun work for him.

Little Ray's chin waggled back and forth like a ball on the end of a stick. "I swear! I don't even know your name, man!"

"I want you to find out who it was."

"What?"

"You're supposed to know the street—that's part of our deal. So show me how well you know it—you find out who tried to do a number on me."

"Hey, man, that's not the kind of contacts—"

"Find out, Little Ray. I will see you right here tomorrow at the same time, and you will prove to me you had nothing to do with it."

"I can't just go down the street asking—"

"A man with white hair. Like an albino. He comes to this place. You find out who he is and I'll find out if he's the one." The pistol nudged Little Ray's chin up. "If I don't see you tomorrow night, I'll get suspicious. You understand?"

"Yes!"

Wager clicked on the safety and stuck the pistol in his belt under the long fringe of the Mexican vest. Little Ray rubbed beneath his chin with the back of his hand and stared at Wager as if seeing him for the first time.

"I figure—and my associates figure—we still got a deal going. If you want to be rich and happy, don't screw it up."

"I won't! A deal's a deal, man, right!"

"Then you show me that all this is just an unfortunate misunderstanding. You tell me tomorrow who that man is."

Little Ray swallowed and nodded, his spray of stiff hair wagging. Wager left him alone in the flat glare from the lights high up the brick wall. When Wager paused to look back, he saw Little Ray gazing with unblinking and empty eyes into the dark. The man rubbed again at the spot beneath his chin, and his shoulders rose and fell as if he had been holding his breath for a long time. Then he turned and walked stiffly back into the Cinnamon Club, his hand holding the scarred doorframe for a moment's support before he disappeared.

• • •

"No more fun and games, Willy. I want him."

"I never seen the man, Wager. I don't know him."

"You know about him. I want him."

"How come you so het up about this dude?"

"He tried to off me."

From his side of the Cadillac's wide front seat, Willy's eyes glinted in the mottled light of the street lamp high up in the trees. "He took a shot at you?"

"Yes. I want him."

"Haw—that makes it kind of personal, don't it? I thought us taxpayers gave you enough coin to pay for that kind of stuff." When Wager did not answer, Willy said, "You don't see no humor in the situation?" Then, "No, I guess you don't." Sighing, the big man asked, "What's he worth to you?"

"No money this time, Willy."

"Say, what?"

"He took a shot at me. I don't put a price on that."

"But, Wager, I'm a businessman!"

"This isn't business."

Willy tipped his panama hat back and dabbed at his broad forehead with a folded handkerchief that wafted a faint scent. "What I hear you say is that Doc was worth a few bucks. But you, my man, are priceless!"

Wager guessed that was about the size of it.

"Um. I thought Black Pride was something. But, man, you got a bad case of Spick Fever." He tucked the handkerchief in his vest pocket. "Maybe someday it'll turn out to be terminal."

"You have something on him, Willy. I want to know what it is."

Once more the bulging figure sighed, then he wagged his head. "Well, it ain't much. But it does hurt to give it away free, you know?" Wager didn't reply. Willy grunted something inarticulate. "Here's all I got: he's new around town and he's up to some hustle. But nobody knows much of what he's into. Whatever his act is, it's got something to do with the strip—he shows up here and there in the clubs."

"What clubs?"

"Well, you know one: the Cinnamon Club."

"What about Foxy Dick's?"

"I don't know. I don't think so. My sources tell me he spends most of his time in that low-life skin joint out east, the Turkish Delights." Willy's eyes glinted his way again. "I reckon you don't care if that's outside your jurisdiction."

"That's right. I don't care. What's he do in these places?"

"If I knew, I could tell you. Whatever it is, he keeps it mighty quiet."

Wager gazed through the tinted glass of the car's windshield at the dim residential street lined with parked cars. On the far corner, a freon streetlamp cast a pink glow that leached the color from buildings and shrubs and showed an elderly couple holding each other up as they stepped slowly across the intersection. Both the man and the woman had white hair. Funny how many white-haired people he was suddenly noticing. "Who's he do business with?"

"Hard to say."

"You tell me he does business. That means he talks to somebody. Who?"

"What I hear, Wager, is that he don't talk to much of nobody. He shows up and orders a drink, sits there by hisself, and pretty soon he leaves."

"And he never talks to anyone? Come on!"

"Once, maybe twice, I hear he talks to this juice man name of Clinton. You know him?"

"The one we popped for killing Goddard?"

"And couldn't hang nothing on. That's the one."

Wager tried to see some meaning in that, but the only thing it gave him was another unconnected item and a sour taste in his mouth. "What's Clinton up to now?"

"Same as ever—sharking money at five percent a day and telling everybody that nobody can touch him. Which it looks like he is right."

Wager started to open the door, but Fat Willy held up a hand to halt him. A diamond on the man's little finger splintered light into a tiny rainbow. "Wager, you got all this for no money, but that don't mean it's free. Come a time I need something that money cannot buy, my man, I'll be collecting."

Wager closed the heavy door. If that time ever came, he'd worry about it then.

. . .

He had been right: at night the wicker-basket doorway to the Turkish Delights gave the place an entry that promised something special for your money. Wager pushed open the gilded door and heard a shriek of laughter, quickly drowned in brassy chords amplified enough to tremble the walls. Through the hazy glow of blue neon hidden somewhere in the ceiling, he could make out a room whose furniture was crowded down to the far end. There, gyrating in and out of a cone of light, a nude girl on a platform jerked her elbows to the loud thud of a jukebox while men shouted "Do it" and someone held up a book of flaming matches at the side of the stage. At this end of the room, the floor was cleared for dancing, and along the right wall, like dark cribs, was a line of shadowy booths. The bar was against the other wall; a scattered row of figures leaned on it, feet on a brass rail, faces catching the chill glow from the stage. A female voice came close out of the shadows, "Hi, you want to sit near the stage or in a booth? You can buy me some champagne in the booth." Wet teeth glinted in the blue gleam.

Another chorus of "Do it" came from the crowd at the side of the platform, and the dancer laughed at the burning matchbook and its column of smoke spinning with her in the hazy cone of light. "Do it!"

Wager ignored the pull of the girl's hand and headed for the bar. "I just want a beer right now."

Her smile turned down instead of up. "Spending big tonight?"

"Maybe later. What's your name?"

"Lolita."

"Maybe later, Lolita."

"Sure, Big Spender."

Her dim shape went back to join three or four girls perched on the barstools clustered near the door. Wager groped through the blue shadows toward the bartender, a slope-shouldered silhouette against the paleness of the bar mirror. The shout of voices rose, "Yeah—right—yeah!"

The nude girl planted her feet near the edge of the platform and leaned back from the waist, legs spread, as a man held the burning matchbook closer to her groin. "Do it!" She motioned the fire closer and a moment later clenched her abdomen to blow out the flame as a cheer drowned out the music and bills were thrust toward her from applauding hands.

"Pussy farts." The man standing beside Wager smiled. He had a pudgy face and a smudge of thin goatee at the very end of his chin. "You don't see that just anywhere—it's a real talent. As good as anything on TV."

"Right," said Wager. "A class act." He ordered a Killian's from the bartender, whose glance said he did not recognize Wager. He handed the man a five and raised his eyebrows at the one-dollar bill coming back.

"Cover charge," said the unsmiling bartender. "For the floor show."

Wager tapped the single toward the slope-shouldered man. "Keep it all."

The bartender smiled one dollar's worth of thanks.

"Has Whitey been in yet?" Wager asked him.

"Who?"

"The guy with white hair. Comes in sometimes with Clinton."

The bartender's eyes blinked once and he said, "I don't know them."

"It's worth something." Wager reached beneath his woven vest and showed a roll of twenties.

"It's not worth anything if I don't know them," said the bartender. He moved toward the waitresses' station.

Wager tucked the bills away and drank his beer. At his shoulder, he felt the interest of the pudgy man. Finally he leaned through the noise of the jukebox to ask Wager, "You come here a lot?"

"No."

"Yeah, I thought I hadn't seen you before. I come here a lot."

"It's a real fine place," said Wager.

"Yeah. And the girls are really nice, too. That one you were talking to—Lolita—she really is good. She can do a hot-and-cold real good."

"A what?"

"A hot-and-cold. Over in a booth. First she makes her mouth real cold with an ice cube, and then she makes it real hot with a cup of coffee. Back and forth like that. It's really a talent. You ought to buy her some champagne and see." He looked past Wager to where the women sat looking bored on their cluster of barstools. "I wish I had enough to go to a booth with her. She really is nice."

Wager peered through the blue light at the man, looking for the irony in his expression that he didn't hear in his voice. But it wasn't there. The small, close-set eyes gazed down the bar with rounded admiration and then blinked and looked at Wager.

"I got enough to buy you a beer, though," he said hesitantly. "Can I buy you a beer?" He held out a hand that was equally hesitant. "I'm Douglas MacArthur Woodcock. No relation to Douglas MacArthur," he explained earnestly. "My dad just liked the name, my mama told me."

Wager shook the soft hand. "Call me Gabe."

"That's a nice name. I don't think I ever met anybody with that name. Pat"—he held up a finger to the bartender—"a couple draws for me and my friend Gabe, here."

A new dancer came onstage and stood laughing and talking with the men at her feet as she waited for someone to put money in the jukebox. She wore a flaring dress with a lot of buttons down the front, and her laughter cut like glass through the deeper male voices. Behind him, Wager heard another female voice rise in self-righteousness, "I told her, 'Honey, he only wants to see two things in your mouth, and one of them's a cigarette.' But she wouldn't listen!"

The bartender set the cold glasses down, his eyes flicking from Wager to the pudgy-faced man. He took the money without a nod.

"Cheers," said Douglas MacArthur Woodcock.

Wager sipped. "So you spend a lot of time here?"

"Sure. There's always something going on. And the floor shows are real neat—the performers are real talented. Better than anything on TV," he said again. And there was still no note of irony, just earnest conviction, like a tour guide afraid Wager might miss the real beauty of the scene. "Since Mama died, I don't have noplace else I want to be. I don't have no family, you see. My dad was killed before I was born," he smiled. "In Korea. He was a soldier, and that's how I got my name."

Wager wondered if he was supposed to say "That's nice." "Have you seen a white-haired man come in? Not gray—white. Like an albino."

"Sure. He comes here maybe two or three times a week."

Someone started the jukebox and a nasal voice loudly moaned about waking up in a cold bed with a hot pillow in his arms. The girl on stage stepped and wriggled awkwardly to the dragging beat and undid two or three buttons. Wager had to lean forward to hear. "Do you know him?"

"No. I thought you did—I heard you ask Pat about 'Whitey.' "

"That's just what I call him," said Wager. "I want to find him—I owe him something."

"Gee, I wish I could help. But I just see him, you know?"

"Does he come in regularly? Does he have any special days he comes in?"

The man thought a moment and then shook his head. "I don't know. I'm here all the time, so it's hard to tell what day it is. He just comes in, that's all."

"Did you ever see him with anybody?"

"No. . . . It's so hard to remember. I think he goes on back. They have a back room where it's not so loud. But you can't see the shows from there."

"Where's this room?"

"On the other side of the stage. But it's for private parties. I've been back a couple times to help clean up, but it's mostly for private parties."

The music ended and the girl on the platform played with the line of buttons, undoing every other one and swinging her hips to some imaginary beat. Someone put another fifty cents in the jukebox to bring a tune with a faster rhythm, and the girl smiled and caught the beat and began working the rest of the buttons as she twirled. The recorded voice sang, "She always pours her beer down the middle because she likes the head."

"You people want another round?" Pat the bartender stood behind Wager and peered at him through the dimness.

Wager nodded and watched the girl undo the last button and shrug out of the dress with her arms upraised, bra and panties glowing pale blue when she pirouetted out of the smoky spotlight to kick her clothes somewhere.

"That's Maggie," Woodcock said. "She's got nice fingers."

"What?"

"In the booth—she uses her fingers, you know? And she's real good. I like it when there's two or three of us there. She'll take two or three of us over and it's real friendly and mellow." Douglas MacArthur Woodcock glanced at Wager and smiled. "It don't cost so much that way, either, and it's lots better than doing it by yourself."

Wager drained his beer. "Here—" He laid ten dollars on the bar. "Have another one." He added, "If you can find out the name of the white-haired man, I'll give you enough to buy a bottle of champagne for any girl here."

The close-set eyes rounded. "A whole bottle? By myself? Gee!"

As he left, Wager saw the bartender's face in the dim light of the mirror. It followed him until Wager reached the door, then the slope-shouldered man moved toward Woodcock and began collecting the dirty glasses. Through the loud wailing of guitars, a woman's voice called after him, "So long, Big Spender!"

• • •

He shaved carefully the next morning, angling the corner of the razor along the welt of flesh that had dried and darkened but showed no signs of infection. It still caught Axton's eye, but his partner said nothing about it. Instead, he laid in front of Wager a handwritten note from someone on an earlier shift. It said, "Word on street is Wager is looking for white-haired man. What's up?"

He looked at his partner. "The word's right."

"Want to tell me about it?"

"If it stays with you."

"That's what partners are for."

Wager told him some of it—the part about the two bums. Max listened closely as he gazed through the sealed windows and out over the stubby buildings toward a distant forest of construction cranes, lacy and graceful in the clear morning light. Wager finished and Axton was silent for a while.

"Gabe, you can't do it by yourself."

"Don't start with that 'team concept' crap."

"It's not that. Well, it will be, if the Bulldog finds out what you're up to. But it's not that with me."

He had a good idea what Max meant, but he asked anyway. "Then what?"

"You went off on your own before. It was wrong then, and it's wrong now. Gabe, honest to God, I can't let it happen again. I shouldn't have let it happen that other time."

"You didn't let it happen. You didn't have much to say about it."

"I didn't tell Doyle about it, either."

That was true. Wager had set up a man to be killed because the law couldn't touch him, and Max knew about it. He knew about it before Wager did it, and he watched in silence when Wager arranged things. The case—the Tony Ojala murder—was still in the Open drawer and always would be. But if the act hadn't been legal, it had been just, and it wasn't his fault that Max didn't see it that way. "You want a medal?"

A tinge of red colored the side of his neck. "I don't want it to happen again, that's all. You know what I think of lynch law."

"I'm trying to find this man, Max. Not lynch him. I want to find him without scaring him off. I'm the only one on his tail, and he's not running because he figures he can handle me. But if we get the whole damned team thumping after him, he's gone."

"You're sure he has something to do with the stripper killings?"

"I'm sure he had something to do with Doc's murder." Wager's thumb dragged along the mark on his cheek. "And

Doc was asking questions about the girls. And the m.o.'s the same. That's all I'm sure of."

Axton shoved a large hand through his sand-colored hair. "You're right—it's a lead, and a good one." He looked sharply at Wager. "What makes you think he's not already running?"

"This." He touched his cheek again. "He's not afraid. Not yet, anyway."

"That is a bullet burn, right?"

"Right."

"Jesus, Gabe. . . . Tell me about it."

Wager gave him the rest of it. When he finished, Max just shook his head and said "Jesus" again. Then, slowly, turning his heavy shoulders away, "That's a shitty thing to do to me, Gabe."

He was puzzled. "What thing?"

"Trying to get your ass shot off. Not telling me what was going on. I'm your partner. You get yourself killed . . . hell, I'll have to break in a new partner. You didn't even think about telling me, did you?"

Wager decided that Max was joking. "Yeah, well, maybe you'll get Munn. He's already broken in."

"I'm not joking! We're partners. That means something to me—it means when I stick my neck out, you'll back me up. The same thing goes for you. But you didn't even give me a chance to stand by you. You knew it was a trap and you went into it and you never even gave me a chance to cover you! What the hell's the matter, Wager, I'm not good enough to be your goddamned partner?"

Max never got angry. Wager, jaw sagging, gazed at the large, flushed face and the blue eyes hot with anger. This angry glare wasn't Max.

"Well, crap on you!" Axton wheeled and bumped into a desk, knocking it two feet into the aisle and tumbling its lamp with a clatter. "I'm due in court." He jammed the lamp upright. "You make up your mind—I'm your partner or I'm not!"

He watched the figure lunge out of the office, shoulders hoisted rigidly around his neck. When he disappeared, the fluorescent lights overhead buzzed sharply as Wager tried to figure out what he had said that had hurt the big man's feelings.

• • •

He still didn't know the next day, and Axton said nothing more. There may have been a touch of coolness in his "Good morning," but it disappeared in the soothing routine of daily reports and queries. Wager's puzzlement was short-lived, too, but for a different reason. When, in the past, someone had laid obscure claim to him, Wager had found no answer to the "Why?" so he tended to ignore it. He had seen in others, especially as a kid, an attractiveness that made people immediately like them. But never in himself. It was an admission he made with neither regret nor longing—it was just a fact: he was not one of those "likable guys" and that was fine. He didn't yearn to be, like he didn't yearn for blond hair or blue eyes. So when someone was hurt because he showed the distance he felt between himself and those who called him friend—or even partner—it surprised him. He did not need that kind of camaraderie, and it surprised him that anyone else sought it from him. But that was their problem, not his; at the deepest, bedrock level of his being, he knew that he needed no one at all, and he was content with that knowledge. If he needed anything, it was only his work.

He scanned the crime report sheet from neighboring agencies, his eye snagging homicides and names that rang familiarly from past cases. Douglas County reported a teenaged girl raped and killed, but it was a strangling, not a small-caliber weapon to the back of the head. Still, Wager jotted it down just in case. Another hit-and-run up in Boulder, vehicular homicide. Deceased and unidentified male found in the woods in Jefferson County; treated as a homicide victim until the cause of death could be determined. From other neighboring counties came lists of burglaries and disturbances that he went over quickly, until one entry in the Assault section stopped him. Douglas MacArthur Woodcock. He had been found, severely beaten, by the Adams County sheriff's office, and was now listed in critical condition at the University Medical Center.

· CHAPTER ·

The ward nurse did not question their jurisdiction. She recognized him and Axton for cops and scarcely glanced at their badges; her nod at their request was only confirmation of what she already knew.

"The other officers couldn't get much out of him, and he may still be sedated. Would you register here, please?"

Wager signed his and Axton's names and the time on the visitor's log, then followed her directions down the wide hall to the third door. Woodcock's bed was surrounded by a clutter of equipment. Most of it stood unused, but a tube ran into his nostril, and his right arm was slung and strapped firmly to his bandaged chest. Another tube ran liquid into his left arm. His swathed head rested in a padded brace that lifted his chin awkwardly, and the purple, egg-shaped lumps and crusted dots of stitching across his face almost hid the pulp that had been his nose. The heavy door thudded softly as it closed, and the man on the bed made some kind of sound.

"Woodcock—can you hear me?"

A stuttered moan between dry, puffed lips.

"I talked to you last night, remember? I asked you about the white-haired man."

One of the swollen lids struggled open and a blood-streaked eye rolled toward the sound of the voice. Even beneath the puffy flesh and the pale-green sheet, Wager could see a tenseness come into the man's body. He grunted, gasped, and tried to grunt again as Axton murmured, "Take it easy—don't try to talk. Just whisper."

A sigh of relaxing effort. Wager and Axton leaned toward the sour, clogged breath. "You remember, Woodcock? My name's Gabe—you bought me a beer."

The answer was more like a breath than words, but they heard it: "Go away."

Wager held up his badge case. "I'm a cop, Woodcock. I want to get the people who beat you up."

"You? Cop?"

"That's right. I want to get the people who did this. Who was it?"

"Uh unh."

"Did the white-haired man do this to you?" There was no answer. Wager leaned closer. "Woodcock—did the white-haired man do this to you?" Behind him, Wager heard the door thump again and the ward nurse's shoes creaked on the floor wax. "Woodcock—you can hear me. Come on, now, we're trying to help you. Did the white-haired man do this?"

"Can't go . . ." The words faded.

"What? Can't what?"

". . . back. Can't go back." In the purple corner of one of the eyes, a tear spilled into the creased and swollen flesh. "Only place . . . Can't go back."

"What's he mean?" muttered Axton.

"No more hand"—Wager's eyes caught the nurse's—"shakes at the bar." He leaned over the man again. "Come on, Woodcock, give me a name. Who did it?"

"Uh unh . . . go way. . . ."

The nurse said briskly, "I'm sorry, gentlemen. Maybe he'll change his mind when he feels better. Sometimes they do."

And sometimes they didn't. A lot of times it was the other way around after the victim had had a week or so of thinking about what else could have been done to him. Wager left a business card on the metal table beside the bed. "Here's my office number, Woodcock. If you change your mind, call that number. Any time of day or night. You hear me?"

The figure lay with its eyes closed and made no answer. The fluorescent ceiling light caught on another drop, like a bead of sweat, squeezed through the oily, puffed slit of eyelids.

On the way to their car, baking in the cloudless sun beside a bright yellow curb, Max asked, "Do you think he'll testify?"

Wager shook his head. "Whitey broke his spirit. The poor bastard didn't have much to start with, and now even that's gone."

"You think it was Whitey?"

"I do. The bartender heard us talking about him."

It was Axton's turn to drive. He pushed the shuddering, underpowered sedan through the weaving traffic and out into the crowded lanes of Colorado Boulevard. "Maybe we should lean on that bartender. Or get the locals to do it."

"I'd like to. But it might scare off Whitey. Whatever he's up to, he's still trying to protect it—he's not running yet." And Wager guessed that the man had not figured that the Taco Kid and Detective Sergeant Wager were one and the same; Woodcock had been beaten as a warning to that scruffy Mexican who had been asking the bartender all those nosy questions.

"He knows you're after him."

"Yes. And I want him to keep thinking I'm the only one interested." He felt Max stifle a comment, and neither man hinted anything about yesterday's outburst. But a few minutes later, Wager added: "When we're ready, we'll nail him, partner."

For some reason, that made Axton very happy.

• • •

Homicide Detective John Lee of the Adams County sheriff's office was not very happy to run across Detective Wager again. He demanded to know what the hell Wager was doing sticking his nose in a case that had no clear ties to the city and county of Denver. "You left Woodcock your goddamn business card, Wager. You told him if he changed his mind, he should call you. The nurse heard what you told him. Now what in hell is going on? If you've got information about a case in my jurisdiction, I got a right to know what it is!"

Newport Beach didn't teach their cops manners either. "I knew the victim, Lee. We were drinking buddies. He gave me some information awhile back, and I dropped by to see how he was doing." It wasn't untrue. And what was Wager supposed to do? Tell Lee he'd been undercover without clearing it first with Adams County? Or even with his own boss?

"Yeah? An informant?" The line was silent while the man on the other end turned over that item. "All right. So why'd you ask about a white-haired man? It sounds like you know something, Wager, and you're looking for corroboration."

Lee wasn't quite as dumb as he looked. "Only a possibility. He and a white-haired man had a beef. I thought that's who it might be. Woodcock couldn't tell me a thing."

Another meditative silence. "And you know nothing about it?"

"Not a thing, Lee. I thought you were Homicide. What are you doing on this case?"

"Crimes Against Persons. That includes Assault. It damn

near was a homicide, though. I've seen people worked over before, but Woodcock got it by an expert. Or a sadist. Whoever did it enjoyed it."

Wager nudged him further away. "Have you come up with anything more on the Angela Williams killing?"

"No. We did find her car in the eastern part of the county. It had been stripped, but we think that happened after it was abandoned. It doesn't seem to be a motive, anyway. What about you? Anything from your end?"

"She's still in the Active file. But that's about all."

"You'll tell me if anything breaks?"

"Of course."

They hung up as cordially as locker mates at the high school gym.

• • •

It took awhile, but he found the man he was looking for. Armed with an old black-and-white police photograph from his thin, dated jacket, Wager had, after a quick supper, wandered from bar to bar in the several blocks flanking the Everready Lounge. The early-evening air was fresh and cool after one of those sudden thunderstorms that scrub away the trash and dust and leave the asphalt sparkling with myriad colored lights and the scrolls of neon glittering cleanly. Sucking a last lungful of fresh air, he turned into another of the small bars, one that offered no exotic dancers or live music, just a jukebox and a cleared space for dancing. From the outside, Tim's Place looked like a doorway wedged into the crack between two larger buildings, but it opened into a long room lit with the pale yellow of clear glass bulbs made to look like candles. Across the open wooden floor that might have space for three dancing couples, he saw Clinton by himself in a booth, carving a pizza. Wager walked straight toward him, feeling a quick focus of attention from the woman bartender and the few customers. Clinton knew he was coming, but he never turned his head.

Police photographs were okay for identification if you looked for things that tended to stay the same over time: the shape of eyes and cheekbones, the lips, the profile of nose and chin. But some people looked very different from their mugshots, and Clinton was one of them. What, in the faded gray tones of the photograph, appeared etched and definitive, in life faded into suggestion. Clinton's profile as he stuck his head forward to let the crumbs and strings of cheese drip onto the plate seemed fleshier and softer in its angles, and the eyes that lifted to Wager, who sat across from him, were set closer together than the photograph of a thinner man showed. But they had the same sleepy insolence as when he had been ordered to look into the lens while the booking number was held to his chest.

"You're William Frank Clinton," Wager said.

"And you're an officer of the law."

Wager lifted his badge case from his coat pocket and dangled the shield's weight over his forefinger. "Detective Wager, DPD, Homicide." He flipped it away again. "I hear you're telling people you walked on the Goddard killing."

"Why not? I'm innocent."

"And Jimmy King took the fall for you."

"Why not? He's guilty." Clinton had a grin that drew back along one side of his face, showing a glint of molars in the yellow light. It reminded Wager of a dog's jaw and he wondered if the man lolled his tongue when he was hot. "That's justice, right?"

"Yeah, it is." Wager looked up at the waitress who asked him if he wanted to order anything, and shook his head. "Tell me about King. What kind of deal was he working with Goddard?"

The cold humor remained. "I got no idea."

"You're listed as a known associate of the victim and the perpetrator."

"So what? You can list me however you want to. I still got no idea."

There were a few times when you could bluff somebody, and a lot of times when you couldn't. This was one of the times you couldn't, and Wager had no leverage at all. Clinton knew it. "All right. What's between you and King will come out sooner or later. But here's something that's a little more important for you: you tell Whitey I'm going to waste him."

Any humor was gone. "Who?"

"The dude with the white hair—Whitey. You tell him what I said."

"I don't—"

"Right, Clinton, you don't. I understand." Wager rose. "But you tell him anyway. Tell him I'm getting close, and I'm going to get him all by myself. For the pure pleasure of it."

He felt Clinton's eyes aimed at the back of his neck as he walked out. Pausing outside the door, he glanced up and down the brightly colored street and half-listened to the tangled rhythms of loudspeakers bouncing through open doors. Maybe Whitey would bite, maybe not; that's what fishing was all about. Right now, Detective Sergeant Wager had to find a quick-change phone booth to become the Taco Kid.

. . .

This time, Little Ray came to Wager. Clarissa had greeted Wager when he walked into the Cinnamon Club, and, seating him at a table away from the runway, gave him one of those puzzled looks that said she should remember him in some other context.

"Is Little Ray here yet?"

"Haven't seen him. What can I get you?"

He told her. "When he comes in, let him know where I

am, okay?" He handed her ten dollars, which quickly disappeared.

"Sure!"

He sat with his bottle of Killian's and ran the brim of his leather hat slowly up the naked girl's pulsating body. First came the long, almost skinny calves, then the equally long thighs, shadowed with stretching muscles that led to rounded hips which seemed too large and too mature for the girlish legs. It was as if that part had developed and left the rest lagging at the edge of childhood. Above the dark triangle that bumped twice each way and then fooled him with a shift to a circular motion, the curving belly stretched taut and shiny in the crimson glow, and the tiny dark spot of her navel bounced with the music like one of those balls over the words of the singalong films at the old Saturday matinees. This was another new girl—Blanche—and Wager's hat brim had moved up to her rib cage, where the pattern of shadows was like the grip of long fingers, when the stage was blotted out by a torso, and Little Ray sat down quickly and leaned toward him.

"All right. I got something for you."

"Good. I been waiting. Let's have it."

"Yeah, well, you can wait a little more. I want to talk something over first."

The dimness that protected Wager also sheltered Little Ray's face. "Like what?"

Little Ray looked down a moment to where his fingers tugged pieces from a wet napkin and rolled them nervously into pale wads. "You know, I really don't know a thing about you."

"You know I talk for people who have clout."

Little Ray pulled another thin shred from the napkin and began rolling it between thumb and finger.

"And you know I've got some son of a bitch worried enough to try and whack me."

"Yeah," said Little Ray. "There is that. . . ."

"So what's your problem?"

The man's gathered hair quivered as he looked over his shoulder at the applauding men stuffing bills into the straps of the girl's sandals. "My problem's this: you keep talking about how big your fucking 'associates' are, you keep talking about how much you can supply. You keep talking about this humongous distribution system—but you haven't given me a gram of anything to sell!"

Wager tipped the shadow of his hat over his face as Cal, the bouncer, squeezed between tables like a looming whale and headed for the stairs to the disc jockey's booth. "You told me you had a good supplier. The guy in the black van."

"Yeah, well, maybe Lazlo's getting the word somewhere that I'm going to quit him. Maybe he's starting to act like a real shit."

So Little Ray's big mouth had caught up with him, and now his supplier was going to cut him off for his disloyalty. "Where do you think he got that word, Little Ray?"

"How the hell do I know?"

"You know. You farted around about how you're going to be the main man at this end of the strip. You think that idea makes Lazlo happy? You didn't keep it a big secret, man."

"How could I? How the hell could I recruit street people and not tell them something? Answer me that!"

"Maybe you started too early. Maybe you were supposed to organize, not recruit." Wager sipped his beer. "So what's Lazlo saying to you?"

"He's upped my price. If I don't like it, I can find another connection. Shit, you know how hard that is when you're dealing big? I mean, I'm not exactly nickels-and-dimes, you know? It takes time to set up a big deal!"

"I've heard."

"Right, yeah, you've heard. All I've heard is promises, and now my supplier says it's double the price or he's cutting me off. Some choice: I work for nothing or I lose my fucking customers! Now how are you going to cover that? What kind of goddamned clout are you going to show me now, man!"

"Raise the price to your street people."

"It's me he's squeezing—the price is the same to Lazlo's other buyers. But double to me. I raise the price to my people, they just laugh and go to one of the others!"

"So pay it."

"What?"

"The price. Pay it. Use his stuff for one more week. My associates will be ready to move by then."

"A week? You're sure?"

"One week and you'll be able to tell Lazlo to stick it." Wager took a long drink. "Where's your next buy from him?"

"Why?"

"I want a look at him. He's competition."

"Oh—" He tugged more shreds from the napkin.

"He's already trying to keep you from splitting. Maybe he's the one who tried something on me, too."

"Like what?"

"Christ, do I have to spell it out for you? The white-haired man, Little Ray—the one I told you to find out about. Maybe Lazlo put him on me because I'm going to bring in competition."

"Naw, he wouldn't—"

"He's got reason to. You think he's going to just say 'Okay, I quit—it's all yours'? I want a look at him. The next time he comes at me, I want to know him!"

Little Ray scratched uncertainly at his headband.

"You think about how much you owe him. And then you think if you're with me or against me. That's the choice, Little Ray—right here, right now. You choose." He leaned back and watched the man sweat.

". . . On the corner of Emerson and Thirteenth. There's a school there—it's dark and nobody's around. Ten-forty-five Thursday night. Lazlo'll set up near the corner so we can see anybody coming. You'll have a hard time getting close enough to eyeball him."

"I'll worry about that. You just be there like always. Now tell me about Whitey."

"I really got nothing to tie him to Lazlo, that's a fact. One of my people—Watchdog—said the guy's not into dope at all. It's something else, something that smells like big bucks, but he's not sure what."

"How's he figure that?"

"He says the guy has some kind of route. Not the same days or times, but the same four or five places. Watchdog's got a lot of curiosity, you know? That's how he got his name. Someday it's going to get him in trouble, but he's good."

"What kind of route?"

"Clubs—discos. Watchdog followed him two, three times when he saw him on the street. He goes into a place, sits down and orders a drink, and then a little later he leaves. He goes to the same places and most of the time he doesn't touch his drink. That's what caught Watchdog's eye—he saw him get up and leave a full one at Barnum's and then do the same thing at The Corral. So he tailed him."

"He didn't meet anybody?"

"Didn't talk to nobody, didn't deliver nothing, didn't pick up nothing. Just ordered his drink, sat and looked at it awhile, and then left to do it again. The guy's either nuts or he's working some scam that I can't figure. But it's got nothing to do with Lazlo. I'll swear to that."

"What places did he go to?"

"Barnum's, and The Corral. And here. I never noticed the guy, though. You can't see for shit in this place."

"Where else?"

"The Palm Room. And Mickey Finn's."

"Not Foxy Dick's?"

"Watchdog didn't say so. He goes out to the Turkish Delights, too, a couple times a week."

"Who does he talk to out there?"

"A couple people. Watchdog didn't see much out there, though. The guy's a regular or something; he goes into a back room."

"What about the Everready Lounge? Did he go there?"

"Not while Watchdog followed him."

It was corroboration, and it was a pattern. But as yet it didn't mean much. Wager tore off a dry corner of his paper napkin and wrote his unlisted home number. "You hang onto this—you only. You tell Watchdog and anybody else you got working for you to check those places and to let you know right away if they see Whitey. Then you call this number and tell me where and when."

"You gonna go after him?"

"You don't really want to know that, do you?"

"No, I guess not." Squinting through the dark at the scrap of paper, he said, "One more week? I mean, my ass is really on the line. One more week, for sure?"

Wager stood and smiled. "Count on it." He left a bill beside his half-empty glass and started out. On the way, Clarissa's face caught the dim red glow from the stage as she stared at him with a puzzled frown.

. . .

He was tired. His eyes burned from long hours without sleep and the cigarette smoke and the glare of headlights that had splintered on the dusty windshield of his Trans Am when he drove home. But he still could not convince his body to relax enough to let him sleep. The feeling of pent-up energy kept tightening the muscles in his shoulders and back and legs, and even a series of savagely quick push-ups and sit-ups followed by a long, hot shower failed to drain off the tension. So he lay in his worn robe in the thin light that spilled across his couch from the city outside. There, hung over a chair on the balcony, were his vest and hat and Levi's placed to air out the musty stink of tobacco smoke. Half-illuminated, they looked like a crouching figure peering in through the glass doors, and it didn't take much squinting for that shine off the leather crown to look like white hair.

He closed his eyes and massaged them until he felt moisture press between the lids. Try as he might, he could picture nothing more than a shadow behind the arm that aimed that pistol at him. No dim oval of face, no color for coat or shirt, no glimmer of hair. The glare of the headlights had partially blinded him, and the blackness inside the car under that viaduct had completed it. The only knowledge Wager had of who the attacker might be was the sure feeling in the center of his chest. There were too many parallels, too many things that happened together not to have some meaning. It wasn't proof, but there was a solid feel to it, and that feeling not only persisted, it grew.

In following the trail of the killer of Annette Sheldon and Angela Williams, Wager had picked up the trail of Whitey. Doc's death was the point where they crossed, and that, too, was at the Cinnamon Club. So was Annette Sheldon. But not Angela. And Whitey didn't go to Foxy Dick's. But he did go to the Turkish Delights. And now Douglas MacArthur Woodcock wouldn't be going there anymore. That had been Whitey's trail, too.

There had to be a tie-in. It had to be lying there as plain as a dead rat on a kitchen table. But Wager couldn't see it. He dragged his thumb along the bullet crease on his cheek, feeling the burned flesh that had dried and was now beginning to crack and lift. He'd noticed when he shaved that those whiskers that weren't seared had begun to punch up against the scab and break through. In the hard glare of the bathroom light, the bristles had looked white. Another sign of Whitey, and this one in the middle of his own face. The downward twist at the corner of Wager's mouth said there was something almost funny in that. Ironic, anyway, and that was good enough for humor. A police reporter once told Wager that instead of a sense of humor, he had a sense of irony. Whatever the hell reporter Gargan meant by that.

Should he put out a police call for Whitey? There wasn't a thing that would stick in court. No fingerprints. No weapon. No witnesses. Circumstantial at best, and not much of that. Circumstantial hunch. There should be a booking charge called circumstantial hunch. It was good enough for the Code Napoleon. Wager had read somewhere about that: you lock up the suspect and the burden's on him to prove his innocence. Here, it was the other way round: you lock the police behind procedural restrictions and it's up to them to prove the suspect's guilt. And, sometimes, even that wasn't enough, not if the procedure hadn't been followed to the last detail. No, he couldn't have Whitey picked up, not even on a seventy-two-hour hold. What good would it do? Wager had to keep the man worried enough to fight but not so scared that he ran. And to do that, he had to offer him another chance. He had to make Whitey think that his problem was getting bigger, but not so big that one more bullet wouldn't solve it.

Yawning, he felt the weight of weariness press his eyelids down, and the couch, with its configurations different from that of his bed, began to offer his body fresh avenues to sleep. On a rising surge of darkness, his half-open eyes once more caught the shape of his hat beyond the glass and from it the faint gleam of pale light.

· CHAPTER ·

Ross and Devereaux were officially off duty at eight the next morning when Axton and Wager logged in with the dispatcher. But they did not go home. Instead, Devereaux, with a satisfied smile, told Wager they'd stay long enough to finish up the paperwork on an arrest they had finally made: Pepe the Pistol.

"You're sure you don't want Max and me to book him in?" asked Wager. "I thought we were all supposed to be a team."

"Oh, hey, Gabe—we are a team. The whole division gets the credit, believe me! It's just that it's only a few minutes more, and there's no sense starting the paperwork all over again. I mean, we're that close to being finished."

At one of the gray metal desks, Ross, his shirt sleeves folded back on his thick forearms, printed steadily with a soft lead pencil on a form that would be sent to the division secretary for typing. Sitting at the side of the desk facing him, the kid tried to keep his face stiff and expressionless as he gave a brief answer to the occasional question. But the flesh around his dark eyes was pinched with worry and he chain-smoked from the new pack of cigarettes that Ross or Devereaux had bought for him.

"How'd you get him?"

"It was Ross's idea. We almost had him that last time, you know?"

"I remember."

"Well, this time we split up. Ross figured the kid must wait somewhere in the project for the patrol car to make its last tour of the shift. Well, Ross let me off a couple blocks from the girlfriend's house and I walked on over. Meantime, he drives over to the mother's house and cruises around. Then he comes past the girlfriend's house about six. Routine patrol, right? Well, maybe ten minutes after Ross drives off, Pepe comes right up the front sidewalk like he's delivering the milk or something—here it is daylight, and he just walks up big as life and knocks on the door. His squeeze opens it and that's when I step around the corner and pop him. 'Police officer, Pepe. Lift 'em high.' He almost shit!"

"He didn't try anything?"

"Nothing. He had the piece on him—.25 automatic." He nodded toward a tangle of plastic bag at the far side of Ross's desk. "But he didn't make a move." Devereaux added, "If the girl hadn't been standing right there, he might have. Maybe he was afraid she'd get hit."

So there sat Pepe the Pistol, object of all those hours of cruising and waiting and searching. Father of one kid, killer of two others. A skinny fifteen years old. He had had a quick childhood. "Why didn't he skip town?"

"I asked him that. He said it was his girl. He was trying to stay out of jail until the baby was born. Then he said he was going to turn himself in, do his time, and come back and take care of them."

"Sure he was."

Devereaux shrugged. "That's what he said. He said if he ran out on her, he wouldn't be any better than the two kids he wasted."

"What's that mean?"

"The girl had been screwing those other two before she started going with Pepe. They gave him some shit about whose kid she was carrying and that's why he put holes in them. They treated her like she was a thing, he said. He didn't want to treat his woman like she was a thing to be used and dumped."

Wager could understand what Pepe felt when he had gone home and dusted off his old man's pistol and come hunting for those who had hurt something in his heart and laughed while they did it. The punishment may have been a little heavier than the crime, but Wager could understand. And he guessed Devereaux did, too. It was, of course, what worried Max about Wager working the Sheldon killing on his own—that he would again go beyond the law with some personal idea of justice. And Wager could not honestly say he would not.

But the kid had made those two pay for their fun and games, and now he'd pay for his honor. All for the sake of his true love, who, when her belly went down, would probably end up dancing at Foxy Dick's or the Turkish Delights, if she was lucky. Well, it wasn't Wager's to worry why or how—not when he was on duty, anyway. Those were questions that came when you couldn't sleep, and you told yourself there were no answers even as you asked them. In the silent apartment when you lay there alone, you might ask why it happened in the first place. What happened to the children? What left them so alone that they had to claim space in an adult world with adult crimes or feel that they had no substance or value? When you were in the silence of your separate cubicle high above the life of the street, you could ask that.

"Does the union know about Ross's free overtime?"

"Hey, come on, Gabe. Don't start that. Ross said the union rules allow for a few uncounted hours, so it's okay."

It was nice to know that the union rules, like the team concept, bent a little when Ross wanted something bad enough. Maybe that's why Ross tried to keep them so rigid for everybody else. Maybe that's what politics did to people, even office politics. "Well, union work or not, you still did a good job," he told Devereaux.

The tips of Devereaux's ears reddened slightly. "Hell, the judge'll probably let the kid off with six months' probation." Then he grinned. "Still, it's nice to finally bag the little bastard."

. . .

That was the way Wager wanted to feel about Whitey. But all he had right now was that gut-tightening pull of a thing about to happen. Exactly when, he couldn't say, but soon: something you've waited for a long time, and you just had to hold the lid on your feelings until it did happen. It was a sense of expectancy that kept him leading Axton back to his apartment during the duty tour to check the telephone answering machine.

"You're a damned Mexican jumping bean, partner. Do you want to tell me what it's all about?"

"It's about Whitey. I've got a lot of people looking for him. One of them's got to spot him sooner or later."

"Your snitches?"

"And a whole stable of street pushers."

"I won't even ask how in the hell you worked that." After a minute, he added, "But I've got to ask what you'll do when you find him, Gabe."

Wager had been turning that over in his mind, too. Both in the way Axton meant and in the way his partner did not know about: the mindless fear that had blown him like an ungoverned wad of dust tumbling away from the blast of Whitey's pistol. "I'm going to watch him." He told Max about the man's route. "Whatever he's up to, it's worth killing people for. I want to get his motive, and then I want to get him."

Max gazed at the heat-whitened city flowing past the cruiser's window and whistled that little half-tune between his teeth. "It's got to be money. He's got to be selling something or collecting something."

"He doesn't have any contacts. He buys a drink and then leaves. And he sits by himself."

Max's large head wagged a time or two.

"I figure Annette Sheldon and Angela Williams knew something about him that he didn't want them to."

Whistle. "But they were never seen together? Whitey and either girl?"

Wager had to admit that was so. "But he was the last one seen with Doc—and Doc was asking questions about Sheldon. That's a connection."

"Well, it's curious and worth following up; but it's not evidence. Not yet. Look, if the call does come in, let me follow the dude. He's the one that took a shot at you, right? He knows you, but he's never seen me."

"You're a whale, Max. He couldn't help but spot somebody as big as you are."

"Hey, come on—I can look small when I have to."

"Sure. Like a small rhinoceros." Wager shook his head and admitted one more thing to Max. "He's supposed to look for me. I put the word out through Clinton that I was after him. By myself."

"You called him out?"

Wager's thumb slid along the faint ridge of flesh on his cheek. "He had the first shot. I figure it's my turn."

"Gabe—"

"Only if he tries something. Just like any other suspect." Max would have to be content with that, because that was as much as Wager would—or could—promise.

• • •

The telephone finally rang a little after eight. Wager had been experimenting with a recipe from a new cookbook, *Tinfoil for Two: Oven Recipes for the Hurried and Harried Single.* This one was supposed to yield a baked Chinese dish in an hour, rice and all, but the rice came out like lumpy oatmeal and the bean sprouts like charred slugs. Wager dumped it and pulled the recipe out of its little plastic binder rings and threw it away. The cookbook now began on page 17; tomorrow night, he'd try Porkchops in Orange Sauce a la Alcoa.

Once, one of his dates had asked him why his cookbooks were missing so many pages, and he told her.

"You mean you try each one in the book and then just tear out the page and throw it away?"

"Sure. If it's no good."

"Why?"

It seemed pretty obvious to Wager. "If something's no good, why keep it?"

She looked around the pale walls of his apartment, empty except for a sword hanging in the middle of one white expanse and a small photograph of a dead tree framed on the other. "That's what you do in your life? Try something once and then toss it away if it doesn't suit you?"

"Why not?"

She had been busy the next couple times he called, so he stopped telephoning. But he still puzzled a little over her attitude.

His favorite quick meal was a can of fried hash with a couple eggs poached in the middle. Splashed with plenty of hot sauce, it was good, and it took only ten minutes. He had just stifled the steaming pan with a lid when the telephone rang.

Fat Willy's breath hissed in his ear. "That Whitey you wanted, Wager. My sources, they have come up with a little info."

"What is it?"

"He's into some kind of juicing."

"Moneylending?"

"That's what I said, ain't it?"

"What did your man see?"

"Nothing. It's what he heard. That dude don't show much at all, but there's these whispers."

"Did you find anyone who owes him money?"

"No. And that is a touch odd, ain't it? I mean, a man in that business, he got to advertise, right? Whitey, he don't advertise. But my man says he's into the vigorish all right. He got something going with your good friend Clinton."

"Did you get a name for him?"

"No. And I ain't gonna ask Clinton. You cops let him run around killing people. Besides, you getting all this cut-rate."

Fat Willy hung up, leaving Wager to gaze at the wall of his apartment where his black-and-gold NCO's sword hung in its scratched scabbard. But it wasn't the sword his mind's eye rested on; it was the image of a man with white hair and an indistinct face.

• • •

The next phone call came just before midnight. Wager, dozing at the edge of wakefulness, had the receiver off the hook before the first ring finished. "Yeah?"

The voice was a tense mutter. "You the dude with all the associates?"

"That's right."

"Well, you know who this is? You wanted me to look for somebody."

"I know. Have your people spotted him?" He reached for his Levi's.

Little Ray's voice relaxed a little. "He just went into Mickey Finn's."

"Where's he coming from?"

"The Corral."

"He hasn't been to the Cinnamon Club yet?"

"I don't think so. Watchdog says he usually starts at one end of the strip and takes them in order."

"My associates will be grateful."

"Next week, right? That's when they start getting grateful, right?"

"You got my word on it. My associates are setting things up right now." Or at least they would be as soon as Wager told Moffett and Nolan where Lazlo and his black van would meet Little Ray tomorrow night.

"And you'll be in touch, right?"

"Didn't you just use my phone number?"

The voice dropped into relief as it realized the fact. "Yeah. I guess I did. Okay—catch you later."

Or vice versa. And if the Vice people wanted to find Little Ray's fourteen-year-old girlfriend, they could get him on a nice statutory rape charge, too. Wager thought Moffett might be interested in that.

He finished tugging on his huaraches and vest and gave himself a quick check in the bathroom mirror before hustling over to the Cinnamon Club.

The place was almost empty. Just inside the entryway, a printed handbill read, FREEDOM OF EXPRESSION!!! WRITE YOUR CONGRESSMAN!!! and in smaller type explained that the State Supreme court had ruled against the clubs and, pending appeal, there would be no more bottomless dancing where food or drink were served. Beside the handbill was a poster: *Bottoms Up—See It While You Can. All Nude Review Still at the Cinnamon Club.*

Clarissa recognized him with a wide smile. "Hi—good to see you again. How about a seat right at the runway?"

Wager said No. "I'm waiting for somebody." He headed for a rear table just inside the door.

She stayed on his heels. "I haven't seen Little Ray yet. Beer? It's a Killian's, right?"

"That's right."

"See? I remember you." She brought it quickly. As his eyes adjusted to the dimness, Wager could see waitresses near the door waiting for the next customer to come in.

Elsewhere, a few stood at tables and smiled and chatted with their regulars.

"You must have a brother." Clarissa poured his beer into a glass.

"Why's that?"

"You look like somebody. In this light it's hard to tell, but you look like somebody I've seen before. What's your name?"

"Gabe."

"Gee, that's a name you don't hear often. Mine's Clarissa," she reminded him.

"I know. You're a good dancer, Clarissa."

"Thanks!" Her thighs, just below the edge of her tight shorts, pressed at each side of a table corner; her tights rode out in a warm curve over the table lip, and she seemed in no hurry to go back to the line of waitresses clustered by the door.

"When do you go on again?" Wager asked.

She glanced at the current dancer who, in a frilly bodice with many ribbons and straps, was twirling a black-stockinged foot in the air like a cancan girl. "Three more performers. Berg—Mr. Berg—moved me to later in the evening," she said with modest pride.

"Congratulations."

"Thanks. But it doesn't mean much on a night like this."

Wager figured there had been a lot of slow nights lately. He put a bill on the table under the curve of those tights. "In case I'm not here to see you dance."

"Oh gee, thanks." Her thumb folded it expertly into her palm.

Mostly on impulse, Wager asked, "Maybe you'd like to go out sometime?"

She smiled a wide thank-you but said, "We're not allowed to date the customers. Club rule."

"No offense meant."

"None taken. Really!" She moved off into the scarlet

gloom and Wager watched a male arm in a flowered Hawaiian shirt reach to tuck a bill into the garter of the girl onstage. Berg himself was trying to get things started among the mostly silent men.

"Let me clean the table for you." Clarissa was back with a bar towel and brushed her hip lightly at his shoulder as she bent across him to wipe at the shiny wood. "Give me a call if you want anything." She smiled again and was gone. Beside his glass was a square of paper about the size of a calling card. It held a neatly typed telephone number.

Wager was on his third slow beer when he saw the man come in and wondered how, in the past, he had missed him. The hair turned pink in the glow from the stage and moved across the black wall like a dying spark. Most of the people whose business depended on contacts made in dark corners wore recognizable hats like Wager's or striking hairstyles like Little Ray's. Whitey didn't need that; his hair caught your eye like a faint, blinking light. If you were looking for him, it was something you wouldn't miss. But if you weren't, then you didn't pay much attention to just another white head out buying what he could from the young girls.

The waitress at the front of the line started toward him and then stopped, called away by a word Wager couldn't hear through the throb of music. A girl farther down the line went instead. He squinted to make her out but it wasn't until a little later, when she stood in the pale glow of Nguyen's bar, that he recognized one of the club lesbians, the one with the long brunette curls . . . the one who had known nothing about Annette Sheldon and didn't want to . . . Sybil—that was her name: Sybil. Wager watched closely as she carried the tray back to the table and took payment. Then she headed back to Nguyen, who rang up the sale. Aside from a brief hello, neither Whitey nor Sybil said much, even on this slow night when the girls were trying to hustle a few more bucks out of their regulars. Instead, she wandered back toward the dressing room to get ready,

Wager guessed, for her turn onstage. It was vague and pointless, just as Fat Willy's man had said, and Wager, still waiting for something to happen, watched the man drain his glass and stand and walk out with a brief nod to Nguyen —who had told Wager he did not know the man.

It was the same at Barnum's. Whitey had his drink and left the place, meeting with no one. It wasn't your normal bar-hopping expedition, but it was what Wager expected. Nothing happened. Nothing. What did occur, and what made Wager drop back into the clusters of strolling night people, was Whitey's unobtrusive skill at checking his trail for someone following him. He paused in front of an unlit display window and, using the shiny reflection, surveyed the figures behind him. Once, waiting for a quick break in traffic, he trotted heavily across Colfax in mid-block and stepped into a pharmacy where, a moment or two later, Wager caught his silhouette at the side of the window, watching. He changed pace quickly, speeding up near a corner as if about to turn into a dark side street, then doubled back to see if any familiar face was trying to keep up. Why would the man, whose stops were routine, be so cautious in going from point to point? As edgy as a whore in church, Whitey stayed with the crowds and with the well-lit sidewalks. And, Wager was sure, the maneuvers were habitual—Whitey wasn't looking for Wager, in disguise or out. He was just being careful. A courier? Delivering what? Picking up what? The pattern of stops and the caution fit a courier. Everything fit except the fact that he made contact with no one. That is, almost no one . . . almost! The people he did make contact with in every bar were almost nobodies, so much a part of the club's landscapes as to be invisible—almost. . . .

Wager, feeling a little bounce of excitement enter his stride, turned from the man who, half a block ahead, had paused again to glance in the window of another closed shop. Across the street and in the next block, rippling light bulbs spelled The Palm Room and above the letters, in brown and green neon, something vaguely resembling a palm tree swayed back and forth through three flickering positions. Wager knew where the man was going, and he knew now who his contact would be: Clarissa had shown him, and Wager had been too damned dumb to see it at the time. Right out in the open and so simple and natural you'd never notice a thing. That had to be the way it was done. And the next question was, "What?" What was Whitey delivering or picking up from the waitresses at each of his stops?

Not looking, but knowing that the man was working his way along the other sidewalk beyond the blur of cars, Wager stretched his legs to reach the flickering sign. Whitey would still be looking behind him while Wager was now in front, and that little twist gave the kind of smile to his lips that brought startled looks from some of the people he pushed by. He turned into The Palm Room and paused under the shaggy plastic fronds that hung from the entryway ceiling. Blinking against the cigarette smoke and painfully amplified noise, Wager groped his way toward the bar and the half-dozen motionless figures watching the woman on stage.

"Can I get you a table?" A girl stood at his elbow and smiled. "My name's Tess."

Wager glanced past her and understood why the men at the bar stared fixedly. A nude girl sat on her heels, knees apart, and leaned back, lifting her breasts toward the ceiling, while her partner, a giant, glistening python, inched its thick body between her legs and up her round stomach in small, rippling moves. Its markings, an intricate pattern of greens and yellows and browns, shone in the spotlight with a clean and primitive sharpness that, to Wager, dominated all that was happening around it, drawing his eyes with the fascination of the substantial.

"Who's that onstage?"

"The dancer's Simba. The snake's Leo. You like snakes?"

"I like the snake better than the broad. No, I don't want a table—not yet. Just some phone change." He looked around. "You got a phone here?"

Without wasting another word, she tossed a hand toward the small white sign glowing in a far corner and turned back to her station.

Wager, an eye on the doorway, waited for the bartender to finish mixing an order and come toward him, dragging his towel along the bar top. "Help you?"

He held out a bill. "Phone change, please."

"Sure."

Taking the handful of coins, Wager stood at the telephone, his gaze toward the door. Placing a call, he listened to the recorded voice tell him the time and temperature over and over until Whitey, unhurried, finally came in. One of the waitresses came forward with a smile and he followed her to a table. Wager hung up and moved in behind them.

From his small table, Wager saw the waitress ask something; the man nodded, both hands empty and forearms resting in front of him.

"Getcha something now?"

Tess was back and Wager said, "Dark beer."

"Heineken's okay?"

"Fine."

Whitey watched the stage, where the python's head was nearing the girl's neck; she had begun to flex her hips to the same rhythm as the snake's measured ripple and the beat of the throbbing drum. Still watching as the waitress took his order, he reached into his coat's left vest pocket and brought out something that his hand half-covered and laid it on the table in front of him. Then he reached for his wallet and pulled out a bill. The waitress came back with the tray and served him; Whitey handed her the bill and Wager saw through the dimness that the table in front of the man was empty of everything except his glass and the napkin it rested on. But Whitey's eyes were still on the stage and, casually, he tucked something away into his right vest pocket. He brings something in his left pocket; he takes something in his right pocket—but Wager hadn't seen what it was. Like watching bumps moving under a blanket, you know something's going on, and you have a pretty good idea of what it is. But exactly how it's happening is still hidden.

The recorded drums ended in a deafening roll and the girl stood, the snake draped heavily back and forth across her shoulders, its long tail dangling between her breasts. The music went into a quick and slightly quieter tune and she paced around the lip of the stage, twisting sharply on the ball of each foot and pausing with each step to show off her body and the snake's and to allow the men to stuff bills into the thongs of her sandals. Whitey sipped once at his drink and stood, shadowed eyes going over the half-empty room. They hesitated when they came to Wager, sitting at the table just behind him, and he felt that little electric tingle that comes when you know you've been spotted. Then the dim face finished its survey and Whitey strode slowly toward the exit as if waiting for someone to follow him.

Wager let him go. He did not know if Whitey recognized him as a cop in disguise or if the bartender at the Turkish Delights had described him as the short Mexican who was asking all the questions and who should have been smart enough to quit while he was in one piece. He hoped it was the latter, but it didn't make too much difference now—Wager had seen all he would be able to see, and there was no need to spook the man further. Finishing his beer, he raised his finger for another. Give Whitey plenty of line—let him stand around outside until he felt safe and went to his next contact. Now was not the time to rush.

The loudspeaker announced Big Bertha and Her Incredible Fifty-Twos, and Wager sat back to enjoy the show. A woman with frizzy blond hair laughed and joked with the men at her feet as they called to her to take it off. She did, one gauzy wrap at a time. She held out the shimmering color as she spun and tossed it into the darkness at the end of the runway, where a pale hand reached to pull the floating cloth to safety. By the second number and Wager's third beer, she was down to three or four transparent veils with her bra and panties saved for the final dance. Tess brought him another round without being asked. Wager sipped until the grand finale, then he placed a bill on the runway as he left.

A small tripod facing exiting customers held a carnival-like sign that proclaimed, *Ladies! Every Tuesday Nite: Don't Miss Won Hung Lo. He Will Amaze and Delight You with His Dancing Anatomy!*

• • •

He was in no hurry; he had more than an hour and spent it shaving off his darkened bristles and changing back into the unofficial summer uniform for detectives: slacks, open white shirt, sport coat whose only purpose was to cover the Star PD holstered on his hip.

At one-thirty, he headed for the Cinnamon Club; ten minutes later, he sat in his dark Trans Am, sheltered by the shadows of a tree that overhung the alley leading to the club's parking lot. A little after two, he saw Sybil and Rebecca pull out of the lot in their shiny ZX. Their address was in his little green notebook from the first interviews, which now seemed so long ago, and he might have waited for them there. But he wanted to be sure of them; he felt the almost quivering tightness in his chest that told him he was getting close, and he did not want to lose them now.

He followed them through the residential streets whose only traffic was the occasional late automobile speeding recklessly through intersections or the bright cab busy taking working girls home after club closings. Ahead, in the middle of the block, the Datsun swung its long hood under the shine of a streetlight and disappeared between concrete piers that lifted an apartment tower over a parking garage for residents. Wager pulled into the only open space along the curb, a fire zone, and crossed the street as he heard the muffled sound of two car doors somewhere in the dimly lit parking garage. He ducked under the traffic bar and found the women waiting for the sharp glow of the elevator lights to bounce down through the numbers to the basement garage.

They heard his shoes and jerked around, fear widening their eyes.

"Police, Sybil." He had his badge out. "Detective Wager. I'd like to ask you some questions."

The hand that clutched her own throat fell away with a sigh, and Rebecca, the one who had the butterflies tattooed on each cheek, breathed, "Shit—you ought to wear a bell around your neck or something."

"Can I come up?"

They glanced at each other. "You're sure this is police business?" asked Rebecca.

"It is."

The elevator arrived with a *ding* and the doors pumped open, spilling light across them. Neither woman entered. "What kind of police business—what kind of questions?"

"It's about the white-haired man. The one you waited on tonight."

Sybil's eyes blinked rapidly two or three times and she was very still. Rebecca, without moving, seemed to draw farther away. "I don't know what you're talking about."

"Sure you do. I want to know what his racket is. I want to know what it is he gave you, and what you gave him."

"Nothing—I don't even know the man!"

"Come on, Sybil. Think about it. You asked him if he wanted the usual to drink, and that doesn't sound like strangers in the night. He handed you something. When you brought the change, you gave him something. It was a delivery and a pickup. Now what was it?"

"You don't have to tell him nothing, Syb. You go to hell, cop—she doesn't have to tell you a thing!"

The elevator doors shut with a slight hiss and the light from the car died with it.

"You can tell me here without being arrested, or you can tell me at the station, Sybil. If I hear it from you here, Whitey won't know where I found out—he's got a half-dozen drops along the strip and it could have been any one of them. But if you're brought in, I'll make damned certain the arrest report gets in the newspaper."

"Arrest for what? What the hell can you arrest her for, cop?"

"Three counts of accessory to murder."

"Oh, Jesus—"

"But she . . ."

"Whitey killed three people, Sybil. And he had a woman phone me and set me up to be wasted."

"It wasn't me! I don't even know your number!"

"Nguyen knew my number. It was probably somebody at the Cinnamon Club—somebody Whitey could ask for a little favor."

"Not me—really!"

"But like I said, he's got drops all over the strip. It could have been any of them. I think that; he'll think that."

The pale blur of her face hung unmoving.

Wager leaned past the taut figure to press the elevator button. "So no hard feelings. Let's just go upstairs and talk about it."

· CHAPTER ·

15

Sybil did not know all of it. She knew the money was good and the work was easy, and she knew better than to ask questions. She'd had an idea—one she didn't let settle into clear belief—that Shelly had worked for the man and somehow crossed him, and was killed for it. She, Sybil, wasn't going to be that dumb.

"It's not being dumb, Sybil; it's being smart—smart enough to know when the game's over so you can still get out while you're not wearing stitches."

She thought about that while her roommate rattled loudly in the kitchen and stuck her head across the divider to ask sourly if Wager wanted coffee, too. Later, he figured that domestic touch was what swayed Sybil his way, because when they were all sitting around the low table with their cups steaming under their noses, she finally began to talk.

"He comes in, I don't know, once a week—sometimes every other week. He brings money and hands it to me. It's wrapped with one of those paper bands that says how much. It's usually a couple thousand dollars, sometimes even more. I take it back to Berg and he writes out a receipt and gives me a hundred. Then I take the receipt back to him when I bring him his drink. I leave it on the table with the napkin, and that's it—that's all I know about it."

"A money-laundering scheme? Is that what it is?"

"I don't know. I get a hundred every time I do it. That's all I know. It's all I want to know."

"Annette Sheldon was doing it before you were?"

"I—I guess so. That's something I didn't ask."

But she had been making a lot more money than Sybil. "Did Berg ever say anything about her?"

"Once he, ah, told me to keep my mouth shut because this man is very hard on people he doesn't like. He never mentioned Shelly's name, but we both knew who he meant."

"Did he tell you she got greedy? Maybe skimmed a little?"

"No. But that would be dumb. The money has that wrapper with the amount on it, and he gets a receipt from Berg."

"What about Angela Williams?"

"I've never heard the name."

Two thousand dollars at each drop—five regular drops every week or so . . . ten thousand a week . . . Walking the streets with ten thousand or more in his pockets . . . no wonder he practiced all those maneuvers. "Where'd the money come from?"

"I don't know. And I never asked."

"What's the man's name?"

"I don't know that either."

He believed her. And he believed that was all she would be able to tell him. Draining his cup, he reminded her not to tell anyone she had talked to him. "This time, I'd know how he found out, Syb. And neither one of us would take it kindly." He thanked Madame Butterfly for the coffee, and then sat for a few minutes in the dark of his silent car while he turned over Sybil's information.

Now he had the motive. Figure—what?—half a million a year gross, maybe three hundred thousand after expenses. And somehow laundered so that the tax showed up as paid and then the money could be used like anybody's savings account—buy a little real estate, a few stocks and bonds, salt it away at a good honest interest rate. Or lend it out again through Clinton. A good setup. Conveniently local, small enough so that it doesn't attract Mafia interest, but still almost as profitable as working for the federal government. . . . It would be worth killing for, if you thought you could get away with it. Whitey thought he could. And so far he was right.

Maybe Annette went with him willingly— "Come on, I want you to meet somebody."

Doc went out of the Cinnamon Club with a pistol at his back, and he tried to leave a message with those two bums. Maybe he even tried to ask them for help, but their eyes were glued to that bill he held out and they never even looked at his whispering mouth or sweating, scared face.

Angela Williams? There was still no connection between her and Whitey, but that would come. Wager felt as certain about that as he felt the grainy weariness that burned under his lids when he rubbed his tired eyes. That one would fall into place, too.

He started the Trans Am and headed slowly back to his apartment through the empty streets. As he passed avenues sloping down toward the South Platte river valley, he noted that the night wind had blown Denver's smog clear and left patterns of lights sprawling all the way to the dark where the mountains lay; there, lights spread in bands and patches up their flanks to blend with the dim stars. Nearer, the streetlights were the sharp blue or pink of vapor bulbs, and, here and there, the softer yellows of curtained windows dotted the blackness. But even as he watched those narrow wedges swing past the car's windows, he wondered what to do next. He knew the man's stops and routes; if the man did not run, Wager could pick him up. But what would that get him besides a laugh when the man was let go for lack of evidence? Wager wanted the man for homicide, not for laundering money; and there was a good chance he could not get him for either. Berg? Lean on Berg until he broke? No tie between the owner of the Cinnamon Club and the murders. . . . Still, Sybil said Berg knew something. If he was squeezed hard enough, he might let something out—there had to be ways to get to him without Whitey knowing.

He was still sketching out various means to pressure Berg as he unlocked his apartment door; in the semidark of his living room, the telephone answering machine's Alert light was a little crimson diamond. Wager, turning on the lamp, pressed the Rewind and Play buttons. The first few seconds of the tape were blank, the sign of a caller who had hung up when he heard the recording. Then came a half-familiar voice: "Wager—this is Moffett. We got that Lazlo dude and a half-dozen street people, too. Thanks for the help." Now Little Ray wouldn't have to worry about the profit margin on his merchandise, not for a few years, at least. He let the tape run farther and then a tense voice, pinched by the tape's distortion, cut in at mid-sentence—the speaker had not waited for the sound of the beep—". . .neth Sheldon. I got to see you. As soon as possible. Call me at the shop anytime. I'll be there. It's important."

He pressed Stop and then ran the tape back and listened again to the anxious voice. Sheldon. Why would the man who almost chased him out of his shop suddenly be so eager to see him?

Wager checked his watch: two fifty-five. The man said anytime, and it was worth a phone call to see what he wanted. Locating the number for the Nickelodeon Vending Repairs, Wager dialed it, waiting through rings that seemed abnormally long. Halfway through the fifth, it broke off, and, after a breath or two, a soft voice said, "Hello?"

"Sheldon?"

"Yeah—who's this?"

"Detective Wager. I just got your message. What's it about?"

"Not over the phone. I can't talk over the phone. You got to come here."

"There? Right now?"

"Yes. How long's it going to take you to get here?"

"Half an hour, forty-five minutes. What the hell is it that can't wait until morning?"

"I can't tell you over the phone! And . . . and if I leave the shop, he'll follow me. . . ."

"Who?"

"The guy you're after. The white-haired guy you're after!"

Wager didn't know if the tiny buzz filling the silence was in the wires or in his mind. He said slowly, "All right. I'll be there."

"Come to the back door—you know, the alley. And come alone!"

"Sure, Sheldon. I'm on my way now."

But when he set the receiver on its cradle, he did not move. Instead, he asked himself a few questions: Where did Sheldon get Wager's unlisted number? How did he know Wager was after Whitey? And exactly why might he want Wager to come alone to a dark alley? I can lead you to Whitey—just meet me in the dark alone. It almost worked last time, why not try again? Sheldon . . . Whitey . . . there was some connection . . . Annette, and now her husband. . . . But maybe this time Whitey would be on the receiving end; maybe this time Wager, dragging his thumb along the small scar on his cheek, did not intend to let somebody drive him into ungoverned terror.

He picked up the receiver and dialed Max's number. A promise was a promise, even at three in the morning.

It rattled half a ring and Max, a cop even in his sleep, was wide awake by the time he said "Hello."

"It's Gabe. I've been invited to another dark alley. Want to go with me?"

"Where do I meet you?"

"I'll pick you up in fifteen."

It was less than that—vacant intersections and empty streets allowed him to shoot the Trans Am across town without stopping. But Max was already waiting, a figure seated on the porch steps of his large old house, caught in the sweep of headlights as Wager pulled into the driveway. Wordless, he got in; Wager backed out and shoved the car through the gears as he worked his way toward the north side and Sheldon's shop.

"Hope I didn't wake up Polly."

"No. She's used to it."

Sure she was. Wager just hoped his partner hadn't told her who called; she'd be clinging to the ceiling if she knew her husband was helping him on another one of his semiprivate expeditions. So would Bulldog Doyle, for that matter. But since Wager had his partner along, maybe the Bulldog would see them as a team.

"What do you think Sheldon's connection is?" Max asked after Wager had filled him in.

Wager had thought a lot about that. But saying it aloud made the pieces click solidly, and he took his time. Besides, talking kept his mind away from that other question, the personal one, the one that had lain unbidden but like a heavy stone at the back of his mind ever since that night under the viaduct.

"It's got to be part of the laundering. My guess is the vending repair service is a dummy corporation—Annette was getting a lot more money than Sybil. She had to be doing more than just transporting."

"Well, that could explain how Sheldon knew you were after Whitey."

"That, too. And a vending machine service is a natural expense for clubs and bars. Repairs, rental, stock—a bar could account for an extra couple thousand a week if IRS wanted to take a close look."

"So Whitey brings in the hot cash and turns it over to the bar owner." Max's voice was a musing rumble. "The owner lists it as income, takes his cut, and then writes a check to Nickelodeon for vending machine service. And that goes on the books as a legitimate expense."

"Maybe with a few refinements, but yeah. And then Nickelodeon covers its income with employees' salaries, overhead, other expenses—all dummy—and hands most of it back to Whitey."

"You think Annette Sheldon started taking a little more than she was supposed to?"

"That's my guess. I figure that's what Sheldon's been trying to hide all this time." Wager added, "But I can't figure Angela Williams. Unless she learned something. Like Doc."

"Well, we'll sure as hell find out." Max watched the streetlights flicker across the hood of the car as it sped down I-70 toward the Seabury district. "Jesus, where does that much money come from in the first place?"

"The usual: dope, prostitution, vigorish, gambling. What's new is the laundry service. Clinton, maybe a few others, provided Whitey with the money; Whitey provided a weekly laundry service."

Max grunted. "Whitey was with Clinton and Jimmy King just before Goddard was beaten to death. And wouldn't it be nice to get Clinton, too!"

"Wouldn't it though."

"What's the going rate for loan sharks?" Max asked.

"Last I heard, it was five percent a day."

"That's a lot of money—those nickels and dimes add up."

The car tilted down a ramp that led them past the looming black curves of the Coliseum. In the distance, cramped by the bulk of the elevated highway above, a grimy yellow sign glowed in front of a truckers' motel; Wager angled north two blocks to the row of small shops that held Sheldon's store. When he was half a block away, he turned off his headlights and slowed to pass the front of the darkened windows. He was not surprised to find no light, no shape standing in the open waiting for them. There hadn't been that other time, either.

Sunk out of sight below the window, Max said, "He told you to come to the back?"

"Yeah."

The cramped voice panted, "I wish to hell you had a four-door."

Wager turned the lights back on and swung toward the alley. Trash cans and telephone poles nudged the space as he steered toward the solid mass of the shops. Maybe a hundred yards down, a faint patch of light spread across the gravel, glittering on fragments of a bottle. Wager let the motor pull them forward slowly and quietly. He, too, sank farther down in his seat, hand resting on his pistol as he eased past the raised door and saw the single work lamp fill one corner of the room with a glow. The rest of the shop was dark.

"We're going past now," said Wager.

"See anybody?"

"Not a soul." He turned off the dome light. "I'll park a little way down the alley." Letting the car coast to a stop, he killed the engine. Max already had his door open; Wager, looking back, studied the shop before he opened his. "I'll cross the alley and go along the wall."

"I'll be behind you. Just take it easy, partner."

"Not too close, Max. Give me plenty of room."

"Right."

He listened for a final few seconds and then shoved his door open to step through the night glow that gave the alley a faint shine like starlight. His hand brushed the gritty stucco of the wall as he carefully worked his way past black, grated windows and garbage cans toward the paleness of the raised garage door. Pausing at the frame, he listened. Nothing. It was as quiet and dark as that viaduct had been, and Wager felt his shoulders draw tight at the vision of that blinding rush coming toward him out of the black.

"Sheldon?" His dry mouth didn't work too well and he called again. "Sheldon?"

No answer.

Loosening the Star PD holstered in front of his left hip, Wager leaned cautiously around the frame. Above the glare of the hooded lamp the shrine to Annette flickered, shadowy and elongated in the yellow splash of a prayer candle cupped in a dark red bowl.

"Sheldon?"

Crouching, he stepped into the shop and glanced toward the dim end of the workbench, where the door led to the front. Empty. Wager squatted to peer at any mass of blackness hiding under the long shelf. Nothing. He snapped off the lamp and waited for his eyes to clear, ears sharp for any sound; now the dim shine of the alley came in the doorway and the yellow circle of the prayer candle danced softly against the ceiling. Slowly, Wager moved toward the far end of the room.

The door leading to the front of the shop stood open; beside it, another door, labeled Men, was tightly closed. He hesitated at the edge of darkness, feeling the crusty surface of a poorly varnished frame beneath his fingers. Then he bent low quickly and ducked forward, stepping to the side as he cleared the door and squinted among the scattered vending machines that made tall black rectangles against the windows.

A muffled *whump* and the red flash of a stifled muzzle. Wager sprawled and blinked and rolled, knowing that the shot came from somewhere to his left, somewhere among those tall, clustered shapes. He held his breath, pistol angled up, until the rattle of shoe leather moved toward him and he rolled again, hard, away from the doorway as a crouching figure moved across the light of a front window and was gone.

He fired once, the noise loud against the walls as the bright flash of his weapon lit up the darkened vending machines. Rolling again, he blinked away the glare of his pistol, only half-aware of a second shot flung his way between two oblong shadows. Crawling, his shoulder cracked into a metal corner and he heard the quick rip of his coat on something, then he was up and crouched in the blackest shadow, breathing lightly through his open mouth as his ears strained to hear through the tingle of that first shot.

Somewhere, somebody was whining.

That's what it was: the high-pitched nasal whine of somebody trying to strangle his own terrified noise.

Blinking, shifting his gaze quickly from point to point in the way that had become habitual on those night patrols in Nam, Wager tried to use his lateral vision to thin the darkness. A scrape—a tiny crackle of grit—over there . . . just beyond his vision. . . . A thin creak like a rusty nail slowly pried from a hole. . . . Wager's pistol, gripped in both hands, turned toward the slightly darker gloom that seemed to gather into stealthy movement.

He didn't see it. He wasn't sure what told him it was coming. A more solid blackness, maybe, or the air mashed in front of it, but a moment before it hit him he ducked his head, catching the plummeting, solid weight of the metal case across his shoulders and curling against the hard gouge of knobs and the sudden, lung-crushing weight. The machine rocked across his humped back and crashed in a splinter of glass and quivering steel, knocking Wager aside before it thudded flat on his leg and wrenched his knee sideways. Wincing against the searing pain of pulled ligaments, he saw a blurry shape lunge toward him. His pistol swung toward the rush of legs and then the man was gone, leaping through the tangle of fallen machines, and Wager, tugging himself from under the angled weight, stumbled after him.

He reached the workroom in time to see Max dart across the opening and hesitate, looking where he had heard the shot.

"I'm okay, Max! Which way?"

Max's arm pointed across the alley and Wager saw a shape dark against the gray of a distant house's wall. It stumbled into something and clattered it into fragments, fell, rolled, then staggered up again into a crippled lurch.

Vaulting the low mesh fence beyond the alley, Wager sprinted after the figure, the ache of his knee suddenly gone. Behind him, he heard Max's large shoes thud into the lawn as the big man angled left to head off the man and Wager, pistol cocked, darted for the shape that started right, saw Max, then turned toward the other side of the house. A light winked on behind a drawn shade and a silhouette bent to peer out a crack. Somewhere in a neighboring yard a dog barked insanely and Wager, feeling a shattered birdbath grind beneath his shoes, swung right as the man hobbled toward the narrow lane that led between the house and the chain link fence.

"Police officer," Wager shouted. He dropped to one knee, pistol balanced in both hands and rock-steady; the barrel traversed toward the shape that halted to jerk its arm up and aim at Wager. "Police officer," he said again. "You're covered—drop it!"

A shot answered him. A spurt of blue-yellow at the pistol end of the silencer frayed into the air as the red of the muzzle speared his way and a solid, quivering thud punched the fence behind him. Wager squeezed the trigger with the even, straight pull born of long target practice.

But before his weapon could buck, a shot blasted from beside him.

A splash of orange light showed the white-haired man peering at Wager down the long shaft of a silencer, then the grass blades flickered in another muffled round and a loud second shot, strobelike, showed him lift back and half-turn with orange eyes goggling toward Max, his revolver braced against the side of the house as a third round shattered the blackness. Then the clunk of a heavy weapon against the earth, and a long, groaning sigh, like no other sound, of life stunned into death.

• • •

The man's ID said Eugene North, but Wager and everyone else in Homicide guessed that a check of fingerprints with the FBI records would turn up a different name. Through the sealed windows behind Sheldon, Wager could see the sprinkled gleams of distant office towers pale gradually as the sky lightened from a still-hidden sun beginning to rise somewhere over Missouri or eastern Kansas. This time, Wager asked the questions, and this time Sheldon did not get mad when he was advised of his rights. He just talked. "I want to get it over with," he told Wager and the small cluster of Homicide detectives that brought a strangely crowded feeling to the early-morning emptiness of the offices. Ross and Devereaux on the duty shift were filling out their forms: the measurements from Max to the victim, the location of known bullet holes, the number of rounds fired by everyone. Max, pale and with dark circles under his eyes, sat with a cup of coffee and answered when he was supposed to answer and kept quiet when he was not. Pacing restlessly between the two groups of his people, Chief Doyle, unshaven and rumpled from the haste of yanking on his clothes, chewed an unlit cigar. He had a rule never to smoke before breakfast, but chewing wasn't quite satisfactory and it irritated him.

"So North made you hide in the men's room?" Wager asked.

"Yes," said Sheldon. "He thought you'd try the door—hear me, maybe—and then he'd get you from the front room. I thought you were going to shoot through the door! When the shooting started, I thought . . ." He swallowed and wiped at the corners of his soft mustache and looked at Wager. "I didn't want to phone you. Honest to God, I didn't want to. But he made me. He . . . he killed Annette. . . ."

"You witnessed that?"

"No—oh no! Afterward . . . before I came to see you people. He called me and told me she was dead and told me to say she was missing."

The organization of the laundering scheme had been just about the way Max and Wager figured it. The business had half-a-dozen phony employees on its books, under contract rather than salary so the Social Security and withholding wouldn't have to be accounted for—one of Annette's touches. The clubs paid the vending repair service, the service paid its "employees'" salaries and expenses into Annette's pocketbook. The Sheldons' trips to Vegas had been courier service—they deposited North's cut in a bank there as one more bit of distance between him and the operation. The Sheldons had been doing all right, but Annette thought they were taking more risk than North and figured they deserved more money for it. She threatened North with the police, and North wasn't the kind to be threatened.

"Did Berg get a cut?"

"I think so. Or maybe he was paying off a loan. Annette told me once that North or somebody had loaned him money to keep the business going. The liquor and stereo equipment, the overhead, the license—all that stuff is really expensive. And then the profits weren't as good as they expected."

What Sheldon didn't know, Wager could guess. Clinton and North helped Berg and the others over a rough spot or two—"Hey, think of it as a friendly loan; take what you need"—until they had Berg and the others owing their souls at five percent a day. Then they offered a way to work the debt off. "What about Angela Williams? Did he kill her, too?"

"Him or somebody working for him." His eyes gazed at the gray rug between his feet. "It was cover, he said."

"What?"

"Cover. I'd told him about you coming by the shop and asking about Annette's money—how much she made and all. That worried him a lot. He wanted you to think that some crazy guy was killing dancers. He wanted cover for the operation."

So Wager had stirred things up all right. Do something, lieutenant, even if it's wrong. And one of those things was another death. "He killed her for that?" And Angela Williams's death was what had stirred Wager's suspicions about Annette Sheldon. So tangled a web of causes that things seemed almost fated, almost as though things really had worked out for the best—except for the dead. But what was Wager supposed to do—nothing at all?

Again the tuft of straight, uncombed hair sprouting from Sheldon's crown nodded. He took off his thick glasses and wiped them on his cuff and Wager was surprised at the amount of baggy flesh beneath his wet eyes. It made him look even older and weaker. It made him look like someone who could be manipulated by a strong woman. Even one who maybe loved him. "He killed Annette for the same thing. Money. She was a good dancer . . . she could have made it all the way to the top. . . ."

And Angela had been a good mother and a good daughter. And Doc a good snitch. Everybody was good at something. Wager would give Detective Lee a call in an hour or so and tell him the Angela Williams case could be closed and Lee would know that Wager was good at solving homicides. And Clinton would still be on the street because he was good at covering himself. Everybody was good at something.

Wager sipped at his coffee and glanced at Max. His partner had been good at shooting. Max had fired three rounds and then called to Wager, and they had stood there as the yard light winked on, showing the broken birdbath and uprooted and scattered petunias, their fragrance thick in the cool air, the scared face at the back door, and the sprawled figure, whose pumping blood slowed to an erratic pulse, then a weary flow, then ceased, even as they watched.

"I thought he hit you," said Max. "When you didn't fire back, I thought he hit you."

They heard the querulous voice from behind the dark screen door, but it didn't register with either man. "Thanks, Max."

"Why'd you yell at him? Why'd you give him a shot at you?"

Because it was procedure. And because he wanted to know if he had the guts to hold his fire. But all he told Max was, "It seemed like the thing to do."

"I thought he hit you," Max said again.

"He tried." Wager remembered the ease and sureness with which he had leveled his pistol and aimed, unafraid. The steadiness of his trigger pull. "You got him before I could, that's all." And it was true.

Max sucked in a long, slow breath that stifled his feelings; they would come later. Alone. Maybe with Polly. Probably not. Those kinds of feelings weren't something you loaded onto your wife. Max would give himself the familiar arguments and he would go about his life because there was no bringing anyone back. He would joke about all the paperwork. He would nod and smile when someone said he had saved the taxpayers' money. He would say "Thanks" when someone told him "Good shooting."

And late at night, in the silence of his apartment, Wager would wake up sweaty and staring and be glad that Whitey was dead and not him. But he would be glad, too, that this time his flesh had stood its ground and done its duty.

Wager turned his attention back to Sheldon, who had not moved. Behind him, he heard Bulldog Doyle's heavy tread as he made another round between the two groups. The odor of the unlit cigar wafted around Wager's shoulder as Doyle leaned toward him.

"Good job, Wager," muttered Doyle. "You and Axton did damn fine work."

Wager looked up at the Bulldog's pale gray eyes over that underslung jaw that had given him his nickname. "Thanks." Then he smiled. "It was teamwork all the way."

Doyle's eyes hardened and he bit into the soggy tip of the cigar. It made a sound like chewed cabbage.